T0356249

HOW TO HAVE A KILLER TIME IN D.C.

HOW TO HAVE A KILLER TIME IN D.C.

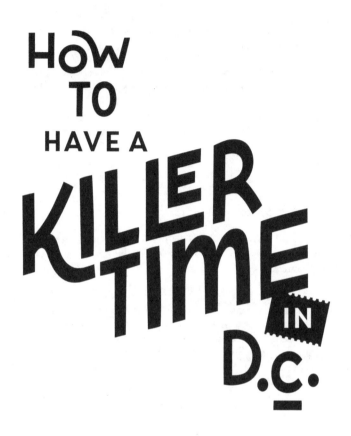

SAM LUMLEY

KENSINGTON PUBLISHING CORP.
kensingtonbooks.com

KENSINGTON BOOKS are published by

Kensington Publishing Corp.
900 Third Avenue
New York, NY 10022

All Kensington titles, imprints and distributed lines are available at special quantity discounts for bulk purchases for sales promotion, premiums, fundraising, educational or institutional use. Special book excerpts or customized printings can also be created to fit specific needs. For details, write or phone the office of the Kensington Special Sales Manager: Kensington Publishing Corp., 900 Third Avenue, New York, NY, 10022. Attn. Special Sales Department. Phone: 1-800-221-2647.

KENSINGTON and the KENSINGTON COZIES teapot logo Reg. US Pat & TM Off.

Library of Congress Control Number: 2024951046

ISBN: 978-1-4967-5355-7

First Kensington Hardcover Edition: May 2025

ISBN: 978-1-4967-5357-1 (ebook)

10 9 8 7 6 5 4 3 2 1

Printed in the United States of America

The authorized representative in the EU for product safety and compliance is eucomply OU, Parnu mnt 139b-14, Apt 123
Tallinn, Berlin 11317, hello@eucompliancepartner.com

To my parents, who looked the other way when I started reading their library books instead of my own.

AUTHOR'S NOTE AND ACKNOWLEDGEMENTS

Thank you, reader, for coming on this trip with Oliver and Ricky and me!

I can't believe the time has finally come to go home and unpack my bags from this adventure. Believe it or not, this trip started nearly four years ago; this book was my pandemic baby, written primarily in the winter of 2021–22, at a time when I hadn't really properly left my house in well over a year. If, while reading this book, you ever found yourself asking why Oliver is a travel writer, that's why—I created him as a sort of proxy, to get to do something I couldn't do at that moment in time.

And I sent him to Washington, DC because it's a place I love, and knew well enough to write about without being able to go myself at the time. I send my gratitude to everyone in the District for hosting me on my imaginary visit, especially the stewards of the very real places that showed up in this book: Ronald Reagan Washington National Airport; Hillwood Estate, Museum & Gardens; the National Building Museum; the Rayburn House Office Building; Smithsonian's National Zoo & Conservation Biology Institute (and the Carvel ice cream concession at the Panda Overlook); and the heroes who keep our nation's capital moving in the Washington Metropolitan Area Transit Authority. To the residents of the District, my apologies for the vehicular mayhem I unleashed on your streets in these pages, and if you happen to hold a Maryland driver's license, I'll say this: Ricky is entitled to his opinion, but I'm pretty sure he wasn't talking about *you*.

Oliver is also meaningful to me as a representation of an Autistic experience that in some (but not all) ways looks a lot like mine, something I haven't seen much in our culture. His autism isn't a superpower, and it doesn't render him broken; he is self-aware, he is capable, he is learning what success looks like to him, and most of all, he is human. If he's a little further along in parts of his life's journey than I was at his age, well, that's my gift to him. If you, dear reader, are Autistic yourself, or love someone who is, I hope that seeing his experience on these pages has been in some small way a gift to you, too.

A lot of authors will tell you in their acknowledgements about all the people who helped them craft their book, all the people with whom they workshopped ideas and swapped pages, and how they'd have gone crazy if they'd had to do it all by themselves. But I'm an Autistic author, so here's the most Autistic sentence you'll read today: I set out to write a book because it was something I thought I could do alone.

Of course, in the end that's not at all true, and over the course of this trip I've been fortunate to cross paths with a small but mighty group of fellow travelers who have made the journey that much richer and the destination far sweeter. I am grateful to Tory Hunter, the first person outside my house to read this book, for giving me the greatest boost my confidence has ever known; to my wonderful agent, Kimberly Fernando, for all the leaps we decided to take together; to my editor at Kensington, John Scognamiglio, and copy editor Rosemary Silva and production editor Robin Cook, for their polishing and their thoughtful questions; and to Kris Noble for bringing the cover to such sweet life.

Most of all, I am grateful to my husband Johnny. I can only aspire to match the depths of his love and support. I could never really have been alone on this trip; he has, in some way or another, been on every page of this book from day one, and I wouldn't have had it any other way.

Okay, time to do some laundry, but I don't think I'll put my suitcase away. I've got a feeling I'll be headed on another trip with my friends soon—I hope you'll join us for that one, too.

CHAPTER 1

The streetcar rumbled to a stop, along with the rest of the traffic on Market Street, right before it would have smashed the hot dogs.

I was disappointed.

For the past few minutes, my managing editor, Drea, had been standing in front of the plate-glass window in the conference room, transfixed by the crumpled car below us. I had allowed myself to be distracted from the wreck by the hot dogs that had rolled neatly onto the tracks, entertaining fantasies of the meaty carnage that would happen when they met the wheels of the streetcar. Now that wouldn't happen, and all we were left with was the much more sobering possibility of actual human injury.

"God, I hope that's ketchup on the windshield," Drea murmured, snapping my attention back to the car. The noise outside had diverted us from starting our meeting when the green sedan hopped the curb and plowed onto the sidewalk, colliding with the hot dog stand. Now the tip of its nose was just out of our view below, fragments of the shattered cart were strewn all over the sidewalk and street, and the vendor who had been working the steam trays was nowhere to be seen. There was a small crater of cracks in the center of the windshield, which was indeed surrounded by splatters of something shiny and red.

My stomach, which had already been a bit knotty, did a few somersaults as I considered whether it was ketchup. I wished I could have stuck with the distraction of the hot dogs. That had been helping. This was not.

"Okay, you guys, I have another meeting in fifteen, so . . . ?"

Ramona had joined us at the window at first—perhaps the first time I'd ever seen her looking at something other than her phone—but the collision hadn't held her attention long.

With one last look down to the street, Drea and I turned and joined her at the conference table. I unscrewed the cap of my orange water bottle and took a long draw to try to compose myself, though I was fairly certain that was a lost cause by now. I usually worked from home, so a rare summons to the editorial offices in San Francisco tended to fill me with a dread of the unpredictable, especially when it was for a meeting with the big boss, the editor in chief; today had been no different, and the scene outside had further thrown me off-kilter.

Ramona tapped on her phone a few seconds longer, then dove right in. "Oliver, we're sending you on assignment. You're ready."

She still kept her eyes locked firmly on the little screen in her hand as she spoke to me. I had a hard enough time reading people, but her inability to untether and fully engage with others took inscrutability to a new level.

On the upside, at least I didn't have to worry about faking eye contact with her—a particular blessing in my still slightly unsettled state after seeing the crash. Not that she didn't expect your full attention to be on her, regardless of her refusal to reciprocate—she had an uncanny ability to sense when your focus was anywhere but firmly on her. As long as your eyes were pointed in her direction, though, they could land on her ever-typing hands, her terrifyingly perfect, severely chic brown bob, her prodigiously pierced ears, whatever. I'd heard it rumored that her eyes were brown, but I'd never actually seen them, and I hoped I never did.

My own eyes—green, bespectacled—were blinking a bit more than usual as I processed her pronouncement, the crash now forgotten. *Wait, really? A feature assignment? Already?*

Drea chimed in from her spot next to me at the table. "I was telling Ramona about the conversations you and I have had about your interest in feature writing, and we agree you've been doing great work with your FOB pieces." *FOB* meant "front of book," the section of punchier, newsier articles, interviews, and short features that made up the first quarter or so of each month's issue of *Offbeat Traveler*. "We wanted to see how you'd do with something a bit more substantial."

I was still blinking, trying to process this turn the day had taken. In meetings like this, I was always kind of expecting the worst, but this was so far in the other direction that I wasn't sure how to respond. Or maybe *this*—achieving my dream of feature writing after just under a year on the job, which frankly felt way too soon—not something as clean and simple as getting fired, was actually the worst. I had thought I wanted to do this, to be able to travel and see the world—but was I ready? How could I prepare when I hadn't done this before? Had I gotten too ambitious and set myself up for failure? I could feel my usual level of anxiety, which I'd say generally hit somewhere around my belly button, rising fast, bubbling up around my chin, headed for my ears and nose. *Save me, Drea! Save yourself, Oliver! Save me, Ramo*—No, that was ridiculous. Ramona wouldn't save me, because she'd never notice I was drowning.

What she would do was forge ahead with the conversation, blissfully unaware. "We're getting desperate pleas from the flacks in Washington, DC, to help them do a so-called 'reset' on the city's tourism. I don't know, I guess there was some brouhaha or something before the inauguration, and the last administration made people get mad when they thought of DC and hotels in the same sentence." One hand released the phone to wave dismissively. "They're struggling a bit. So you get to go and put a happy face on our nation's capital. No political stuff. Just, like, restaurants and museums and boutiques. You know, the usual deal. Drea has the details."

With the buck passed to her number two, Ramona swiveled in her chair back toward the plate-glass window, which she still didn't care to look out of, crossing her legs and tapping out an emphatic message on her phone that may as well have been a curt GTFO to Drea and me. We were dismissed.

"Don't worry. I have a detailed itinerary," Drea said, as if she had read my mind. She steered me along the outskirts of the bullpen toward her office two doors down from the conference room. "You'll be fine. It really is just talking up a lot of local merchants, plus one or two of the less controversial museums. We have you in a new boutique hotel, which, of course, you'll include in your piece, and everything's really accessible by Metro—you know how they love their subway. Nothing too . . . offbeat," she said wryly, rolling her eyes at what a misnomer our magazine's title had become in the decades since it had been absorbed into its first media conglomerate, then passed from owner to owner.

"I also have a photographer you'll be working with," she continued as she settled into the chair behind her desk and I took the chair across from her. "He's actually an old friend of mine from Howard. His name is Ricky Warner. He's a really fun person—I think you'll hit it off. And he's lived in DC a long time, so he can help you find your way around. He's willing to give you plenty of his time, so you guys should be able to work together most of the time you're there. It'll be really simple, and you'll have a great time. Do you feel okay about this, Oliver?"

Talk about a loaded question. A therapist had explained to me once that some people feel anxious only at the outset of a new situation, like the first day of a new job, but once they feel comfortable in that environment, they can take any new wrinkle, like a new assignment, in stride. I had no idea what that must be like. For me, new is new—and though my job wasn't new to me, this assignment very much was—and new is terrifying, any opportunity an opportunity for failure. But I wanted to tell Drea what she wanted to hear, and hoped that saying it would make me believe it, so I exhaled as many of my nerves as I could. "Yes, I think so. When am I leaving?"

"You leave on Tuesday of next week. I have you flying out of Oakland, into Reagan. You can get on Metro at the airport and take it more or less directly to your hotel—be sure to include that part in your story."

She passed me a folder with a printed itinerary, a map of the Metro system with the stops and transfer stations between the airport and the hotel highlighted, a Metro timetable, lists of contacts, and clippings and press releases from the places I would be visiting. She'd share everything with me electronically, too, I knew, but she knew that I liked to have things on paper to study and that I'd want to start on the BART ride back to Oakland.

This would be okay. I was maybe not as convinced I was ready as Drea and Ramona wanted me to be, but I had said it, so I would believe it: I could do this.

"Of course you can do it, Oliver," my mother was saying.

It was Monday evening, the hours ticking down until I headed to the airport, and I was still having second thoughts, or maybe third or fourth thoughts—it had been a mentally taxing few days—about my readiness for this next step in my nascent career. We were sitting at the table on the deck, and through the window to the kitchen, I could see Aunt Julie and her wife, Deb, washing and drying the dinner dishes. Julie and Deb lived in the downstairs flat of the old high water house that my parents had inherited from my grandparents, but they came up for dinner with my mom and me several times a week.

Spring had finally gotten to the point where the sun was still out at this hour, but it was dropping fast, and a cool breeze and a hint of marine layer were coming in off the Bay.

Breeze or no, I was starting to sweat, and my hands were clammy as I fidgeted with my napkin. "I really don't know. It involves talking to so many people I've never met before."

"You do that all the time for the things you write now. I've heard you do interviews over the phone. You hate the phone, and you still do great with those conversations, so what makes you think you can't do it now?"

"When I do that, I have my questions given to me by someone else. This time I had to come up with them myself. What if they're stupid?"

My mom looked at me, deadpan. "Oliver. You spent nearly a week, including all weekend, doing research. I'm sure the questions you came up with are much better than 'What's the travel toothpaste you can't live without?' which I *know* is one of those questions you've been told to ask before. It's listening, that's all. You're a great listener. Ask your question, listen to what they say, then follow the conversation from there."

I considered this. "Okay, what about this photographer person? I don't know anything about him, but I'm supposed to spend practically all my time with him for four days. How am I supposed to do that?"

"You know Drea speaks highly of him, and Drea's your friend, right? She wouldn't put you in a situation she didn't think you could handle, so I think it's safe to assume he's a nice person who you'll get along with fine." She gave me a funny look, waggling her eyebrows. "Maybe you'll even . . . *like* . . . each other."

I could never really tell what people thought of me, but I thought Drea liked me. I knew I liked her; she was the only person at work I'd felt comfortable telling about my autism, and since then, she'd looked out for me. If my default instinct going into new situations at work was that I was going to mess up and get fired, I could usually reassure myself that Drea would give me enough information that I wouldn't mess up, and that even if I did, she wouldn't fire me anyway.

As for . . . *liking* . . . this photographer person, this Ricky—well, that seemed like wishful thinking on my mom's part. I wouldn't even know where to begin with something like that. I had tried once, while I was at Cal, and it had gone nowhere; Benjamin Chao and I had circled each other for two years, constantly finding ourselves sitting next to each other in classes or in social settings but barely ever exchanging more than a sentence or two. He was cute, and we were able to establish that we were both gay and Autistic, but if we'd had more in common than that, we'd never sussed out how to find out. I figured that was about what I could expect—even if the pang I felt around my rib cage when I told myself that said I wished it were otherwise.

Julie and Deb came through the open kitchen door, Julie flicking the switch to turn on the lights strung over the deck as she stepped out. Deb waved as she headed toward the stairs down from the deck to the door to their flat below, but Julie dropped into the chair next to my mom.

They looked so alike and so different at the same time: the same small noses, the same high cheekbones, the same natural golden highlights in their hair, shot with gray on my mom and intertwining with a pink streak on Julie; but where my mom was covered against the breeze in a sensible cardigan, Julie's tank top put her tattoos and the tangle of silver chains around her neck on display.

This was my cue to leave. Julie and my mom had "sisterly business to discuss"—code for idle girl talk—and I had a bag to finish packing.

"Hey, kiddo," Julie said as I got up. "Have fun on your trip. I know you've got a lot of stuff you're supposed to do, but if something goes wrong, don't sweat it. It'll give you something else to write about. Hell, maybe you should even *try* to get lost or something. Shake it up! Live a little! This is a big opportunity, but also a good chance to be young and dumb and have fun."

"Thank you, Aunt Julie," I said politely. "I'll remember that."

I could hear her laughing, not exactly at me, but at my love of organization and sticking to schedules, as I went inside and headed up the stairs to my room in the attic. I had to grin, too. She wasn't wrong, but I would try my hardest not to follow her advice.

As I entered my room, I tapped the screen of my phone on my dresser and saw that I had gotten a text from an unfamiliar number. I swiped it open. It read, **Hey, Oliver, this is Drea's photographer friend, Ricky. Looking forward to working with you. I'll meet you at the airport tomorrow, and we can get started right away. Look for this mug.** Below this was a photo, a self-portrait, I supposed, but more well composed and shot than the average selfie.

I studied the photo. It was closely cropped around his face. He was smiling broadly, showing off straight white teeth and deep dimples. Thick eyebrows arched mischievously, and under them his dark eyes twinkled and crinkled at the corners as he looked at something up and to the left. His skin was a deep golden brown, and his hair was shaved nearly bald on the sides of his head, exploding into a small mop of loose dark brown curls on top.

I could feel myself getting flustered again as I pored over the photo, and I decided to blame my mom. Why did she have to put *that* idea into my head? Why did he have to be so . . . *hot*? I felt a flash of the familiar dullness in my chest, dread at the idea of another attraction I didn't know how to act on.

I was also feeling the prick of rising sweat again as I debated whether I had to respond or not. I checked the time; it was 7:48 p.m., so it would be 10:48 p.m. on the East Coast. I decided that, even if Ricky wasn't still up, the polite thing was to respond and figure he'd see it in the morning.

Thanks! My flight gets in at 4:56 p.m., so I'll see you shortly after that, and we can take Metro to my hotel, I typed, wondering if I was being too formal by being so exact with the time. Certainly he wasn't getting a selfie in return. He'd have to wait to find out what I looked like tomorrow. It was the only chance I'd ever have of having the upper hand with someone who looked like *that*. I clicked his picture again to enlarge it. Yep, I was definitely sweating.

A distraction was needed. Really, it was the picture that had been the distraction; I had things to get done. I threw the phone down on my bed and added a few neatly folded shirts to my half-packed duffel bag, counted pairs of socks and underwear again, decided that one extra pair of each was cutting it too close, and added a couple more. Then I caught myself. What did I think I was going to do with this guy that I would need multiple changes of socks and underwear a day?

I rolled my eyes at myself and put most of the new additions back into the drawer. I laid out the clothes I planned to wear tomorrow on top of the dresser and set my blue canvas Vans neatly on the floor below, ready for the airport security theater shuffle, and moved to the bathroom to pack my toiletry bag.

I packed everything except the items I'd need the next morning and wandered back into my room as I brushed my teeth. I glanced as casually as I could down at the phone on my bed to see if there had been another text, growing even more resentful at my mother when I saw that there wasn't. Why had she gotten me thinking of this like some kind of setup when it was nothing more than a professional engagement to work with someone? I was sure that was all it was to this Ricky person, who probably already had lots of his own friends and a girlfriend or something.

That's right, Oliver, I told myself. *Assume he's not even an*

*option. It's not like you need the headache of trying to figure out
what to do in that situation again anyway. Or the heartburn.*

Grabbing Drea's folder from my desk, I plopped down on
the edge of the bed and pulled out the travel itinerary I had
prepared for tomorrow, even more detailed than the one she
had given me. It read:

- 5:00 a.m.: Get up and go for a run
- 5:45 a.m.: Get home, shower, and get dressed
- 6:10 a.m.: Breakfast
- 6:35 a.m.: Walk to MacArthur BART
- 6:54 a.m.: Catch the Orange train toward
  Berryessa/North San Jose
- 7:09 a.m.: Exit the Orange train at the Coliseum
  station
- 7:18 a.m.: Catch the spur line from Coliseum to
  Oakland International Airport
- 7:27 a.m.: Arrive at Oakland International Airport
- 8:35 a.m.: Depart Oakland International Airport on
  United, with nonstop service to Ronald Reagan
  Washington National Airport
- 4:56 p.m. (EDT): Arrive Ronald Reagan Washington
  National Airport, walk to National Airport Metro
  Station
- 5:32 p.m.: Catch the Yellow Line train toward Mt.
  Vernon Square
- 5:46 p.m.: Exit the Yellow Line train at the Gallery
  Place–Chinatown station, locate platform for Red
  Line trains
- 5:54 p.m.: Catch the Red Line train toward Glenmont
- 5:58 p.m.: Exit the Red Line train at Union Station,
  walk to hotel

I closed my eyes and flopped backward onto the bed, trying
distractedly to memorize the various colors and terminal sta-

tions for my train rides, trying not to picture Ricky's shining eyes laughing up at me from my phone, and failing at both tasks.

Nothing like an early morning run, when you could be alone in the world for the last little while before the darkness lifted and the day began, concentrating on nothing but breathing and moving, to refocus your mind. At least, this was what I was trying to tell myself on Tuesday morning, but honestly, my breathing and moving were pretty automatic after so many years of covering the same route day after day, and my mind was free to wander.

Thankfully, my brain had moved on to a new preoccupation: the logistics of my travel that day. I had checked into my flight the previous morning, exactly twenty-four hours before departure, and gotten my seat assignment, a window seat in economy, in a mid-pack boarding group. So I'd be part of the herd shuffling onto the plane, wrestling for overhead bin space, although as a not very tall person, I had a habit of deferentially putting my duffel bag under the seat in front of me—I didn't need the foot space as much or the hassle of reaching up to the bins. As I steered from the light puddle of one streetlight to the next on autopilot, I visualized the process: queuing up at the gate, trudging down the Jetway, finding my seat, tucking my bag at my feet, wrestling the seat belt into submission (how do they always get so tangled?), and then probably closing my eyes and praying my seatmate wouldn't be a talker or a total armrest hog or smell too strongly of anything. This was doable. I visualized myself doing it all and making it out alive.

The person and the assignment waiting for me at the end of the flight? Best not to get ahead of myself; it was a nearly six-hour flight, after all. If I paced my visualization correctly, I wouldn't get to that part until we were halfway to DC, and by then there would be nothing to do about it, except maybe channel my panic into the crossword puzzle in the in-flight magazine.

I had been winding through mostly residential streets in this reverie, but now I was rounding the corner onto 51st Street, which expanded to six lanes right here as Highway 24 fed onto it and it approached Telegraph Avenue, where it was lined with shopping centers and storefronts. Time to be a little more aware.

There was usually very little traffic out during my predawn runs, even at this major intersection, but I still liked to be vigilant. I didn't run with headphones, partly for this reason, although mostly it was because, as much as I liked listening to music while doing mindless things, I wasn't a big fan of putting things on my head or face.

On this Tuesday morning, it was even quieter than usual. There was a soft hum coming from the freeway behind me, but no cars exited onto the street. I reached the corner at Telegraph and scanned to each side; no cars were coming from either direction. An extra-short block down Telegraph to my left, Claremont Avenue angled down to terminate its descent from the Berkeley Hills. I saw no headlights coming down Claremont, either, but I noticed that it was unusually dark. A series of streetlights seemed to have gone out over there all at once, and the cloud cover blocking out the moon didn't help.

I had the light and began to jog across Telegraph. As I stepped off the curb, I caught a flash of movement out of the corner of my eye and became aware of the slap of tires and the whoosh of air being sliced by something large, the distinctively droning near silence of an electric car approaching fast.

I jerked my head toward Claremont in time to see a sleek sedan, a Moonshot MS-100, speeding toward me, running a red light from Claremont onto Telegraph and hurtling forward. The car's headlights were off—no wonder I hadn't seen it coming down that darkened stretch—but through the windshield, the driver's face was faintly illuminated by the telltale glow of a phone, his eyes cast downward, and I could see in its ambient light that he was using it with both hands.

I had a split second to react as the car careened into the lane, coming straight toward me, and a burst of adrenaline propelled me forward in a sprint long enough for me to clear the lane as the car blew through its second red light in a matter of seconds.

In a daze, I spun on my heel in the middle of the crosswalk to watch my near-death experience drive away under the streetlights of Telegraph Avenue. I wheezed out a winded "Hey!" knowing the driver wouldn't hear it and would never know what had nearly just happened. Shaking, I turned back and finished crossing the street.

I needed to get back home. I tried to tap into the adrenaline to start running again, but I was coming down from the jolt and quickly had to slow to a haggard walk. I panted and fumed the rest of the way.

What was with all these vehicular disasters lately? What had that driver been doing? It occurred to me that the phone-addled individual behind the wheel probably hadn't actually been doing the driving. The Moonshot, with its Silicon Valley sheen, had quickly become an "it" toy for wealthy Bay Area techno-snobs and eco-show-offs, but behind the glowing promises of fully autonomous driving pumped out by the company's attention-hungry CEO-slash-pitchman, Kelso King, there had been ugly rumblings that the car wasn't ready for prime time. I'd seen stories of allegedly self-driving Moonshots driving themselves through guardrails and off hillsides, into a marina and very nearly into the Pacific, and, in one memorable case, through a Starbucks drive-thru at thirty-five miles per hour, with nobody inside the car.

Now it seemed these stories of disaster had almost added me to their ranks. How could the self-driving system be allowed to operate without headlights? Why was it ignoring traffic signals and speed limits? Should I be calling the cops on this guy? I had no license plate number, no idea where he was going—in the darkness, I hadn't even been able to tell what color the car was. There was nothing to be done but try to get over the anger, be grateful I was safe, and resolve to be extra careful when I saw a Moonshot headed my way in the future, assuming I'd be able to see it coming.

I didn't begin to feel even halfway human again until I had showered and had my first sips of orange juice. My mother sat with me, nursing a cup of coffee, while I had my breakfast. I decided not to worry her by telling her what had happened. She surprised me by asking if she could walk with me to the BART station and see me off.

"Indulge your old mother," she said. "Going off on your first big assignment is like the grown-up version of your first day of school, and I want to see it."

I agreed, and soon I was shrugging my father's old green utility jacket over my blue button-down oxford, grabbing my duffel, and meeting my mother at the door.

It was still mostly overcast and cool as we walked down the street, but I knew the sun would break through by late morning, giving my mother a beautiful spring day to enjoy. My weather app had told me that Washington would be having a beautiful spring day, too, but I'd be trapped on a plane for most of it. Fortunately, the rest of the week promised to be every bit as nice.

"So," my mother began, "have you thought through your trip today? Ready to do this?"

"Yep," I said, trying to be breezy and not get ahead of myself by visualizing the scary part. In my visualization I figured I was still somewhere above Nebraska, still thousands of miles from having to meet new people and trying to take my career to a momentous, terrifying new level, but no need to tell my mother that.

"I know it's helpful for you to have your itinerary," she said gently, falling back into the old role of pep-talking coach she had so patiently cultivated when I was younger, "but don't forget that once you get there and start to feel comfortable, it's okay to let things happen a little more organically."

I gave her a sidelong glance. "Et tu, Brute?"

She laughed lightly. "You maybe don't have to take it as far as what Aunt Julie said . . . What was it? 'Be dumb and have fun'? But you only have to rely on your tools as long as you need them. Your itinerary is like training wheels on a bike. Eventually, you can ride without them, right?"

"I never got my training wheels off," I pointed out.

"Well, maybe that was the wrong metaphor, but you know what I mean."

After a few steps in silence, she abruptly changed the subject. "So, Aunt Julie and Aunt Deb have been talking about moving to Sacramento, and last night Julie told me they're pulling the trigger. They want to be closer to Aunt Deb's parents, and they found a place there and will be moving next month."

I took this in. My aunts had moved in years ago, in the aftermath of the one-two punch of the loss of my grandmother—my mom's mother, who had lived in the downstairs flat before—and my dad within three months of each other. I guess Julie and Deb thought we needed them then and Deb's parents, in declining health, needed them now.

"Now we'll actually have to find tenants," I mused. Ugh, strangers living right under us. Could we count on them to be quiet? Not to smoke in the yard or burn their cooking or run the washer and dryer at night, when I could hear them as clearly as if they were in the room with me, even though I was as far from them as was possible in our house? Julie and Deb were family, and they knew how to live with us.

"Well-ll," my mom said, drawing the word out, "I was

thinking maybe you'd like to move downstairs. A little independence, but still close to me?"

"Huh. I wouldn't have thought of that."

"Not that I'm trying to get rid of you! I was just thinking, you've got your degree, you have a job, you're doing well— maybe this is the next step. And maybe you need a little more privacy sometimes. Maybe I do, too."

"What do you mean, privacy?"

I wasn't sure if I was asking about her privacy or mine, but she chose to focus on mine. "Oliver, you're an adult, and it's fine if you want to date or invite friends over, and I'm sure if you did, you'd rather not have your mother in your hair."

"It's nice of you to think that, but where are these dates and friends coming from?" There was that lonely pang again.

She sighed. "They're coming from you paying more attention to how people talk and act around you. I know you don't want to hear this from your mother, but you're a nice, smart, cute boy, and people respond to that. They want to get to know you. Remember when we went out to dinner last week? That waiter was falling all over you!"

I thought back. The waiter had struck me as an incredibly absent-minded individual, constantly coming around to top off my water when I had barely had any. My main takeaways from the experience had been a bloated feeling and an urgent need to get home so I could pee, not flirtatious thoughts of the person who had put me in that position. Maybe I did need to pay more attention, but, I realized with dismay, I wasn't sure what it was I was supposed to pay attention to.

"Or, I don't know," she continued, "you could invite some of your coworkers over. It wouldn't be a bad thing to get to know them better."

We had arrived at the entrance to the MacArthur BART station. The first wave of morning commuters bustled around us as my mother wrapped me in a hug—something only she was allowed to do—and I tried not to blush.

"Anyway, think about the apartment," she said as I turned toward the entrance. "We can talk more about it when you get home. And remember what I said about being open to changing things up if you need to. Have fun, and stay safe!"

I gave a little wave and headed for the turnstile, sighing a little to myself as I turned away from my mother. Why was she throwing all of this at me *now*? I had other things to worry about than an apartment—like sticking to my itinerary, the only way I knew how to make this trip a success, everybody's advice to the contrary be damned.

CHAPTER 2

"We've been cleared for departure. Flight attendants, arm doors. Cross-check."

Getting through the airport, to the gate, and onto the plane had all gone according to plan. I had stashed my duffel at my feet, settled back into my window seat, and closed my eyes to shut out the quiet, slow-motion jumble of the rest of the passengers jockeying for overhead bin space, climbing over one another into their seats, trying to negotiate their children into closer seats or other people's children into seats farther away, and making inane requests of the flight crew just because they could. My kingdom for the ability to comfortably use headphones or earbuds, but such is my lot in life, I suppose.

I wasn't into the chaos, but I knew that once everyone was strapped in and the plane started to taxi and the tightly controlled choreography of the safety spiel began, I wouldn't be able to look away. As we lurched away from the gate, I opened my eyes, ready for the show, and became uncomfortably aware that the person sitting in the middle seat next to me seemed to be staring very intently in my direction.

I didn't want to turn and look and end up eye to eye, so I focused downward and fumbled around as if I was looking for the safety card in the seat-back pocket and did a quick glance out of the corner of my eye. The knee to my left was a woman's, clad in jeans, with ballet flats on the feet sticking out below. Her hands fidgeted in her lap; there was fresh pink polish on her nails. That was as much as I could tell from this vantage point.

Well, that wasn't entirely true. My nose told me that although it was not yet nine in the morning, she had managed to find an open airport bar, or maybe she had pregamed before leaving home. And she was laser focused on me. Great.

She seemed about to make her move, but at that moment the flight crew launched into the safety presentation. I watched raptly as they swayed up and down the aisle, miming the proper use of seat belts, oxygen masks, and life vests and doing that two-handed, two-finger point toward the emergency exit doors that only they are allowed to do unironically. I meant for my body language to make it very clear how important I found this information, and I suppose it worked, but as soon as the floor show was over, she made her move, ducking into my field of vision so aggressively that I couldn't pretend not to see, although I didn't yet meet her eyes.

"Ollie Popp? That *is* you, isn't it?"

I winced. I hadn't heard that one in a long time, but I found I didn't hate it any less now than I had as a kid, when my classmates would sing it at me to the tune of the fifties pop song "Lollipop."

"*Oliver* Popp, yes," I replied and felt a jolt of recognition as I looked up and her face finally swam into focus. "Elise?"

"Yeah!" It was a little huskier than I remembered, but the breathy laugh of Elise Perkins was unmistakable.

I laughed a little, too, reflexively. I hadn't seen Elise Perkins in about seven years, but in my memory, she was surrounded by laughter, a bright, happy, gawky, goofy sun around whom others had orbited and in whose light we had basked. She had been a year ahead of me in high school, and we'd been teammates on the quiz bowl squad, my one extracurricular activity. She had been our team captain in her junior and senior years, and it had never occurred to any of the rest of us that anyone else could be. We hadn't been close friends, but she was the type of person who, if she knew you and she saw you in the hallway or out at lunch, would always have a smile and a warm greeting for you. I wasn't sure, but I thought she might also have been a captain of the swim team, and she had been an officer in the Black Student Union. She racked up an impressive résumé of AP test scores, was valedictorian of her class, headed off to MIT in a blaze of glory, and I hadn't seen her since, until now.

Now she was sitting next to me on a plane, a grown woman with a little less baby fat in her cheeks and a little less light in her eyes but the same bright smile on her lips. Her top half was ready for a comfortable flight in a soft-looking baby-blue turtleneck sweater, and despite the early hour and the suggestion of booze on her breath, she was perfectly coifed and groomed and seemed to have added a little more poise to her arsenal of charms.

"What are you doing here?" we asked each other in unison, then burst out laughing again.

"You first," I said.

"Just a work trip to DC," she said. "You?"

"Yeah, me, too. What are you doing these days?"

Her voice dropped, as though her answer was a secret. "So, you've heard of Moonshot Motors, right? Electric cars, Kelso King, self-driving, big hype, blah, blah, blah? I'm on the team developing the autonomous driving software."

I flashed back to that morning's near miss and might have blanched a little, but she seemed to take it as a sign that I was impressed.

She continued, "My specialty is AI, you know, artificial intelligence, machine learning—that's what I studied at MIT. I'm working to make it so that the cars don't make the same mistakes twice—or at least not too many times. At this point, I feel like I should point out that the stuff I'm working on is, like, five years more advanced than what's on the road right now."

"I should hope so," I blurted out. She gave me a quizzical look, and I explained, "I nearly got run over this morning by one of your cars, and I'm pretty sure it was driving itself. It was speeding and running red lights, too."

She sighed and lowered her eyes to her hands in her lap, which had resumed fidgeting nervously. "I'm sorry that happened to you. It's been happening a lot, to the point that we don't even understand how it can be happening so much."

"Hey, I'm okay," I said. "I didn't mean to sound like I was accusing you of anything. Some kind of weird coincidence, I guess."

She flashed me a sad half smile. "That's the party line: they're coincidences. See, I'm actually going to testify in front of a House committee as a representative of the self-driving team. This congressman, Dean Randall—he represents a big, old-school car industry district in Michigan, so not like he's biased or anything—he wants to introduce regulations on how self-driving features are tested and rolled out to consumers. Basically, a bureaucratic framework that the legacy automakers are already used to, but that will slow down us Silicon Valley upstarts so they can catch up."

She was growing more animated, but there was still a hard edge to her voice. "So anyway, I get to be the face of progress and try to explain away all these problems and say we don't need any oversight or regulation. Typical techno-libertarian BS."

"It seems like you're a little conflicted," I said.

"I mean, the thing is, none of this is really my job," she said. "And really, I'm not the only one making this case—we have a whole team going to testify, including King and a bunch of muckety-mucks. I'm mostly there to explain the technology, how we develop and test it, that kind of thing.

"Honestly," she said, grabbing my arm and leaning in conspiratorially, her already hushed voice dropping even lower, "I'm pretty sure the only reason I'm one of the witnesses is because I'm the only woman, and the only person of color, on the self-driving team."

"They're tokenizing you?"

"Yeah, ain't that a kick in the head?" She laughed again, even huskier this time and more unpleasant.

As we had been talking, a flight attendant had been coming down the aisle with a tablet, taking drink orders. Now she had reached us, and she asked if I wanted a beverage. I ordered a water. She turned to Elise, who ordered a Bloody Mary and gave me a wink as she handed over her credit card.

I had already smelled something on her breath. She clearly wasn't drunk, but she seemed to have a mind to get there. This was not the kind, ebullient Elise I had known in high school. I wondered sadly how she had gotten to a point where she seemed so unhappy.

But as soon as the flight attendant moved on and Elise turned her attention back to me, it seemed as though I had been mistaken. The clouds had parted, and her eyes shone.

"I'm going to have some fun while I'm in DC, though," she declared, as if willing the subject to change. "I've got an old friend to look up while I'm there." That sounded nice enough, but her meaning became clear when she mouthed the words *booty call*. I laughed self-consciously.

"So, you said you were on a work trip, too," she said. "What are you doing?"

I felt a momentary surge of pride, followed by immense anxiety that I was a fraud. When I'd run into acquaintances and answered this question before, I'd always downplayed my job: *Oh, I'm just writing little stuff that nobody reads.* But this time, I could truthfully say what I'd always wanted to say, even if it didn't seem quite true yet and wouldn't until I saw the results in print. I said it anyway.

"I'm a travel writer. I'm doing an article for *Offbeat Traveler* on the latest tourism trends in DC."

"Ooh, sexy!" Okay, now I was embarrassed, but she seemed very impressed. "So, like, you get to go to all kinds of restaurants and museums and stuff for free, right?"

I nodded as the flight attendant returned with our drinks. Elise took a deep pull on her Bloody Mary. Licking her lips with satisfaction, she came up for air. Then, as though she had been hit by a lightning bolt of inspiration, she grabbed my arm again and turned to me. So much arm grabbing—I was glad I had my jacket on, but still tensed at the touch.

"A writer! A journalist! Omigod. We're putting on a press event tomorrow night. Trying to get out in front of the hearings, you know? You should totally come. Even if you don't write about it or anything, it'll be fun and we can hang out."

I did not have room in my schedule the next day for some PR event that had nothing to do with my assignment, but before I could figure out a tactful way to say so, Elise had popped up in her seat, drink still in hand, craning her head wildly as if looking for someone.

She spotted her prey. "Joey!" she called, a little too loudly, to a man sitting across the aisle and two rows behind us. A baby murmured nearby at the sound, and someone behind us hissed, "Shhhh!"

I could feel my face flush with embarrassment, but Elise seemed not to notice that she was making a scene. Still facing backward on her knees in her seat, she took another swig of her drink with one hand and with the other beckoned the man to get up and come over to us.

"Joey, this is my old friend Ollie—Oliver, sorry—and he's a journalist, and I was telling him about our event tomorrow," she said once her colleague had joined us, bracing himself with an arm against the overhead bins and hunching slightly to have a more direct line of sight to us. He was maybe a couple of years older than me, with a neatly trimmed beard and prematurely thinning hair, fastidiously dressed for business travel in pressed slacks and a lightweight gray sweater over a collared shirt. His eyes lit up at the word *journalist*, and he gave me another appraising look, practically licking his lips.

He reached across the row to shake my hand. His offered palm was velvety soft, with an unnatural hint of damp, making me think of moisturizer. Internally, my skin was crawling, but I maintained my outward composure, even though he held on to my hand longer than I was comfortable with. "Oliver, it's a pleasure to meet you. Joseph Harris, Moonshot Motors media team—you can call me Joey." He gave a mock-annoyed look at Elise. "What outlet are you with?"

"Uh . . ." I was still thinking unpleasant thoughts about the horrors of lotion, so it took me a beat to process the question. I wasn't sure if the honest answer would be the right one, but Elise swooped in to save me.

"He's with New American Specialty Media. You know, *Motor Mania*, *Business Daily*, all kinds of stuff we want to be in." This was technically true; NASM was *Offbeat Traveler*'s parent company. I was impressed that Elise knew this and had been so quick to use it.

"Oh, that's *great*," Joey enthused.

I gave him my email address in automatic response to his request, and he promised to send me the details and put me on the list to get press credentials to enter the event, though I didn't want to introduce even a hint of this complication to my itinerary.

A flight attendant down the aisle had been giving Joey the evil eye, and the poor elderly woman in the aisle seat next to Elise, who had been resolutely feigning sleep since takeoff, was struggling to maintain the façade, the corners of her mouth twitching with displeasure, so I was relieved that Joey returned to his seat and didn't linger any longer.

"Ooh, you better watch out," Elise whispered to me as he left us. "He's gonna email you an invitation to more than our little event." I gave her a puzzled look, and she returned it with a slightly bleary-eyed puzzled look of her own from over the rim of her cup. "Oh, sorry. Have you not come out yet?"

"Oh, wow," I stammered. That Bloody Mary had really loosened her up. "Uh, yeah, I guess so."

"Thank *god*," she said. "I was so worried in high school that you were going to stay in your little shell forever."

"So, wait," I said, still trying to catch up. "You think he's interested in me?"

"Duh, Oliver. That handshake? I thought he was writing something dirty in your palm with his fingers, it lasted so long. And you saw him checking you out."

My mom was right; I really did need to pay closer attention. But in my defense, he had distracted me by flaunting his moisturizing regimen in my face, which was definitely a turnoff now that I considered him in this new light.

Our conversation faltered for a moment while I mulled this over. Elise downed the last of her drink and wedged the empty cup into the seat-back pocket in front of her, exchanging it for the in-flight magazine.

"Oh, goody, look. If it isn't my benevolent overlord," she said, waving the cover toward me. Kelso King, the CEO of Moonshot Motors, flashed a blindingly white, too-perfect smile through the windshield of an MS-300 sports car. He was wearing aviator sunglasses, his hair blowing in a way that no person's hair had ever actually blown while driving a convertible, and there was a similarly artfully wind-blown blond woman with oversized shades of her own in the passenger seat next to him, pouting through artificially plumped lips. *Get ready for a sexy eco-getaway!* the cover copy extolled. *Oof.*

I asked Elise, "Is he really as hands-on as he wants everyone to believe?"

She rolled her eyes. "We get our marching orders by reading the same tweets as everyone else," she sighed. "He'll tweet something like, 'I've asked my team to make sure our cars could drive themselves to the top of Mount Everest with no human intervention,' and we'll just be like, 'Girl, what? Bye.'" She waved the magazine dismissively, almost clocking her possum-playing neighbor in the face with a corner of it.

"It's ridiculous. He's so fake. I met him once, and I guess I'll meet him again when we brief tomorrow, before our testimony, but no, he's not hanging around with engineers or in the factory, like he claims he is."

I pulled out my own copy and studied the photo. "Those teeth look pretty fake, too," I observed.

"Oh god, you should look up a photo of him two years ago. Night and day. They're veneers. It's his girlfriend there, the queen of fillers. She's got him doing that, too."

As I flipped through the pages to find the article, I asked, "What's her story?"

"She's so weird," Elise said. "I mean, I haven't met her, but everything I've heard or read about her is bizarre. They supposedly met when he hired her to do a spiritual cleansing of his house after his last divorce. As far as I can tell, her only real job is being an influencer on social media—lots of inspirational, meaningless words, with pictures of expensive stuff that happens to be tagged so you, too, can buy it."

I found the article, which, in true airplane magazine fashion, turned out to be an ad-choked two-page spread toward the back of the book, despite the cover treatment. It was mostly about how Moonshot had set up what they termed "Independence Hubs" at several major US airports, which I gathered were essentially car rental kiosks, with an all-Moonshot fleet, that had done away with human employees. They then passed these savings along to their customers by charging exponentially higher daily rates than anyone else's for the honor of driving away in an electric status symbol.

There was another photo of King and the woman, whom the article referred to only once and only as "Mimi." If she had a last name, it was apparently assumed that we already knew it. In the photo, she was daintily dropping a small Louis Vuitton bag into the trunk of the MS-300, while King unplugged it from a sleek freestanding charger. The merest sliver of pavement was visible in the foreground of the photo, while behind the action was a breathtaking vista of desert and mountains. The caption identified this as the Independence Hub at the Palm Springs airport, the smallest of their six locations and apparently built largely at Mimi's insistence.

Elise had been scanning the article, too, and, as if reading my mind, said, "She had him build that one so all her friends could use it when they fly in for Coachella. They have a place out in Palm Springs, too, but no way are they renting a car like the rest of us schmucks. They get picked up from the airport in a limo wherever they go."

"Gee, the article really wants us to know how rich he is," I observed. "All these phrases . . . 'maverick billionaire,' 'tycoon with a Texas twang,' 'endless resources.' "

"That one's especially rich," Elise snorted, then caught herself. "Ha! Pun intended."

"Where did his money come from? Is it all the car company? I thought you guys were losing a ton of money."

"Okay, so I actually know this," Elise whispered conspiratorially. "Nobody else knows. You know how he presents himself as this, like, man of mystery, right, and wants everybody to think he's self-made? Total hooey." She leaned forward as she spoke, riffling through her seat-back pocket and coming up with a slightly crumpled napkin, which she smoothed on the edge of her armrest. "Do you have a pen? I don't want to say it out loud."

I pulled a pen out of the inside pocket of my jacket, clicked it open, and handed it to her. She pulled down her tray table to create a writing surface, and cupping her hand over the napkin to shield it from the still closed eyes of the woman next to her, she wrote a single word: *oil*.

I whispered, "That seems kind of at odds with what he's doing now. Was he himself involved, or was it a family thing?"

"Both. King isn't his real last name. He's been really secretive about it, but I think he's hoping if it ever comes out, he can say he started building electric cars to ease his troubled conscience. But I'm fairly certain he's still heavily invested in the old family firm."

"If nobody knows about this, where did you hear about it?"

She winked at me. "If you do get a—ahem—*personal* invitation from your new friend Joey and decide to go, you should probably know beforehand that he's a horrible gossip. So don't do anything with him you wouldn't want everyone, including your mother, to know about. Now, how he knew about this little tidbit, I'm not sure."

Writing about Moonshot Motors and Kelso King was not in any way related to the purpose of my trip, but I filed this information away as interesting and potentially useful in the future if I got really ambitious and wanted to try a little moonlighting at another NASM title. Joseph the PR rep might not be so loose-lipped in a strictly professional setting, but if Elise was right, could I Mata Hari some juicy tidbits out of Joey the over-moisturized flirt using these wiles I apparently had?

Elise had drifted back to her in-flight magazine, so I entertained myself with this outlandish scenario of questionable journalistic ethics as I flipped my own copy to the crossword. I whizzed through the puzzle, completing it on the "across" clues, then sat back and closed my eyes to recover from the drains of the morning: the early morning scare with the runaway car, the trip to the airport, all the people and noise and smells of the airport, even reconnecting with Elise.

As I dozed off, the last thing I was aware of was the flight attendant making another pass for drink orders and Elise requesting another Bloody Mary.

* * *

I slept longer and more soundly than I expected. By the time I woke up, we had started our descent into National Airport. I opened the shade on my window and watched the Virginia countryside turn into outer suburbs, then to suburban sprawl as we dipped lower and lower.

As the wheels hit the runway and we were pushed back into our seats by the force of the flaps coming up from the wings to slow us down, I realized that I hadn't given much thought to visualizing the rest of my day, or the next several days, or to my imminent rendezvous with the photographer, Ricky.

My brain still slightly scrambled from sleep, I tried frantically for a moment to run through the rest of the day's itinerary in my mind, curling my fingers inward and raking my fingernails roughly through the sweat in my palms in an effort to jolt myself into alertness. I realized with dismay I'd have to wing it for a bit, until I was on the first leg of my Metro ride and could look back at my notes and get my bearings. Not my preferred way of doing things, but, oh well—here went nothing.

CHAPTER 3

Elise and I chatted a bit as we waited to deplane and as we trooped up the Jetway into the terminal. She put my number into her phone, texted me so I'd have hers, and promised we'd hang out at the Moonshot press event the following evening, which she seemed to take as a given I'd attend. I wasn't sure what more we had to talk about, and I already had my schedule mapped out, so I'd have to figure out how to beg off, but right now I had other things on my mind.

I was distracted, trying to gather myself for the rest of my day, so I was a bit relieved when Elise peeled away from me in the terminal to find a restroom and I was left to make my way to baggage claim, where I had no bags to claim but a photographer to meet, in solitude.

I'm a fast walker, so navigating through airport terminal traffic was always a bit like looking for the right gaps between the cars in a game of *Frogger*. As I weaved and bobbed, I was struck by a revelation that opened up a pit in my stomach: by not sending Ricky a picture of myself, I'd made it so that he wouldn't recognize me, and *I* would have to approach *him*. Stupid, stupid, stupid!

I slowed my pace a bit. Did I have to pee? Yes, I did. Luckily, you're never too far from a restroom in the airport, so I ducked into the next men's room I encountered and tried to relax myself from the tension I felt rapidly rising from my stomach to my chest. I blew out a couple of forceful breaths before the corner of my eye caught the guy at the next urinal staring at me like I was crazy.

I finished up and moved to the sink to wash my hands. I didn't want to stare at myself in the mirror in this crowded bathroom, but I stole a few glances as I lathered and rinsed. Did I look crazy? No. Maybe a little flushed. I exhaled forcefully a couple more times, this time through my nose, as I dried my hands and rejoined the flow of bodies moving toward the terminal exit.

I felt a little disoriented, more aware than usual of my body, my extremities, more conscious of their movements, which made those movements feel more forced, less fluid. *Get it together, Oliver.* I kept up the deep breaths as I moved more slowly and carefully than usual past the security checkpoint toward the baggage claim. Within a moment, I was back to earth, feeling almost normal. Only a little low-grade panic to make sure I'd be extra awkward when I found Ricky.

I started scanning as I entered the baggage claim area. It was too soon for my flight to have a carousel, but a couple of the belts were moving, disgorging luggage from other flights. There were crowds around them, but it stood to reason Ricky wouldn't be among those. I gave the periphery of the room a good sweep, checking out the people slumped in the rows of chairs or leaning against columns or along the windows facing out to the arrivals pickup lane.

It took two passes around the chairs for me to pick him out. He was sitting next to a large older woman, almost hidden behind her, and for some reason, he had sunglasses on even though he was indoors. He was wearing a utility jacket a lot like mine, but black instead of green, over a black-and-white-striped T-shirt, dark-wash jeans, and a well-worn pair of black leather boots. As I walked toward him, he shifted uncomfortably in his seat, his arms crossed with one hand raised to support his chin, crossing and uncrossing his legs.

He noticed me once I was within a few yards, and he stood and pushed his shades up onto his head, breaking into a somewhat more guarded, shifty-eyed version of the smile I had seen in his picture last night. "Oliver?"

What a relief. He had figured me out, even without knowing what I looked like. "Yeah, it's nice to meet you. Thanks for sending a picture—"

"Do you have any bags you need to wait for? No? Okay, this way." He gave my arm a small tug as he pushed past me, and started walking rapidly down the walkway along the front of the terminal. Caught off guard, and trying to ignore the sinking feeling that this was not going to go well, *at all*, I spun around and hustled to keep up.

What was up with this guy? He wasn't much taller than me, but he was making long strides and I was nearly at a jog when suddenly, with a quick look over his shoulder, he slowed down. I almost walked right into him.

He turned to me. "Sorry about that," he said with a grin. "While I was waiting back there, I realized I was in a direct line of sight from the American ticketing counter, and I noticed someone working behind that counter that I . . . wanted to avoid. But I think we're in the clear now."

"You have enemies?" I asked, baffled.

"I don't know if I'd go that far," he chuckled. "Just someone I kinda ghosted on a while back. I mean, it would be confusing, wouldn't it, if you saw someone who was supposed to have taken a once-in-a-lifetime fellowship in Helsinki casually sitting twenty feet away from you?" He winked as he said this.

Aha. Ricky was every bit as hot as his picture had suggested, and I had caught myself using his butt, which looked really good in those jeans, as my North Star when I had been trying to keep up with him, but maybe he was also kind of a flake.

A short distance ahead, an overhead sign indicated a pedestrian bridge to the Metro station and a parking garage. Ricky, who had started to ask me about my flight, was walking with less urgency but no less confidence, and I was supremely confused when he passed the turn to the bridge. I came to a stop, and he turned and gave me a quizzical look.

"Don't we want to go this way?" I asked.

"Oh, no. I'm parked a little farther down. That goes to garage C. I'm in B."

"Parked? We're supposed to take Metro . . ."

"C'mon," he urged, starting to move forward again. "Sorry, I had some errands to run while I was in Virginia, and I needed to drive. It'll be quicker anyway."

I was scrambling to keep up again and felt my panic creeping back in. "I thought I mentioned taking the train. I was specifically told to take the train from the airport. I need to include it in my story!"

"Hey, it's okay. You can take Metro from the hotel to the airport when you're leaving, if it's that important. It'll be the same trip, only backward."

Plus column: hot. Minus column: flaky, didn't follow directions, took us off our schedule, a little flippant about it. The minuses were adding up. At this point, whether he was hot or not was clearly irrelevant. The big question was, Would I be able to work with him? Or would his chaos jeopardize my chances of feature writing before I even got started?

I needed to ground myself and be ready to draw a firm line to keep Ricky on track the rest of the evening. As we walked toward the parking garage, I unzipped my duffel and rooted around until I found the folder with my printed itinerary and contacts, with a master schedule at the front, followed by tabbed dividers for each day of the trip. I flipped to today's tab.

"You know we have a seven-thirty dinner reservation, right?" I called to Ricky's back as he rounded the corner into the pedestrian bridge to garage B. "We have to be at this,

this"—I searched the paper with my finger for the name of the restaurant—"uh, Edible Revolution, *on time*. The restaurant is having a PR rep meet us there right at seven thirty."

"Aye, aye, Cap'n," he said with a mock salute, then added, "Drea sent me the same itinerary she gave you. Don't worry, we won't miss anything. We'll go to the hotel, check you in, and we can walk to the restaurant from there."

We were in the garage now, and after zigzagging through a few rows of cars, Ricky moved between two, fishing in his pocket for keys. I went around to the passenger side of the one to his right, a gray Corolla, but he turned his back to me and unlocked instead the passenger door of the car to his left. He straightened back up and looked around for me.

"Oh, there you are," he said as I trotted around the Corolla, trying not to blush at my mistake. "No power locks," he explained as he rounded the front of the car to the driver's side. "You can toss your bag in the back seat."

This was easy to do, as the windows were down and there was no pillar between the front and rear windows, creating a wide opening. The car was a low-slung two-door, very old but in good condition, painted in the gleaming reddish-copper color of a penny that's no longer brand new but hasn't yet tarnished to brown. The interior was upholstered in vinyl of roughly the same color as the exterior, and as I settled into my bucket seat, I groped over my shoulder for a seat belt before realizing that without a pillar, there was nothing for it to attach to. Ricky nudged me with an elbow and waved his own lap belt at me to clue me in.

I didn't drive, but anything that could be identified and categorized always caught my attention, and I was pretty good at car makes and models. This one was unique. I flipped through my mental Rolodex and came up with what I thought was the right answer, but with a question mark attached.

"Corvair?" I asked.

"Very good," Ricky said, sounding impressed, as he turned the key and the engine rumbled to life behind us. "A '66. My grandfather bought it new. I beat out all the other grandkids and two of my uncles in a drinking contest to get it when he died. I think you're the first person I've given a ride to who knew what it was right away."

"Your grandfather's prize possession and you leave the windows down in an airport parking garage?"

He laughed, pulling the sunglasses down from his hair to his eyes, as we pulled out of the garage into the late afternoon sunlight. "A car this old? That's not, like, a Ferrari or Mustang or anything remotely popular? Who's going to steal it? Trying to find buyers for the parts would be more trouble than it was worth."

He merged onto the George Washington Memorial Parkway, and within a moment we were gliding along the edge of the Potomac, the river occasionally blocked from view by a greenbelt and a buffer of trees basking in the same sweet spring warmth that whipped and wrapped around us through the open windows. We passed through a knot of traffic fighting its way onto the north- and southbound on-ramps for I-395, and then the Washington Monument and the domed roof of the Thomas Jefferson Memorial burst into full, unobstructed view across the river as we crossed a bridge over one of its many inlets. Ricky followed the signs for a left-hand exit toward Arlington National Cemetery and the Arlington Memorial Bridge, then navigated through a traffic circle onto the bridge, passing between a pair of granite pillars that perfectly framed a dead-on view of the Lincoln Memorial at the other end.

Ricky had been driving meditatively, shifting through the gears as traffic dictated but otherwise keeping both hands draped loosely on the steering wheel, but as we crossed from Virginia into the District of Columbia, he turned to me and asked, "Is this your first time in DC?"

"No, I came when I was in eighth grade," I replied.

"Oh, yeah, school trip?"

"No, my parents brought me. Public schools in California can't afford to schlep all those kids all the way across the country."

"I suppose they wouldn't, would they," he mused. "So did your parents take you to all the museums and stuff?"

"Yeah, we did the Mall and the Capitol and Mount Vernon. My dad was a teacher, so he wanted me to have the type of trip a school would have taken me on."

"And now you're back, on your own as an adult, to do glorified PR for a bunch of restaurants and hotels and overpriced stores? From the obvious to the banal . . . I could show you the *real*—"

"Look," I interrupted. "This is my job—and your job, too, I might add. This is a big opportunity for me, and I don't want to mess it up. I need to do what I was told to do, and I'd really appreciate it if you'd help me with that." I felt the blood rising in my face. I didn't like talking this way to anyone, much less someone I barely knew who I had to spend the next several days with. But I was tired, and Ricky seemed determined to make all my plans go sideways.

"I get it," he said, briefly raising his hands from the wheel in surrender. "And this is an opportunity for me, too. Drea really did me a favor by hooking me up. I don't think a little spontaneity or serendipity could hurt our story, but if that's the way you feel, I'll toe the line."

Our story? This seemed awfully chummy, but I decided to overlook it. "Thank you," I grumped.

We were silent the rest of the way across the city to the hotel, though I caught him sneaking curious looks at me at a couple of stoplights.

Ricky dropped me at the entrance to my hotel, the Monument, and went to park in the underground garage. When I gave my name at the desk, the clerk summoned a manager, who gave me some flowery words of welcome and asked if his colleague from the marketing department could have a bit of my time that evening to tell me about this new hotel's finer points.

"I have a dinner reservation soon," I said. "I don't think I'll be back much before nine." I was hoping that this would be much too late for the marketing manager, but I was assured that she would meet me in the hotel bar, the Quarry, at nine. I guess even the marketing folks had to work long hours at hotels.

Ricky rejoined me in the lobby with his camera bag, and we rode the elevator together to the sixth floor. As we entered my room, it became clear that the management had chosen this spot for me very intentionally. Directly ahead, through the floor-to-ceiling, room-width windows, the curtains had been pulled back to reveal a dramatic view of the Capitol dome.

I hung back in the little sitting area by the door with my duffel for a few minutes while Ricky took photos of the room. The decor was mostly tasteful, modern, and generic, with the sole nods to the hotel's theme being a textured wallpaper behind the headboard of the bed that sort of mimicked the look of weathered granite and a truly tacky pseudo-Warhol print of the Lincoln Memorial in the bathroom.

As I waited, I hungrily eyed the perfectly arranged mass of pillows and blankets on the bed. Suddenly I was very tired, but there was still a good deal of work ahead, so once Ricky finished taking photos, I tossed my duffel down on the chair next to the bed, gave it one last, longing look, checked my notes and directions one last time, and followed Ricky back out of the room to head to the restaurant.

I hoped that the walk to the restaurant would perk me up. The weather did its part; it was still softly warm as the sun began its descent. Ricky wasn't much help, however. Aside from a comment that he should come back up to my room after dinner to take some pictures of the view after it was dark and the city outside was lit up, he seemed mostly lost in thought.

It wasn't a long walk, and we arrived within a few minutes. Edible Revolution occupied a glassy corner on the ground floor of an office building along the edge of Chinatown. There were healthy crowds in the dining room and at the bar, both of which seemed to be decorated with antique farm implements and dimly lit by retro, Edison-style light bulbs with overturned milk pails for lampshades.

I approached the host stand. "I'm Oliver Popp," I told the young blond woman behind the desk. "You should have a seven-thirty reservation under either my name or under *Offbeat Traveler*."

She tapped into her tablet. "I've got it—Oliver. I have a note here to let Crystal know when you arrive. I'm texting her now. She does PR for us."

She had maintained an impressively steady stream of typing on the tablet as she had said this, but now she raised her gaze and took me in. "What is *Offbeat Traveler*, anyway? Is that a travel Insta? I *love* those—I'll totally give you a follow."

I was trying to respond, but her eyes flickered away and practically did a cartoon double take upon landing on Ricky's hotness behind me as she tore on. "Wait, is it one of those gay travel accounts? That is *so cute*—and you guys are an adorable couple. Aww, yay!"

I was sure I was deep red by now, and Ricky was grinning widely, but before I could stammer out a correction, we were descended upon by a woman in a flaming fuchsia wrap dress, who introduced herself as Crystal. She could have been Ramona's sister, with an eerily similar, but blond, intense bob and the same intimidatingly poised carriage. Where Ramona focused only on her phone, however, Crystal aimed the same terrifying laser beam of attention straight at Ricky and me, talking a mile a minute as she led us to a table in the corner where the restaurant's two windowed walls met.

"Oliver, it's so nice to meet you! Is this your first time dining with us? Your first time in DC?" She didn't wait for me to answer any of her questions. "That's great. I work with all the locations operated by the Revolutionary Restaurant Group, and we're so excited to welcome you to our newest dining experience. We're really thrilled with our concept—totally farm-to-table, of course, but the amazing thing is that many of our meats and produce are grown from stocks *directly descended* from those cultivated by our nation's founding fathers in the eighteenth century! Isn't that incredible? And wait until you taste it—you won't believe how much better they had it, how fresh and rich everything tastes. We've put together a tasting menu for you tonight, so you can try a little bit of almost everything, and I've made sure you'll be totally taken care of by one of our best servers, and I'll be here if you need absolutely anything, or if you need any questions answered at all, okay?"

How she wasn't gasping for breath, I couldn't tell. I'm pretty sure I was totally glazed over as she finished this spiel, but Ricky was ready with a question. "Wait, descended from the animals and crops raised by the founding fathers? How on earth can you tell?"

She gave a sparkly laugh in response to this, but her eyes were cold and hard. "We work with incredible farmers throughout the mid-Atlantic. Believe me, these heirloom cultivars and bloodlines have been highly prized and carefully documented over the centuries. I swear, you'll be able to taste the history!"

At this, she got up from the table, as if to forestall any more impertinent questioning of the historical agricultural record, and glided away. Ricky shrugged at me, and I couldn't help but give him a smile.

"Hey," he said to me, "I feel like I got off on the wrong foot a little bit. I'm sorry about the Metro thing. I didn't mean to throw you off or anything."

His face was glowing golden in the dim yellowish light, his brown eyes fixed softly on me. "It's okay," I said. "I'm sorry if I was a little snappish about it. You're right, I was thrown off, but you were also right that there will be other opportunities to get the Metro experience for the story."

"Thank god we've made up," he said, a grin creeping onto his face. "Imagine what it would do to our lives as gay travel influencers if we'd kept fighting."

I laughed but cut myself off at the approach of our waiter, who was carrying a tray of drinks.

"Good evening, my name is Carlos, and I'll be taking care of you tonight," he said.

He had approached from an angle where he could see more of me than he could Ricky, but as he started setting down the glasses, he noticed Ricky and I could have sworn he gave a small start. Ricky, too, had seemed to stiffen slightly at the sound of his voice and the mention of his name.

When Carlos spoke again, his voice was noticeably frostier. "I'll have some starters for you momentarily," he said, then departed abruptly.

I raised an eyebrow at Ricky.

"Another enemy?" he said feebly.

"Our gay travel influencer lifestyle is *really* going to be in trouble if we keep running into your exes everywhere," I said sternly, hiding behind the joke to fish for confirmation of what I had suspected, hoped, and feared all along.

"What can I say?" he said. "I've traveled around." He gave himself a rim shot on the lip of one of the Mason jars Carlos had brought.

There were nearly a dozen glasses of varying types on the table between us. Ricky started shuffling them around, positioning a couple at a time off to the side on a corner of the table for photos, next to a bud vase with a single peony. Carlos had also left a card that enumerated the different drinks he had brought for us to sample.

"Um, slight problem," I said to Ricky as I scanned the card. He grunted as he snapped a series of photos, and I continued, "These are all alcoholic, and I don't really drink."

"Some writer you are," he muttered, his eye still to the camera.

"Yeah, well, will you help me? You know, taste them, and give me some words I can use to describe each one?"

"Okay, give me a sec," he said. As he finished his last set of photos and set the camera down, he grabbed a martini glass with a pink concoction.

"According to the cheat sheet," I told him, "that is their version of a cosmopolitan."

"Their version? What could they do differently to a cosmopolitan?" He took a sip. "It tastes like a cosmopolitan."

"It says that the vodka is made in small batches from some of their founding fathers grains."

"Well, then, it tastes like a very patriotic cosmopolitan."

"How about a description I can use in my article," I said.

"Zingy, refreshing, perfect for the influencer desperate to change the subject from his tawdry past and keep his scam going." There were those twinkling, mischievous eyes again.

I had to laugh. Maybe this week would be okay.

While the historical roots of the food seemed like a dubious, unverifiable gimmick at best, I had to give Edible Revolution credit for a delicious dinner made from undoubtedly fresh ingredients. It was a few minutes before nine o'clock by the time we made it back to the hotel for our meeting with the marketing manager in the bar.

I noticed a line of four gleaming Moonshot MS-100 sedans in the semicircular driveway in front of the main entrance. I couldn't seem to shake these cars today, but the reason for their presence began to make sense when, on our way across the lobby to the bar, we bumped into Joey, the Moonshot PR rep I had met on the plane that morning. He beamed when he saw me.

"It's Oliver, right? Are you staying here, too? What a coincidence! Our whole team is camped out here." He cut his eyes to Ricky and gave him a disdainful appraisal. "Who's your friend?"

"This is Ricky Warner, the photographer I'm working with on my piece. Ricky, this is Joseph . . ."

"Harris," he reminded me, brightening a bit but still offering Ricky a decidedly unenthusiastic handshake. "So we'll see both of you tomorrow night, then, right? I'll send you the details as soon as I get back to my room—which will be right this minute, I'm so beat. Wish I could join you for a—"

He was interrupted by a large entourage sweeping into the lobby. Leading the charge was Kelso King himself, tall and fit and smiling in his trademark rich Texas rancher look of denim, suede, and Stetson, his blond girlfriend, Mimi, wrapped in a scarlet-red faux fur coat at his side. The men and women trailing behind them looked like a mix of lackeys, lawyers, lobbyists, and other DC power types.

"Wow, you really meant the whole team," I whispered to Joey.

"Absolutely," he said, his eyes following them reverentially as they swept through the room. "They're in the presidential suite on the top floor."

Mimi had stopped to accost a middle-aged woman coming out of the elevator with a small dog in her arms. "Oh my goodness, what a precious puppy!" she cooed. Her voice was very strange, breathily girlish but incredibly loud, projected as though she were a seasoned stage actress. "What is puppy's name? What are puppy's pronouns?"

I couldn't hear the woman's reply. King tipped back his head and laughed, the sound carrying almost as much as Mimi's voice had, and the retinue pressed forward into the elevator. Joey scampered off with a wave to join the other hangers-on.

We made it to the bar, where the bartender had a message waiting that the marketing manager had needed to go home for a family matter but would meet with me over breakfast in the morning. This was fine by me, but Ricky suggested we stay anyway and get some photos of the bar and soak up the ambiance for a bit.

As we settled in at a high-top table, he asked, "What's this event tomorrow? Who was that guy?"

"I ran into an old friend on the plane this morning. She works at Moonshot Motors, the electric car company."

"I get it now—whoa, that was Kelso King."

"Right, and she introduced me to that guy, Joey, who's on their PR team, and invited me to this press event they're putting on tomorrow night to distract from their congressional hearings. They assumed I'd go, but I haven't had the heart to tell them I can't."

"Why not? I mean, it's not our primary focus, but it seems like there could be something interesting there—maybe even another story. We could do a little digging on the side."

"On the side?" I gave Ricky a skeptical side-eye. "You don't think I should try to get one feature under my belt before taking on something completely outside my area of expertise? And what about our itinerary? I think we have enough to do."

He shrugged. "I bet we could find some wiggle room in the itinerary. Doesn't it have us going to Georgetown or something? We don't need to do that."

I raised an eyebrow at him. "We don't?"

He raised one of his own thick brows right back as he continued, "And it seems like you've got a couple of good ins with this company, between your friend and this guy Joey, who was not happy to see me with you, I should point out, since I've been made out to be so fast and loose this evening."

"Yeah, the way he was looking at you, I thought he was another one of your exes," I said.

"No, he was clearly into you and saw me as a threat. Hope I didn't get in the way of anything there."

I flushed. "You think so? Um, I don't know. He seems nice enough, but . . ."

"Not your type?"

My type? What was my type? Was Ricky trying to feel me out? I sensed the need to tread very carefully here, but my tired brain wasn't fully keeping up. "He seems a bit . . . corporate," I said unconvincingly.

"Ah, so you like the rough-and-ready, independent sort, huh?" Ricky grinned, peacocking a little, puffing out his chest and throwing back his shoulders, tossing me a wink.

Oh, boy. I hadn't been trying to lead him on, but had he sensed that I was comparing Joey to him? And that he had come out ahead? Did he like it, or was he just being playful? Or was this flirting? Was he flirting with me? Was *I* flirting with *him*? I felt myself losing control of the situation very quickly. I tried to get the upper hand back.

"Elise thought Joey was into me, too. She thought he'd invite me to more than the event."

"Who's Elise?" Not the direction I thought this gambit would take us, but I'd take any distraction I could get.

"She's . . . over there," I said with surprise. For there, across the bar, was Elise Perkins herself, seated at a table next to a man, their heads leaned in close together. Was this the rendezvous she had mentioned on the plane?

They were far enough away, and the light was low enough, that I couldn't make out a whole lot about the man. He seemed to me to be somewhat older than her. He was dressed in a suit, the jacket draped over the back of his chair, the tie loosened and askew. Their bodies were close, but their body language didn't seem happy.

Ricky looked over his shoulder at the pair. "Who's that with her?"

"I don't know. She mentioned getting together with a friend in DC on the plane. They don't seem too happy to be together, though," I said.

"No, they don't. And he looks familiar, but I can't place him—and no, he's not someone I've dated."

All this talk of dating. I had wanted to change the subject, to regain control over my suddenly overactive hormones, but it kept coming back, and darn it if Ricky wasn't really attractive and surprisingly fun to be around. I blame it on how tired I was, but it slipped out: "Are you dating anyone now?"

He looked back at me with surprise but answered seriously. "No, I'm not. What about you?"

"No," I said.

He crossed his arms on the table and leaned toward me. "So what's the scene like out there in San Francisco? You've seen what a small world it can be here."

"I live in Oakland, not San Francisco. And I don't really know what the dating scene is like. I haven't dated that much." Or at all, but no need to tell him that.

"Why's that?" His eyes were soft, and his face was doing that glowing thing again. Soft lighting was this man's best friend.

I searched for a suitable answer but came up blank. I gave a half smile and what I hoped was a nonchalant shrug. "Busy with other things, I guess."

"Well, I'm sure the right person will come along at the right time for you. Someone you'll really want to be a gay travel influencer with," he said.

I wondered if he was opening a door for me, hoping I'd

walk through, but decided that I was much too tired to get myself into any more trouble tonight. "I think right now bedtime is the right time for me."

We made our plans to meet up again in the morning, after breakfast, and headed toward the elevators, where he would go down to the garage and I would go up to my room. As we left the bar, I glanced back for one last look at Elise, wondering why she seemed so shrouded in sadness.

CHAPTER 4

I woke up Wednesday morning feeling a little silly. Things had gotten too personal too quickly with Ricky the night before. We were professionals working on a job together, and I'd started to go giddy with some kind of middle school crush, succumbing to my mom's hints and eagerly buying the wares of a shameless charm merchant who probably didn't know how to turn it off, and who didn't seem to realize how important this story was to me. Today I'd stay focused on the task at hand.

As promised the previous evening, the hotel's marketing manager joined me for breakfast in the atrium to give me details and spin I could use for my article. As far as I could tell, the hotel's location was both its strongest selling point and its biggest weakness: located in a peculiar little wedge of the city between Union Station and the Capitol, it was close to transportation and many attractions, but the immediate neighborhood was oddly quiet and featureless, comprised mostly of government and corporate office buildings. Rooms like mine, with its unobstructed view of the Capitol, commanded a premium; the other views on offer were incredibly uninspiring.

I went up to my room to brush my teeth and grab my jacket, and by the time I returned to the lobby, Ricky was waiting for me, his camera bag slung over his shoulder.

There were dark circles under his eyes, and his posture was loose-limbed. He was clearly not a morning person. "D'you think I could filch a cup of coffee from the breakfast room?"

I shrugged and waited while he went to steal his caffeine fix.

We set out walking at a leisurely pace, working our way at right angles through the urban grid toward the Gallery Place–Chinatown Metro station. It occurred to me that yesterday Ricky's physical movements and bearing had almost seemed calculated to show off his lean, lithe physique; this version was still lithe, but more in the manner of a drowsy cat slinking toward a sunbeam. Yesterday's black utility jacket had been replaced today by a lightweight gray nylon bomber, and the way his upper body curled into the jacket for warmth, one hand in a jacket pocket while the other clung to the coffee, added to the feline impression.

He noticed me studying him and asked, "Did you sleep okay? The bed in that room looked awfully comfy."

"Yeah, it was pretty nice," I responded. "Did you get enough sleep? You seem tired."

"Nah, I'm good. I got on a call with a friend on the West Coast after I got home, and maybe stayed up a little too late. I'm ready to get to work, Cap'n," he added with a sleepy grin.

Our destination was Barracks Row, a small commercial strip in one of the oldest parts of the city, between Capitol Hill and Navy Yard. It had a heavy concentration of restaurants and a smattering of galleries and performance venues; we'd be dropping into several of these this morning, mostly before they opened for the day, so that we could get photos and talk to the proprietors without getting in the way of their business. By lunchtime, we were slated to make our way on foot from there to the nearby Navy Yard neighborhood, which fronted the Anacostia River and had been heavily redeveloped in the years since the baseball stadium had been built there.

We took Metro from Gallery Place to L'Enfant Plaza, where

we changed trains and headed to the Eastern Market station. By the time we emerged from the station, a few steps from the intersection of Pennsylvania Avenue and 8th Street, which marked the northern end of Barracks Row, Ricky's coffee seemed to have worked its magic. He was walking taller, chatting and joking as we headed to our first stop, a restaurant serving diner-style comfort food with a few hipster touches.

We were greeted with homemade Pop-Tarts, Tater Tots, biscuits and gravy, and a thick slab of generously frosted chocolate cake. Ricky snapped photos of this bounty while I chatted with the owner, jotting down a few notes on my pad. Once photography was done, I sat down and goggled nervously at the spread, wondering how I was going to do this at five more restaurants in the next two hours.

"Just try a bite or two of each," Ricky whispered when the owner had gone to the kitchen to get me some water.

"This seems so wasteful," I muttered.

"If it makes you feel better, tell yourself that the kitchen crew will eat what you don't."

"Is that true?"

He shrugged. "Probably not, but you can tell yourself that if it helps."

If delusion was what it took to do the job, then call me Cleopatra, queen of denial. I sampled a little bit of each, making notes about each bite in my pad, although I couldn't resist eating more than a couple of the Tater Tots. Ricky grabbed the Pop-Tart after I had taken my bite and took it with us when we left, polishing it off as we walked down the street to our next stop.

Moderation would get you only so far when you were required to do a lot of it, and I was grateful for the break when, three restaurants later, we detoured onto a side street to stop in at an art gallery. Although we had intentionally arranged with the owner to be there before regular business hours, he had decided that he wanted the place to appear bustling in the photos and had gathered a troupe of friends to stand around and pretend to be absorbed in the art. A jazz combo played sullenly in a corner; the musicians looked even less thrilled to be up at this hour than Ricky had a couple of hours earlier. The gallery owner kept a huge smile plastered on his face throughout this whole performance. The artifice in the place was suffocating—or maybe I was too full of rich food.

"That was grim," I said to Ricky when we were finally back out on the sidewalk.

"Is the glamour already wearing thin?"

"Maybe a little. Or maybe I'm just nauseated at the idea of looking at food two more times, then walking three blocks and switching from breakfast to lunch."

We were back on 8th Street now, and Ricky stopped short in front of a pet store, staring through the plate-glass window. "Kittens!" he exclaimed, turning to go through the door.

I caught him by the sleeve of his jacket. "We have another restaurant to be at in two minutes. What are you doing getting distracted by kittens?"

"I thought you said the thought of more food was nauseating. And besides, how many restaurants is someone going to eat at on this one street if they're taking in the whole city? Why would they want to visit this street to begin with? Kittens, that's why. C'mon, look at them!"

Before I could stop myself, I looked. And darned if those weren't some of the cutest kittens I'd ever seen. And then I looked at Ricky and saw the hopeful, impish look twinkling in his eyes and followed him into the store.

I opened my notepad to my list of contacts and pulled out my phone, typed texts of apology to the next two restaurateurs that we wouldn't be able to make our appointments, and looked up to see Ricky holding a fluffy Siamese kitten up to his face, nuzzling it so happily it seemed like they were both purring. I melted on the spot. So much for professionalism.

* * *

After a rejuvenating kitten session and the walk to the area around the ballpark, I had found I was ready to face food again. We had kept all our Navy Yard appointments so far— we had sampled two casual, tourist-friendly eateries and now we were at a sports bar. I was nursing a ginger ale while Ricky gave me descriptive phrases for a flight of craft beers.

"You know, I'm not exactly complaining," he said, "but I don't usually drink this much on the job."

"Think of it as a perk of working with me."

He grinned over the rim of his glass as the foam rose to his lips. "They keep adding up."

I ignored this, as my attention had been caught by one of the television sets above the bar. It was too early in the day for most major sports; a couple of the sets were tuned to highlights shows and one was showing golf, but in true Washingtonian fashion, one was set to C-SPAN. It was this one that I turned to now, after catching a glimpse of the suddenly ubiquitous Elise Perkins.

They were showing the congressional hearing about Moonshot's self-driving cars. The Moonshot team were seated in a row at a long table, with Kelso King at the center, facing the panel of committee members. Several of the people around King were familiar from the elevator entourage in the hotel the previous night. Elise was at the far end of the table and was on-screen only when there was a wide shot of the hearing room, but she stood out because, aside from her, both sides of the room were very white and mostly male.

One of the committee members, identified on the name-plate in front of his microphone as Mr. Randall, seemed to be doing most of the talking. The Michigan representative Elise had mentioned yesterday, who was in the pocket of the Big Three. When a response was requested, King was supplying it, although he occasionally gestured down the table to one side or the other, toward one of his compatriots, as if begging for the blame for his company's sins to be shifted elsewhere.

"You've gone native," Ricky said, leaning into my side a little to draw my attention. "Six TVs, plus the charming company of yours truly, and you're glued to friggin' C-SPAN."

"It's the Moonshot hearing," I said. "I saw my friend Elise." The camera returned to a wide shot of the chamber and held there for a moment. "See, there she is, at the end of the table."

"So she is. And I could be wrong, but isn't that congressman the guy she was with last night? The one with the orange tie and too much hair product."

I tried to look, but the camera cut back to Representative Randall, and the man Ricky had pointed out was seated too far away to be in the shot.

"Do you recognize him now? Remember his name?" I asked.

"No, but maybe we'll see him again. Seems like a conflict of interest to go on a date with someone you'll be testifying in front of the next day."

"Not only that, but how the heck does Elise know a congressman?"

We watched for a few more minutes, but Randall and King remained the twin centers of attention, with no more glimpses of the rest of the committee or witnesses, and presently we had to move on to our final stop in the neighborhood, an ice cream shop.

After a brief chat with the owner, I was gifted a cone with a bright green scoop of "US Mint 'n Chip," which I carried as we walked to a nearby riverfront park for our final set of photos. Ricky wanted a carefully staged photo, with most of me cropped out but my hand holding the cone up in front of the railing of an overlook of the river. I felt very stupid posing like this, and before he had gotten a satisfactory shot, I had to stop him.

"The ice cream is melting all over my fingers."

"Well, lick it off. Lick the back of the cone to stop the melting, but keep the front clean for the shot."

I obliged, and to my horror, he kept shooting, the lens of the camera following the cone up to my face.

"Wait a minute, don't take a picture of me with my tongue hanging out!"

He pulled the camera down to look at the screen and scrolled through the photos, grinning. I leaned in to look and saw that he had indeed taken several photos of my tongue. "You are not, under any circumstances, to submit any of those for publication," I said as he fended off my attempts to reach the DELETE button on the camera.

"Fine, I'll save these for personal use."

"Eww. That's even worse!"

He laughed and moved next to me at the railing while I resumed eating the ice cream. He had me feeling very self-conscious about doing so, but it was still dripping onto my hand, so I carefully avoided looking at him as I ate.

"So now we definitely have to go to that Moonshot thing tonight, don't we. We have to corner Elise and demand to know about her hot congressional hookup. We could make a fortune selling the scoop to the *Washington Post*," he said.

"I am pretty curious," I admitted. "About the whole thing, I mean." I told him about my near miss with the self-driving Moonshot the previous morning, and what Elise had told me about the company's alarm around the frequency of these dramatic errors.

"Jeez, you might have the beginnings of a pretty meaty story there."

"Yeah, but it's not the story I'm supposed to be writing," I pointed out, scratching at a nervous little itch popping up on my arm.

"Would it make you feel better if I told you I ran the idea by Drea already, and she said we should go for it?"

"What? When? You did not. No she didn't." I clutched at my sleeve as the nervous little itch started doing a full-fledged anxiety samba up and down my arm.

He pulled out his phone and searched for Drea in his contacts. He started the call and put it on speakerphone while it rang. In a moment, Drea's voice came on.

"Well, hey, boo! I didn't expect to hear from you again so soon. You have an update already on your progress with—"

"Hey, darlin'," he interrupted. "I'm here with Oliver, who doesn't believe me that you gave the go-ahead to look into this Moonshot thing."

"Oh! And a hey, boo, to you, too," she said to me. "Yeah, Ricky told me last night that you had some good connections. And he doesn't even know this, but I spoke to my counterpart at *Motor Mania* this morning, and he was very excited. Everything Moonshot is superhot right now. So if you think you can chase both stories at once, you've got a ready taker and my okay."

"See?" he said to me, rubbing his fingers together to make the sign for *money*.

That's nice for you, I thought, but I was not at all convinced I should be trying to chase two stories at once.

Ricky aimed his voice back at the phone. "It's gotten even better, too. We've got some sexual intrigue to add to the mix."

"Ooh," she said. "Wait, sexual intrigue in the story or between—Wait, am I still on speaker?"

"Yes, you are, and byeee," Ricky said hurriedly as he cut the connection.

I gave him a deadpan look as he put his phone back in his pocket. For once, he was the one who was blushing. "Did you call her last night to gossip about me?" I asked.

"No," he said indignantly. "I called her to catch up because we're old friends. Not everything is about you."

"Uh-huh," I said, trying not to smile.

I could see that he was trying not to smile, too. He gave a mock-exasperated grunt and said, "Finish your ice cream and I'll walk to the Metro station with you, Mr. Thinks It's All About Him. You go back to the hotel, I'll go home, and I'll be back to pick you up for the event at six."

I was waiting at the curb outside my hotel when Ricky pulled up in his copper-colored car at six o'clock.

I had brought one tie with me, just in case, and I was wearing it now, and I had exchanged my sneakers for a pair of brown leather derbys. Getting into the car, I saw that Ricky had similarly altered what he had been wearing before: he still had the gray bomber and slim black jeans from this morning, but he had swapped in a white shirt with a skinny tie under the jacket, and he was back in his black boots. He looked effortlessly stylish and cool.

I was wondering if I could give him a compliment on his outfit without making one or both of us feel weird, but he beat me to it. As he pulled away from the curb, he reached over and playfully flicked the end of my tie, saying, "You clean up okay. Looking good."

"I look like I'm wearing my dad's clothes," I responded, blushing, which was exactly what they were.

He laughed lightly and drove on. Moonshot Motors was pulling out all the stops to wine and dine the press—including many of the political reporters covering the Capitol Hill hearings, I gathered—and our venue tonight was Hillwood Estate, a museum deep in Northwest Washington, near Rock Creek Park. We drove up Massachusetts Avenue, then around Dupont Circle to Connecticut Avenue.

"This is actually a worthwhile place to go for your travel article, too," Ricky commented as he drove through downtown. "Hillwood is interesting. It was one of the homes of Marjorie Merriweather Post, the heir to the Post Cereal fortune. She was married a bunch of times, but one of her marriages was to the US ambassador to the Soviet Union in the 1930s, and while they were over there, she started buying up art and treasures from Imperial Russia that the Soviets were getting rid of—you know, Fabergé eggs and stuff. She endowed the place as a museum for her collection after she died. It's an impressive sight."

"That does sound perfect for the article," I agreed. "And look at you, playing tour guide."

We were through the Dupont Circle commercial district by now, and as we continued northwest, Connecticut Avenue was lined with large trees, large houses, and large, expensive-looking apartment buildings. In a moment, the trees and buildings cleared, and we crossed a high bridge.

"Okay, Mr. Tour Guide," I said. "What's below the bridge?"

"Rock Creek," Ricky answered. "The last neighborhood we passed through was Kalorama, home of the rich and powerful—your Woodrow Wilsons, your post-presidency Obamas, your Ivankas and Jareds. And up here ahead of us is Woodley Park." He adopted a singsong cadence, gripping a pretend microphone in one hand. "And on your right, the world-famous National Zoo!"

"I thought the world-famous zoo was in San Diego."

"Well, sure, but at least our zoo is free to get into, so you'll always get your money's worth."

He continued to point out landmarks as we proceeded. Down that street was Washington, DC's earliest extant house, built by one of George Washington's right-hand men; on that corner was possibly the first strip mall in the US, now home to a tiny Target but still lit by its original 1930s neon sign.

As we turned off Connecticut Avenue onto Tilden Street, about half a mile from Hillwood, we were greeted by a commotion. In the middle of Tilden's wide, grassy median was a mass of people shouting through megaphones, ringing cowbells, and waving signs as they walked in circles around a wrecked

Moonshot sedan that had been parked in the center of the action.

"Looks like tonight's event has attracted some fans. We should probably stop," Ricky said, easing the car to the curb. We got out and crossed the eastbound lane to the median.

As Ricky began snapping photos, I scanned some of the protestors' signs: I DIDN'T SIGN UP TO BE A GUINEA PIG. MY KID'S LIFE IS WORTH MORE THAN YOUR STUPID CAR. IF YOU DON'T WANT TO DRIVE, TAKE THE BUS.

The woman carrying this last sign noticed Ricky's camera and hurried over to us. "Are you with the press?" she asked breathlessly.

"Uh, uh-huh," I stammered.

The woman turned back toward the crowd and hollered, "*Melba!* Somebody get Melba!" She turned back to us. "Melba is our press liaison."

A short, round woman in a polyester tracksuit hustled over, huffing and puffing slightly, as if her body couldn't keep all its energy in and had to let a little out in short bursts. "We've got some press here," the other woman told her, and Melba's face lit up under her tightly curled gray hair.

"What outlet are you boys with? The *Post?* The *Times?*"

I had to think for a second before I remembered. "Uh, *Motor Mania.*"

"The car magazine? I thought those were the propaganda arm of the automotive industry." Her eyes narrowed, and she held me skeptically in her gaze.

"Oh, no, ma'am," I said, deciding an earnest approach might be best. "I'm doing an investigative report on the problems with Moonshot's self-driving system, so a counter perspective is very important. What brings your group out here today?"

"Well," she said, her body releasing some tension as she swept the scene with one arm, "as you can see, we have people expressing a number of concerns about this half-baked 'system,' as you call it. Many of us are simply motorists concerned about being forced to share the roads with an untested, unsafe technology. There are a few disillusioned former Moonshot owners here, who realized the flaws in the system after too many close calls or even crashes. That car there belongs to one of our group, who was almost killed. There are even victims and family members of victims of crashes with these cars. Here, I'll introduce you to some people."

She walked us deeper into the group, dragging people out of the circle of marchers by the elbow to come talk to us. The man who owned the wrecked car, a physician, detailed the injuries he and his wife had sustained when the car had plowed straight through a T intersection into the front of a dry-cleaning shop after failing to distinguish between the sky and its reflection in the shop's windows. One woman wept as she recounted her seven-year-old daughter's near miss from being sideswiped while riding her bicycle—on the sidewalk. Another man, who introduced himself as an ethicist, went on at length about other motorists' lack of consent to participate in what amounted to a large-scale trial run for an untested technology and about the National Highway Traffic Safety Administration's dereliction of duty in failing to provide oversight.

While we were talking to this man, Melba had scurried over to a folding table set up along the edge of the median, returning with an armload of press releases and pamphlets.

"Here's some information to help with your story," she said, passing them to me in a messy stack. "I'm the contact person on the press releases, so you call me if you need any more information, honey."

The letterhead on the press releases identified the group as LOCOMOTO, which was apparently a tortured acronym for the League of Concerned Motorists. I sifted through the stack as we crossed the median back toward Ricky's car. The group's strategy seemed to include issuing a press release anytime there was an incident involving a self-driving Moonshot in the DC metro area, of which there had been many.

There were also several releases and a pamphlet touting their relationship to a computer scientist, Dr. Lila van Veldt, who claimed to have been involved in developing Moonshot's proprietary self-driving system but now believed it wasn't safe for its intended use.

I showed these to Ricky. "Dissension in the ranks," I said. "And maybe someone Elise has worked with, since that's her department. Another thing to ask her about."

CHAPTER 5

The Hillwood Estate, which included extensive gardens, several outbuildings, and the centerpiece redbrick mansion housing fine and decorative arts treasures, was tucked away in a quiet, upscale residential neighborhood off Tilden Street that bordered Rock Creek Park. You entered through a wrought-iron gate and followed a winding drive to a parking lot by the visitor center, which you could go through or bypass to walk up to the main house via a grand, lushly landscaped forecourt with a circular drive.

There was a row of six Moonshot MS-100 sedans, in the company's signature midnight blue paint, fanned out in the driveway as we approached the mansion. Several guests were circling the cars, peering inside to note that none of them were equipped with steering wheels or even with front seats. When we got our demonstration rides in these specially customized cars later that evening, we were apparently meant to feel as though we were being ferried in spacious luxury by an invisible chauffeur.

Passing by the cars, we encountered a table, where we were checked in and given badges to wear that identified us as being from *Motor Mania*. I hoped that this didn't mean other guests would be approaching us to talk cars; once things progressed beyond identification, I tended to get on shaky ground very quickly. I was realizing that I already felt a little shaky; too late, as always, I discovered that the noise from the protest had left my nerves hummingly taut.

Moving beyond the registration table, we entered the house into a vast, grand entry hall filled with milling guests and Moonshot employees. There were cocktail tables to stand around and a bar set up in one corner, and waiters were moving deftly through the crowd with trays of hors d'oeuvres. Unidentifiable inoffensive music tinkled softly above a low din of chatter and laughter and clinking glassware.

I was instantly very aware of how crowded the room was, and my shakiness turned to something much worse. I felt my chest constrict, and my hands began to fidget at my sides, the fingers opening and closing into my palms. My eyes began to glaze over, as if preparing to recede into their sockets to shut out a scene I couldn't handle. My mind started revving up, not racing yet but picking up speed. *That's a lot of people. So many people . . . so many people. So many people, so many people, so-manypeople . . .*

"Cripes," Ricky muttered, taking in the room, and then he turned to me and started to say something else but interrupted himself. "Hey, are you okay?"

"Um," was all I could manage. *Oh, crud,* I thought. *Not now. Not here.*

Ricky grabbed me by my elbow and quickly maneuvered me along the outskirts of the room toward one of the many doors opening off the central hall. He hailed one of the waiters and asked in a low tone, "Is the entire museum open to us?"

"I think so," the woman replied, and he pulled me through the doorway into a small vestibule. A couple of our fellow guests had already found their way here and were conversing quietly in a small knot in the corner, so Ricky steered me through to the next room, which turned out to be a large butler's pantry.

Where the room we had initially entered was classically ornate, the pantry was modern and spare. It had been renovated, perhaps in the 1950s, with sleek steel cabinets in institutional green and a chrome-edged Formica countertop. Glass-fronted upper cabinets displayed different china patterns, but the overall effect of the room was smooth, shiny, and clean—almost soothingly so. I felt my breathing slow again and my fists unclench.

Ricky wasn't saying anything, but his palm was pressed gently against the small of my back, and though I wasn't ready to fully look at him, I felt his brown eyes resting softly on me. I tried again. "Um. Um." *C'mon, Oliver, you're almost there. Push it through your chest.* "Um, I'm okay . . . Thank you."

He let out a breath. "Let's stay here for a minute, then," he said. "Maybe go over and look at the kitchen, too. We've got a dual purpose here tonight. We can start with this and work our way back to the other thing. Stay here for a second. I'll be right back."

I steadied myself on my feet as he ducked back the way we had come. He returned a second later to hand me a plastic tumbler of water. I clutched the cup gratefully in both hands, sipping some water as we moved through the pantry to the door to the kitchen. There was a cordon across the doorway, so we couldn't go in, but we could look in to see the massive restaurant-style stove and the array of space-age mixers and blenders and other gadgets lining the counters. I leaned against the doorjamb and slowly finished my water.

"I'm okay," I repeated finally, straightening out. "Just got a little overwhelmed for a second."

"Yeah, I could see that. Maybe we should look through some of the exhibit rooms for a bit, then go back and get some of that food in you."

That sounded good to me, so I followed him onward. While many of the rooms in the mansion had been preserved to appear as they did when Ms. Post lived there, showcasing the art, furniture, and priceless baubles as they had been used as the backdrop to her daily life as a Washington social doyenne, others were configured as galleries, with glass display cases set into the walls and vitrines dotting the center of the rooms. Here, the treasures took center stage: intricately detailed porcelain figures, hand-painted decorative china, clocks inset with rare gemstones, silver, gold, and the glittering Fabergé eggs. Almost everything had a royal provenance, from the tsars of Russia to the extravagant prerevolutionary French monarchy.

It seemed that none of our fellow guests had wandered beyond the rooms immediately adjacent to the entry hall, so for most of our tour, we were alone. Ricky had clearly been here before, and he surprised me with the knowledge he was able to pull seemingly out of nowhere about eighteenth- and nineteenth-century decorative arts. As he pointed out pieces, he kept leaning into me, and he stayed close by my side as we moved through the space, his head sometimes almost touching mine when he tilted it toward me to say something.

I would normally recoil from so much bodily contact, so much invasion of my personal bubble. Maybe my guard was down from the near shutdown earlier, but I barely noticed it now, and when I did, all that struck me was how good he smelled and how cool and collected he had been when I had needed it.

I almost didn't want to go back to the party, but finally, after we had made our way through several of the upstairs rooms, I said, "We should go down and find Elise."

"And some food," he reminded me.

He led the way down the stairs and flagged down the first passing platter of food as we landed back in the hall. "Shrimp cocktail, m'lord," he said, handing me a small plate and keeping one for himself. He cast an eye around the room to the other servers bustling about. "Hope you like shrimp," he said. "Looks like everything is shrimp based."

"I can deal," I said. I was scanning the room, too, looking

for Elise and coming up empty so far. I pulled my phone out of my pocket and texted her: **Are you here?** It took me a moment after I had resumed scanning to notice that my Moonshot PR contact, Joey, was giving me a little finger wave, trying to get my attention. Oh, brother.

"Your boyfriend is calling you," Ricky said out of the corner of his mouth, elbowing me a little.

"Goody. Maybe he can help us find Elise, anyway," I muttered back, navigating through the crowd, feeling, to my relief, mostly okay in spite of the crush of other bodies.

"Oliver, there you are!" he beamed as we neared. "And, of course," he made a show of ostentatiously reading Ricky's name badge, "Rocky, what a pleasure to see you again."

"I'm sure," Ricky smirked, nodding to the man standing with Joey.

"Hi. Brian Knox, *Washington Post*," the man said, offering me his hand. "*Motor Mania*, huh? That's cool. So you get to drive all the new stuff? What about that new Corvette, right?"

"I, uh, haven't had a chance to drive it," I stammered. "I'm kind of freelancing, doing this piece on Moonshot for them."

"Ah," he said, turning his eyes to Ricky with a look that I couldn't quite interpret but that gave a vague sense of history between them. "That explains it."

"I'm going to go get something to drink," Ricky said to me. "You want anything? Another water?"

"I could stand to freshen up myself," Brian said, turning to follow him. Uh-oh. I smelled another of Ricky's lovelorn "enemies." And now I was left alone with Joey.

"Are you enjoying yourself so far? Isn't this a spectacular space? I've heard there's a ton of priceless trinkets upstairs," he gushed, laying a hand briefly on my arm. I tried to convince myself that I couldn't feel his lotion seeping through my jacket sleeve.

"Yeah, I don't think I would have found this place otherwise. It's really great," I said, distracted, and not merely from the lotion. The corner of my eye caught Brian and Ricky standing together by the bar, talking animatedly. "Have you seen Elise? Elise Perkins?"

He gave a furtive look around and leaned in close. "She's not here, and if she's smart, she won't step foot out of her hotel room for the rest of the week. If Mr. King can forget she exists by then, *maaayyy-be* she'll be able to keep her job."

"What happened?"

"Well, I shouldn't really say, but I guess it's all a matter of public record anyway. In her testimony today, she stabbed all of us in the back and completely embarrassed herself, that's all."

"What did she say?"

"They were asking her about how we push updates to our autonomous software suite out over the air, and some wise guy decided to ask if the servers could be hacked and if the updates were secure enough to prevent hackers from messing with them. And she had the nerve to say that could happen!"

Okay, Mata Hari time. I forced myself to look Joey in the eyes, feigned my best engrossed look, moved closer and grabbed him by the arm to mirror his body language, and gasped, perhaps too excitedly, "And could it? Could that really happen?"

He smiled and moved even closer, tilting his head dangerously close to mine. "I mean, I don't really know, but between us and off the record, I assume if she said they could, then they could. But she should know better than to say so!"

"Wasn't she under oath?"

He waved his hand dismissively. "Anyway, then it got really embarrassing. This guy tried to follow up with some grandstanding about our duty to our customers and the public, and she says to him, 'What about your duty to your wife and kids? What about your duty to me? Who do you have a duty to?' and basically screams, on the Congressional Record, about how this guy has been having an affair, *with her*, and she gets all hysterical, and they have to call a recess and escort her out. It was a total circus. What a whack job."

So much for our scoop. "Who was the guy?"

"Beats me, I can't tell those politicians apart. It'll probably be all over the Internet by now, though."

Ricky had wandered back over, putting another cup of water into my hand. Joey gave him an annoyed glance, then looked at his wristwatch. "Mr. King will be coming out in a few minutes to give his remarks," he said. "I'd better go see if he's prepped, and if I can figure out where Mimi disappeared to."

We watched him hustle away, then I turned to Ricky.

"So, Brian, huh?"

"What? Oh," he said. "Look, at least three-quarters of the people in this room are based out of Washington. I've probably worked with half of them, or at least with their publications, at one time or another. That's all."

"Sorry to impugn your honor," I said.

"I mean, I did hook up with Brian once," he said with a wolfish grin, "but that was years ago. He's married with kids now."

I punched him lightly in the ribs and pretended to kick his shin, and he laughed.

"Anyway, I saw you getting touchy-feely with that PR prick. Were you trying to flirt some dirt out of him?"

"I was, but I didn't really get anything that the rest of the world doesn't already know." I recounted his tale of Elise's fall from grace.

"Well, the hacking is a new angle to follow up on," Ricky mused. "And we'll find out who her mystery man was, although if he actually is a congressman, I'm sure his office will have him on a media lockdown."

"Maybe you used to go out with his chief of staff or something and can get us in that way."

"Don't joke about that if you're not ready for it to be a very real possibility," he said from under an arched eyebrow. I had to catch myself before I audibly gulped, both at the smoldering intensity of his look and at its implication.

From across the hall, by the entrance, came the insistent clinking of a spoon on a glass, followed by an exhortation for everyone to proceed outside. A small riser had been set up on the driveway, at the end of the row of Moonshot sedans, and Kelso King stood here now, footlights at the corners of the riser illuminating his broad smile under the brim of his Stetson. He raised his hands to silence the chattering crowd.

"Howdy, y'all," he drawled. I had heard it said that the more he felt he needed to charm an audience, the thicker King's Texas twang became. Tonight he was practically dribbling molasses. "I know you've been hearin' all kinds of scary things about my Moonshots and their amazin' self-driving capability, and y'all *know* it cain't all be true, right? So I'm happy you're here with us tonight to get a look for yourselves—that's all I can ask you to do, ain't it, is jedge for yourself?—and experience this marvel of modern technology. I think you'll find it's safe, relaxin', hell, maybe even fun! You can even take your drink with ya, I don't care, and the cops won't, neither!" He hoisted a highball glass, sloshing a little brown liquid onto his hand, and the crowd chuckled, though I wondered if he really thought his cars were somehow exempt from open-container laws.

He passed the spotlight to a member of the PR team, who explained that we would be called in pairs to take our turn getting a demonstration drive along a pre-mapped route. We could continue to enjoy Moonshot's hospitality while we waited our turn, but we had to listen for our call, because there would be no second chances if we missed it.

The first six pairs of riders were called, and the crowd watched and snapped photos as they glided down the driveway into the dark in their shiny blue electric chariots.

"They all had their headlights on, right?" I asked Ricky when he returned from chasing the last car down the driveway for a photo.

"I think so. I'm sure all the cars will be on their very best behavior tonight."

"What happens if something goes wrong?" I asked. "Is there some kind of manual override? Or do we have to bang on the windows like a couple of trapped monkeys while we barrel to our deaths?"

"Boy, you really don't trust these things, do you?"

Ricky led me over to the head PR person, who was still standing next to the platform on the driveway. When he asked her about safety, she pulled up a video on the tablet she was holding, and passed it to me.

On-screen, a woman driving a Moonshot reached to the giant touch screen in the center of the dashboard and tapped a large steering wheel icon in the upper corner to activate the self-driving system. The screen was taken over by a series of large red numerals counting down: 3 . . . 2 . . . 1. As the system took over, we were treated to close-up shots of the woman's hands coming off the steering wheel and her foot rising from the accelerator. On-screen text indicated that the wheel and pedals, which used electronic linkages, were now disabled so that the system would stay in control even if the driver accidentally moved the wheel or stepped on one of the pedals. In order to take over, the driver had to once again press the steering wheel icon on the screen. After another countdown, she was once again in control. The image shifted to show a button on the back of the right-hand steering wheel spoke; this, the on-screen text informed us as a pink-nailed finger decorously pushed the button, allowed for an emergency override, which eliminated the countdown and gave the driver immediate control.

"See," the PR rep said, pointing to the screen. "You can be in control at any time. Now, since the cars we're using tonight are specially outfitted without steering wheels or pedals, you can't exactly take over, but in an emergency, the touch-screen control on the dashboard has been reprogrammed to bring the car to an immediate stop."

"So we have to push a button on the dashboard from the back seat?" I asked skeptically. "That seems like an awfully big impediment to reaction time."

She looked at me wearily. "I really don't think you need to worry about it. It's perfectly safe. I can tell you something else that might make you feel better, too, but it has to be off the record."

"Okay," I said.

"We cleared the route with the DC Metropolitan Police, on the off chance anything happens. They have instructions not to be conspicuous out there or anything, but to have a couple of patrol cars nearby, and if you use the emergency override, the car will notify police dispatch. So if something goes wrong, help should be seconds away. Okay?"

"I guess so," I said. Maybe I was still a little jittery from earlier.

"It's great," Ricky assured her. "He's just a nervous passenger."

"And he works for a car magazine?" we heard her mutter as we headed back inside to get more shrimp.

Several minutes later, the first of the Moonshots came back up the driveway, and the next pair was called. When the third of the cars returned, it was our turn. Joey held the rear door open, and we climbed into the back seat. Ricky made a show of snuggling up to me as we settled in and, right before Joey shut the door, said loudly, "Isn't this intimate!"

I laughed and pushed him away, reaching for my seat belt. "That was uncalled for."

"Fine. When we get back, I'll tell him what a bad kisser you are and how I couldn't wait to get out."

"Wouldn't you like to know."

"We could find out . . ."

"I could be wrong, but I think we're supposed to be working right now," I said, ready to stop this train before it left the station. How did he always get me to go along with him in his flirtations? Somewhere down in my gut, I knew the answer to this, but I was determined that it would stay down there where I could pretend to be oblivious to it.

The Moonshot had already whirred and purred its way down the driveway, out of the museum grounds, and through the neighborhood down to Tilden Street. The map on the giant screen in the center of the dashboard showed the route we'd be taking, following Tilden across Connecticut Avenue, where it merged into Reno Road and wound its way up to Nebraska Avenue. From there, the car would be really put to the test by going through a convoluted traffic circle to turn onto Wisconsin Avenue, headed down toward the National Cathedral.

Reno Road was a quiet street lined with comfortable homes on large lots. There were occasional streetlights, but there was also a near-continuous cover of trees overhanging the roadway, blocking much of the light. Within our silent cocoon, we were lit mostly by the screen, helped only a little now and then by the light from a house or a little bit of street light peeking through from overhead. It was, darn that Ricky, an intimate darkness.

I had thought I'd calm my nerves and keep Ricky at bay by jotting notes in my pad, but I found myself only twiddling with the stylus, no thoughts willing to interrupt my discomfort, then finally giving up and setting the pad down next to me on the center seat. The car was, as Ricky had predicted, on its best behavior. It waited patiently at red lights, came to smooth complete stops at stop signs, and dutifully obeyed all posted speed limits.

I was fidgeting with the ends of my sleeves and staring out the window, trying to ignore the warmth radiating through the darkness from the seat next to me, threatening as always to break down my defenses. Finally, I looked over at Ricky, who was lounging in the corner where the seat met the door, his body angled toward me, his arm along the top of the seat with his hand behind my headrest, watching me intently with a smile. "If you forget about the fact that there's no driver, this is pretty nice," he said.

At the mention of the lack of driver, I looked forward through the windshield. "It is weird, isn't it," I said. "It feels like somebody forgot something very important in this situation, but everything's working normally anyway."

"Hmm," he murmured, his fingers walking over the top of my headrest.

"I mean, what's the point of this? What are people supposed to be doing with this time if they're not driving? More work? Consuming more ads on social media sites?" I swatted at Ricky's hand, which had fully breached the headrest and was toying with my collar. "What are you doing?"

"Answering your question," he purred, tracing a finger from the collar along my jawline to my earlobe. I was surprised to find that I still didn't mind the touch—surprised, and alarmed.

"What's your endgame here?" I asked finally.

His finger, which had started to twirl a lock of hair behind my ear, suddenly went still. His eyes darkened, and his face turned serious. "Do you really want to know?"

"Probably not," I gulped. Outside the window, the National Cathedral loomed into view, imposingly lit against the night sky. "Wow," I said, hoping to change the subject back toward a topic that I could tell myself had something to do with my work, like the architectural landmarks of our nation's capital, instead of one that I couldn't, like my growing suspicion that this man actually did want to kiss me in the back seat of this car, and that I would maybe be okay with it if he did.

"Yeah, God's cool," Ricky said, his eyes twinkling. "See, you keep getting flustered and trying to distract me, and it's so cute and maddening and it makes me want to push your buttons even more. I'm sorry," he chuckled. "It must seem like I'm torturing you a bit, huh?"

He dropped his arm and pulled down the armrest between us, then raised his hands in surrender. "No more funny business."

I considered whether this was a positive turn of events or not. Shortly after the cathedral, the car had turned briefly onto Massachusetts Avenue, then onto Garfield Street, back toward Connecticut Avenue. We were once again surrounded by trees and gracious homes, increasingly interspersed with apartment buildings as we neared the denser core of the Woodley Park neighborhood.

I decided to lay my cards on the table. "Look," I said slowly. "I'm not *not* open to funny business. But I'm only here for a couple more days, and I don't have a lot of experience with attractive, flirtatious gentlemen who seem to be interested in me." God, I hoped I hadn't misread that one. "And I'm just trying to understand what the plan is here."

"My plan," Ricky said, "which so far is going flawlessly, is to have fun, get to know you, do our work, and see what happens. Is that too loosey-goosey for you?"

"It probably shouldn't be, but it kind of is," I admitted. He probably thought his plan sounded light and breezy; to me, no matter how much I wished otherwise, it sounded too messy and distracting to be tempting.

Connecticut Avenue was now passing by outside. We were well lit now by streetlights and bright storefronts and the head- and taillights of the light late evening traffic around us. Ricky had a thoughtful look on his face. "What about this," he said. "What if we do our work tomorrow, and then afterward, I take you on a date?"

Holy cow, a date. I had just been asked on a date. A boy I liked, liked me enough to want to go on a date. I was briefly tongue-tied, then, lifting my eyes to Ricky's, finally said, "I'd really like—"

For an instant, the city lights ahead of us disappeared from my peripheral view. Within that space of less than a second, all I knew of the world through the windshield was fleeting darkness, a thump, a thud, a dull shattering, the wave of shadow briefly rolling noisily across the glass roof overhead, horns around us, yelling. In the first confusing moment that the light returned to the windshield, it glittered a red kaleidoscope, refracted through a spiderweb of cracks.

Everything inside my head immediately turned to white noise, but through it I heard myself yell, in an odd, high-pitched voice, "*What was that?*" as Ricky lunged for the dashboard and tried frantically to hit the emergency stop button on the touch screen. As Ricky made contact with the button, the tires locked to a screeching halt. I was grabbed by my seat belt, and Ricky braced himself against the dashboard to keep from being pitched into the windshield.

He wrenched the door open and tumbled out of the car into a sprint. I followed dazedly, the fuzzy world swimming around me. We had to retrace our route by nearly half a block. Sirens were already sounding down the street, coming toward us, by the time we reached the spot where all other traffic in our lane had stopped. Illuminated in the glow of headlights, a broken figure lay in the street. Ricky reached them well ahead of me, knelt down, took a look, got back up, and tried to catch me before I could see, but somehow, despite my fog, he wasn't quick enough. I saw.

I saw that our car had hit a person.

I saw that our car had hit Elise Perkins.

And I saw that Elise Perkins was dead.

CHAPTER 6

Ricky had his arms around me, trying to shield me from the horrific sight in the street. We stumbled backward until my heel caught on the curb and I went down, slow enough to catch myself into a sitting position on the edge of the sidewalk, but fast enough that pain radiated through my tailbone as it made contact. I wrapped my arms around my knees and stared at a point on the ground just ahead of my feet, rocking slightly backward and forward.

Elise. Elise. Elise. Oh my god, Elise, where did you come from? Where did you come from? Omigod, where did you come from, Elise?

Ricky knelt down in front of me as the scene behind him exploded into a burst of red and blue lights and a swarm of bodies, official, unofficial, moving, shouting, one dead. His voice swam through the crowd to me. "Oliver? Oliver, can you hear me?"

I can hear you. I can hear you, but I can't talk right now. I can't talk, can't move, too busy feeling every part of my body turn to lead, except the brain. I can hear you, but my brain has decided to go to fifty other places at once, none of them here, so I can't talk right now.

A pair of police officers had come up behind Ricky. "Sir? Sir?"

He turned, still crouching. "I'm sorry, I think my friend is in shock, and I don't want to leave him. Is it all right if I stay here and give my statement?"

They assented, and he moved to sit next to me on the sidewalk. One of the officers knelt in the street, and the other remained standing. I could hear every word of their questions and Ricky's responses as he related what had happened, who we were, what we had been doing, how I knew the victim, but none of the meaning filtered through.

The number of people kept multiplying. An ambulance pushed slowly through the snarled traffic, and a team of Moonshot employees, summoned perhaps by our use of the emergency override, protested loudly that they needed to inspect the car, not answer police questions. Passersby on the sidewalk debated whether they had seen anything, whether the police would want to take their statements, how long they had to wait. I couldn't filter any of the noise or voices into separate channels; it all tumbled and jumbled between my ears as I tried and failed to will myself to become numb to it.

I had no concept of time, but it seemed like Ricky was talking to the police officers for hours. Cold started to prick the insensible skin on my face and, still talking to the officers, Ricky leaned over and put his arms around my immobile body and rubbed my arms for warmth, though I couldn't feel a difference.

The scene wasn't cleared, but the commotion was waning by the time the officers left Ricky alone with me on the curb. He had stopped rubbing, but he still had his arms around me, and he rested his head on my shoulder.

"I'm sorry, Oliver. I'm so sorry. They asked if you needed an ambulance, but I said I'd take care of you. I hope that was okay." He seemed to know not to expect any response. "They were nice enough to send somebody to go get my car. Then I'll take you home with me, okay? You can go to sleep, and it'll be all right."

I couldn't say a word, but a red light was blaring inside my head. How did he think he was going to get me into a car? I couldn't stand, couldn't even move. Maybe I never could again. Maybe I was a permanent fixture on this sidewalk now, Washington's newest monument, a memorial to the misunderstood, oft-forgotten American Autistic adult.

When the moment came, it took Ricky and two police officers to lift me and wrangle my locked limbs into the car in an almost convincing seated position, slumped against the door and held in place by the lap belt.

"Are you sure he doesn't need medical attention?" one of the officers asked. "I don't know if I feel right sending him off like this." They were walking around the car with Ricky, so I couldn't clearly hear his response through the closed windows of the car, but among the snatches I caught, I could swear the word *Autistic* left his lips.

He knew? I mean, clearly he'd have realized something was up with me, but he knew it was that?

Ricky was intensely focused on the drive to his apartment, although it turned out that he lived very close to where we had been, just on the other side of Rock Creek Park. The drive across the park was pitch black along a narrow, curvy road, emerging into a quiet neighborhood of neat row houses. I had no idea what time it was, but it seemed that the city was mostly in bed, with few houses adding light to our way.

We navigated a few turns through the neighborhood, then turned off the road into an alley and crept along the fences of the backyards, which were punctuated by narrow driveways into which only the smallest cars could fit. Ricky had to make a multiple-point turn into what I guessed was his own driveway to make up for the lack of power steering in his car. "I'm not really supposed to park here," he said as he shut off the engine, "but I think it'll be fine for tonight. It will make it easier to get you inside."

He got out, unlocked and opened a ground-level door next to the garage, reached in to flick on an outside light, then came back to the car and opened my door. I was still stiff, but the manipulations getting me into the car, plus the passage of time, had loosened the shutdown's grip on my body. With Ricky's arm around my waist, I was able to clumsily plod into the house.

The space was small and dark, and I was still pretty oblivious to my surroundings as Ricky led me through to a bedroom—his bedroom. He sat me on the edge of the bed. "Can you stay sitting like that for a minute?" he asked. "You should have some water."

"Mmmm," was the best response I could muster.

He left and quickly returned with the glass. Slowly, shakily, I was able to drink, first in small sips, then in thirsty gulps. I closed my eyes and lolled my head forward as I finished, finally free of the leaden feeling in my limbs, turning instead to a floppy pile.

"Yeah, let's get you in bed," Ricky said. He carefully removed my glasses and set them on a nightstand by the bed. He loosened my tie, pulling it over my head, then unbuttoned my shirt, taking me down to my T-shirt. I flopped backward, and he went down to the floor and took off my shoes and socks. He stood, considered me for a moment, then muttered, "What the hell." He undid my belt and managed to get my pants out from under my butt and over my noodle legs, then grabbed me by the ankles and rotated me ninety degrees on the bed. I heaved myself into a roll until I was on my face, then did the worm up to the pillow.

Ricky chuckled as he pulled the blankets over me, then sat for a moment on the edge of the bed, looking down at me. He raised a hand and held it above me for a second before laying the palm on the back of my head, gently running his fingers through my hair.

"Good night, Oliver," he said softly, rising. He crossed to the door, turned off the light, and left the room.

I was already very nearly asleep. The dark stillness of the room filled my head, now also suddenly still and dark. As I drifted off, a light flickered at the back of my mind, distant and dim, and right before it went out, it whispered to me, so softly I almost didn't hear it: *Elise didn't scream. She didn't make a sound.* . . .

CHAPTER 7

It took me a moment to orient myself when I woke up Thursday morning. Ricky's apartment. Ricky's bedroom. Ricky's bed. I felt the soft flannel sheets on my legs and peeked under the covers. He had gotten me down to my boxer briefs and undershirt. *Yikes.*

I pulled myself up to a sitting position and took stock of the small room. There were two windows along one wall, but they let in little light. Craning my neck to look through the nearest one, I saw that they opened to a crawl space underneath the front porch of the row house, only getting what light they could from a narrow opening several feet away. A few plastic dinosaurs and palm trees and small rocks created a little tableau in the bare ground outside at window level. We were in the basement.

The furnishings around me were spare and functional: a nightstand with a lamp, an armoire, a dresser. The bed had no headboard, but four thick pillows and a fluffy white duvet added a bit of softness to the room.

Three of the walls were bare, but the one opposite the windows was covered in an artfully arrayed patchwork of photos, some framed, some stuck to the wall with putty in groups that resembled a starburst or that cascaded down like a river through a canyon of frames. I searched for my glasses, put them on, and got out of the bed and padded over to see what Ricky liked to keep around him in his most private space.

Many of the framed photos were landscapes, street photography, and staged scenes and portraits—the products, perhaps, of assignments for college photography courses. The more casually displayed pictures were mostly candid snapshots, less polished but more personal. Groups of friends at college parties (was that Drea laughing with a red Solo cup in hand?), family backyard gatherings, a few photos of Ricky smiling with his arms around one man or another—mementos of the relationships that had gotten beyond the casual phase, I theorized a touch jealously.

In many of the photos, Ricky was seen with an attractive, middle-aged white woman; I could tell from their shared smile that she was his mom. A serious-looking Black father, who shared his thick, expressive eyebrows, appeared less frequently, and from the other people in those photos, I guessed that his parents were no longer together, and that his father had remarried and had a considerably younger daughter with his current wife. Amid the photos, a framed diploma from Howard University, awarding a bachelor of arts degree, magna cum laude, to Tariq Andrew Warner, leaned against the wall atop the dresser.

Outside the room, I could hear the occasional clatter of Ricky in the kitchen. Searching for my pants, I found my clothes and shoes in a neat pile on the floor by the foot of the bed. I pulled the pants on and slowly opened the door, then crept quietly from the bedroom to see if I could snoop some more before I ran into Ricky.

From the bedroom, I emerged into a small living room. The opposite corner of the room opened into the kitchen, which formed a sort of hallway to the front door to the apartment. Ricky must have been all the way down by the door; I couldn't see him, but I could hear him moving and humming to himself. I could also smell fragrant herbs and hear the sizzle of something cooking on the stove, and soft music was playing from a vintage console stereo on the far wall of the living room.

One corner of the room was set up as a home office, with a laptop on the paper-strewn desk plugged into two monitors. Two cameras sat on the desk, beside the laptop, and a third hung from its strap off a corner of the desk chair. The rest of the wall next to the desk was occupied by a floor-to-ceiling bookcase overflowing with books, mostly well-loved paperbacks. A pretty green lamp sat on the corner of the console, bathing the room in warm golden light, and a TV was mounted to the wall above the stereo. A comfortable leather armchair sat in the corner across from the TV, a floor lamp next to it for reading and a soft blanket thrown over the back.

I was a little surprised at how tidy the place was, and although it was small and a bit dark and none of the furnishings were anything fancy, it felt homier than I would have expected of Ricky, although I wasn't sure why that was.

I was standing over the stereo, inspecting the sleeve for the record spinning on the turntable, when I noticed Ricky leaning against the corner of the wall into the kitchen, his arms crossed, watching me with a smile. He was in a black tank top and a pair of fitted gray sweatpants, his curly hair tousled, a cup of coffee in one hand. I began to remember some of the less traumatic events of the previous evening, and I marveled at the idea that the gorgeous person standing in front of me had actually asked me out—and I was mortified at what he had seen me become.

"It's kind of like seeing a teacher outside of school, isn't it," he grinned.

"Hi," I said.

"Hi, sleepyhead. I was about to come wake you up. I made breakfast."

I followed him into the kitchen, finding my eyes yet again glued to his butt. On a small table against one wall were two plates of home-fried potatoes and omelets. I could see asparagus sticking out of my omelet, and it looked like there were chunks of mushroom suspended in the egg. It looked delicious. I sat down, and he went to get me a cup.

"Coffee? OJ?"

"I'll have juice, please," I said, then was struck by a thought. "Where did you sleep?"

He laughed as he poured the juice. "The armchair pulls out into a bed. Were you worried?"

"Just wondering."

"You had my room all to yourself. I hope you made good use of the opportunity to go through my drawers and learn all my secrets."

"What are you talking about? I didn't do any snooping . . . Tariq," I said with a sly grin.

"You got that from my wall. You're too much of a straight arrow, man. You've got to be ready to get your hands dirty to answer the real questions, like what kind of underwear I wear or if I even wear any at all. I'm disappointed."

I had been able to tell through his sweatpants a minute ago exactly what kind of underwear he wore, but I wasn't about to tell him that. "I didn't want to invade your privacy too much after you were so good to me . . . you know, last night. But I did look at your photo wall, so maybe I learned a little bit about you."

"Like what?"

"Like I'd guess your parents are split up and you mostly grew up with your mom."

He looked at me evenly over the rim of his coffee cup. "Very good. My parents divorced when I was three, and I grew up with my mom about fifty miles south of here, in Virginia. My dad moved to North Carolina after the divorce and got remarried."

"So did you get to see him at all?"

"Sure, I spent school breaks and parts of the summer with him. But we had a kind of tough relationship—I mean, I know my dad loves me, but part of why he and my mom split up was because he had a sort of crisis of conscience about being with a white woman. He remarried a Black woman, had a Black baby with her, really wanted to feel connected to that part of our culture, so I was always a little out of place—with my mom's side of the family, too. I mean, *Tariq Andrew*? There's an identity crisis waiting to happen. In Virginia I was Ricky, but my aunts and uncles and cousins always knew I was really Tariq. And in North Carolina I was Tariq, but they all knew I was really Ricky. So I didn't feel like I fit anywhere.

"Part of why I went to Howard was to try to connect with my dad. He went there, and his father did, too. And I loved it and I loved the people and I got a lot out of the experience. At first, it did make him really happy and proud. But then when I was a sophomore, I came out, and he struggled with the idea that I was dating boys for a bit, and then once he got used to it, he was a little bothered that I was sometimes dating *white* boys."

"Jeez," I said. "Seems like you can't win."

He shrugged, taking a forkful of potatoes. "Like I said, I know he loves me, and mostly our relationship is great. But I decided at some point that I could feel like I fit into the world by simply liking myself and being proud of myself, and not letting other people's complicated inner struggles dictate how I feel about myself. So I'm doing okay."

"I guess it's easy enough to like yourself when you're as likable as you," I said, blushing a little at being so mushy, but apparently unable to stop my mouth. "Good at making breakfast, too. No wonder you get all those guys to come home with you."

"Wow. Rude. I'm thirty years old. I think I'm allowed to have some basic life skills at this point."

"You're thirty?" I hadn't tried to do any math, but knowing

that he'd gone to college with Drea, I had at least subconsciously known he was older than me. But this was a bigger age gap than I'd expected, and something about being thirty sounded like being at a different stage of life.

"Yeah, is that a problem? What are you, twenty-six? Twenty-seven?"

"I'm twenty-four," I grimaced.

"Okay, I wasn't too far off. What else should I know? What's your story? What kind of place do you live in?"

"I live with my mom," I said, growing even more embarrassed that I was not only so young but also not independent enough. I added quickly, "I'm moving into my own apartment soon, though."

"Living with your mom is nothing to be ashamed of. Is she your only parent?"

"Yeah, my dad died. When I was sixteen." I forked some omelet into my mouth. "He was riding his bike and got hit by a bus."

Ricky's face drained of color. "Oh, lord. And last night— Oh, jeez, Oliver, I'm really sorry . . . you had to see that. Oh, god, are you okay?"

I looked up from my plate, taken aback. I hadn't consciously made the connection before. "I'm okay. It didn't really occur to me before now."

"Sorry," he mumbled, lowering his head into his hands with his eyes cast down.

"No, really, it's okay," I said, poking his arm with my fork. He looked up at me, and I waggled my eyebrows at him in reassurance.

"I guess I should explain about last night," I continued. I had an uneasy, unplaceable feeling that he already knew, but I felt like I had to tell him anyway.

"Only if you really want to. There was plenty of good reason to have a big reaction to what happened."

"No, I want to. I think I can relate to feeling like you don't fit in anywhere. I felt like that a lot growing up, too, because I'm . . ." He had been looking at me, his brown eyes soft, but now he seemed to sense that I needed him not to, and he lowered his eyes to his plate. I did the same and took a deep breath. "Autistic. I'm Autistic."

He thought for a moment, chewing, and when he had swallowed, he asked, "What does that mean for you?"

Usually the question was just, "What does that mean?" Or worse, "What is that like?" I hated those questions. I didn't know how to answer; they presupposed that I could draw some comparison to an experience other than my own. This question, the difference in phrasing seemingly so minute, hit me powerfully. Ricky wanted to know how it shaped my humanity, how he could use the knowledge to know me better.

I had to think for a moment. "Well," I began slowly, "in part it means that a lot of the time when I'm with other people, I can't pick up on what they're thinking, or what they're feeling, the way that you might be able to, and I have a hard time gauging how they're reacting to me. And that causes a lot of anxiety. And sometimes the anxiety builds up, and especially if I'm tired or overstimulated or there's a lot going on, it keeps building and building until my body shuts down."

"Like last night."

"Like last night," I confirmed.

"I'm sorry if I contributed to your anxiety. I hope you feel now like you know what I think of you." He was back to soft eyes across the table at me. "I like you a lot, Oliver."

I felt my face flush again, and I looked down at my nearly empty plate with a heavy feeling in my chest. I sighed. "I like you, too, but here's the thing. This is my first feature assignment. My first time traveling like this. That's a big deal by itself, but now I have a second feature to work on, and we witnessed a death, and it feels like a lot. So maybe I should focus on the work right now, try to get back on track with our itinerary, and you and I should just be friends."

"Is this because I'm too old for you? God, I knew once I hit my thirties that this day would come eventually, but I wasn't ready for it to be so soon," he said in mock horror.

"No, really. I'm sorry," I said, my eyes still downcast.

"Don't be sorry. I'm sorry I joked about it. If this is what you need . . . okay."

"Are you upset with me?"

He smiled softly. "No, I think I understand. Anyway, we'll always have last night—you know, the earlier part of last night. And I technically *did* get you out of your pants, so . . ."

I threw my last potato at him, and he held up his hands, laughing, "Hey, no homo, brah. That's how guys who are just friends talk, right?"

"Right." I gave him an exaggerated eye roll.

We lapsed into silence for a moment while I finished my orange juice and he sipped his coffee. I pondered whether I was being honest with him—with myself—or if I was pushing him away purely out of fear. The work was why I was here, after all. Ricky was distracting me from my work. Distracting me and making me feel good, more at ease than I'd ever felt with another person, making me laugh and smile and feel safe, even in the face of tragedy and horror. But it was a distraction nevertheless. Never mind that every time I'd looked at him and felt that familiar pang in my chest of fear that I'd always be alone, he'd returned some look or comment that immediately made the fear dissolve.

Finally, he spoke. "I suppose we also need to talk about the other part of last night."

I wasn't sure what to say. When I tried to think about it, it came back only as sense memory: the sounds her body had made against the car as it hit her, the red glow through the windshield after. And climbing up from somewhere beyond the back of my mind, the thought I had been left with as I had fallen asleep—of the sounds she *didn't* make.

"Oh. That," I finally said, sensing the need to give Ricky a response.

"I'm afraid the police still want you to make a statement. We should go over and do that this morning. Do you think you can?"

I was suddenly aware again of how far we had veered from my schedule since yesterday morning. Now I didn't have any clothes to change into, I didn't entirely know where we were, I didn't even know what time it was. Panic rose in my voice as I protested, "But we're supposed to be in Georgetown this morning!"

"Georgetown for a travel article? C'mon, really, like every article ever written about DC hasn't already kissed Georgetown's white ass. I think this is more important, don't you? Elise was your friend. You owe it to her to help them determine what happened."

"Determine what happened?" I echoed. "As in they think it wasn't an accident?"

"I meant determine how she came to be in that place at the time of the accident. Do you not think it was an accident?"

"Well . . ."

I wasn't sure if my nagging little thought meant anything. Maybe when you're hit by a car, you don't even have time to react. I don't know why it bothered me so much. But if Elise wasn't coming to the Moonshot event, if she should have been laying low to preserve her job after an embarrassment, why had she been all the way across town from her hotel room, so close to where we were? What had she been doing there?

Ricky looked at me, puzzled. "Oliver? Where are you?"

"I'm here. It's just that I realized when we . . . when the car hit her, she didn't make any sound. No scream, no yell, nothing. And I can't understand why she was even there to begin with."

"I hadn't realized about the sound, but I think you're right. And that's a great question—why *was* she there? We should go to the station now. I'm really curious if anyone knew what she was doing before the accident. We can ask what they found out."

"But what about Georgetown?"

Ricky put his elbows on the table and leaned in very close to me with his chin resting in both hands, a dreamy grin on his lips, his left eyebrow cocked wickedly. "Oliver. Sweetheart. You have to know that I was *never* going to Georgetown with you."

The DC Metropolitan Police Second District station was a long, low, two-story building faced in red brick and located a block off Wisconsin Avenue, very close to where we had been driven past the National Cathedral the previous evening. Ricky had given a case number, which the officers last night had provided, to the receptionist behind the front desk, and we were waiting in side-by-side plastic bucket chairs to be called back to give my statement.

"Are you nervous?" Ricky asked, noticing me shifting around in my seat.

"No, just getting used to the shirt." I had showered at Ricky's apartment, and I was wearing my underwear, socks, pants, and shoes from yesterday but had borrowed a T-shirt. We were close enough in size that it fit without issue, although Ricky seemed to favor more closely cut clothes than I usually wore.

It had gotten a little better as I'd gotten older, but I'd always had sensory issues with wearing clothes that weren't mine, and the shirt was resting on my skin like an unwelcome parasite, or maybe a boa constrictor closing in around my torso to squeeze the life out of it. And yet, every once in a while, I'd catch a whiff of Ricky's scent on it and wish I could welcome the impending fusion of cotton and skin.

"You look great in it," he said, as if that was my worry, his eyes lingering on my chest for a moment too long. "I might have to let you keep it, in fact. I think it looks better on you than on me."

"Thanks," I mumbled, trying not to squirm.

"Mr. Popp?" An officer appeared, the one who had taken Ricky's statement the night before, although I confirmed this only later, as I had been too out of it to have taken note at the time. He introduced himself as Officer Sanchez and ushered us to two chairs beside a desk in the open-air bullpen beyond the reception area.

"Are you feeling better today?" he asked me.

"Yes, thank you."

Ricky leaned forward. "It's okay if I'm here, right? Like, if I have to be related or something to stay with him, uh . . . I'm his fiancé, okay?"

"You don't have to be related, but congratulations, Mr. Warner," Officer Sanchez said distractedly, shifting piles of folders and forms around on the desk and reaching for a pen. I elbowed Ricky in the ribs, and he stifled a grunt.

"Now, Mr. Popp," Sanchez said, looking up as he arranged a blank form in front of him, "this is simply a witness statement. You're not suspected of anything. You're not in any trouble. I'm going to take down what you tell me to add to our report. As much detail as you can provide, please."

"Are you going to tell me not to leave town or anything like that? I'm only supposed to be here for two more days, then I have to go home to California."

"No, you're free to go home. It seems apparent that this was an accident. In the unlikely event that there was any kind of trial in the future, you might be asked to come back to testify, but I don't expect that to happen."

He asked for my full name and address and where I was staying, then asked for a description of the events of the previous evening. We went over my account of the collision from several different angles, each new approach making me more uncomfortable that I couldn't be more detailed, but she had seemed to come from nowhere, and it had all been over before it had really registered.

Finally, he was ready to move on. "I understand from Mr. Warner that you knew the victim, is that correct?"

"Yes. Elise Perkins. I knew her in high school, then we saw each other for the first time in several years on the flight here the other day."

His brow furrowed. "So you wouldn't say you knew much about her current life, work, lifestyle, anything of that nature?"

"No, only what she told me on the plane."

"What day was that?"

"Tuesday."

"And when had you last seen her prior to that?"

I tried to count backward. "Seven years ago?"

"And how many times had you seen her since the flight Tuesday?"

"Well, I saw her on television Wednesday morning . . ."

"And at the bar," Ricky reminded me.

"That's right, and from across the room in our hotel bar Tuesday evening. But I hadn't spoken to her other than on the plane."

"You say you saw her in a bar," Officer Sanchez said, his tone growing more pointed. "Did you have any indication that Ms. Perkins had a problem with alcohol?"

"Uh . . ." I wasn't sure how much to say. I decided to tread carefully. "At that time, I couldn't see what she was drinking or if she even had a drink. From what little I could see at that distance, she didn't look visibly impaired. Do you suspect that alcohol may have contributed to the accident?"

"Candidly, sir, we do have reason to believe that Ms. Perkins may have been intoxicated, yes."

I took this in. "Does it really matter? I mean, isn't the more important question why the car didn't detect her and avoid hitting her?"

"Well, that doesn't really fall within our jurisdiction, Mr. Popp. That's a matter for NHTSA to investigate, and I understand that they plan to."

"Another question, Officer. Would you say that you would typically expect a person being hit by a car to scream or yell or make some kind of sound?"

"Perhaps, although if they didn't see the car coming or if they got the wind knocked out of them, they might not be able to. Did Ms. Perkins make any sound?"

"No, she didn't. I'm also wondering if any witnesses have been able to shed some light on what Elise—Ms. Perkins—had been doing in that area prior to the accident. She was staying at a hotel a considerable distance away, close to Capitol Hill."

Officer Sanchez riffled through the reports in the open file folder at the top of one of his stacks. "Yes, sir, Ms. Perkins was last seen approximately twenty minutes prior to the accident in a bar on Connecticut Avenue, having a drink with another woman."

"Who was that?"

"We haven't been able to determine that, sir."

"Which bar was it?"

It seemed to strike Officer Sanchez that I had turned the tables on him. "I don't think I'm at liberty to say. Mr. Popp, do you have a problem with the idea that Ms. Perkins's death was accidental?"

"Frankly, I think I do." I was surprised by how boldly I had pumped Officer Sanchez for information, and by how blithely I was pressing on now. "I'm bothered by Elise's presence in that neighborhood at all. I'm bothered that she wandered into the path of that particular car in that particular place at that particular time. I'm bothered that the car didn't stop for her. Was it tampered with? If it didn't have time, how was she moving so fast? And why? Maybe I didn't know enough about her, but none of this is adding up."

Officer Sanchez eyed me coldly. "You're right, sir—it sounds like you didn't know much about her. I'll grant you that there are some interesting coincidences in this case, but we don't have anything to suggest that it was anything but an accident." He put down his pen, rose, and extended his hand. "Thank you for your statement, Mr. Popp. We'll be in touch if we need anything further from you."

I stood and took the offered hand, which he then extended to Ricky. "Congratulations, again, Mr. Warner, Mr. Popp." As we turned to go, he sat back down in his chair, then barked out a laugh and called to us, "Hey, are you guys gonna hyphenate your names? Popp-Warner! Ha! Get it?"

We both turned and looked at him blankly.

"You know? The peewee football program? Ah, forget it."

I shuddered as we continued out the door. "You had to tell him we were engaged," I said to Ricky in a low voice. "Which, by the way, will definitely never happen now, not now that I've heard that."

"Yeah, that's pretty grim," Ricky agreed, then brightened. "Or all it means is we can't hyphenate."

"I can't with you," I said, rolling my eyes.

"Good thing we're just friends," he said, unlocking the passenger door of his car for me.

"Yeah, that's going swimmingly."

As we settled into the car, Ricky asked, "Where to?"

"Georgetown, I guess, right? I don't have my notepad on me . . . or my itinerary or any of my contacts. Maybe we should go back to the hotel first."

"Or," Ricky said, "maybe we should canvass the bars on Connecticut Avenue to try to find out more about Elise's second mystery friend. Or see if we can get in to see her congressman boyfriend. Which one did you say that was again?"

"I didn't. I haven't even looked it up yet. Are you really this desperate not to go to Georgetown? How many ex-boyfriends do you have there?"

"Hey, you were the one turning all detective back there. You don't want to follow your hunches and see what you can find out? I thought you were a reporter."

"I'm a lifestyle journalist, not a reporter, and I'm trying to write a travel article, which you are also being paid to contribute to. Remember?"

"But you are curious, right?"

I chewed my lower lip. I thought back to what I could remember of my itinerary. Georgetown *had* sounded pointless. And I was bothered by Officer Sanchez's disinterest in what had happened to Elise. And Ricky had that eager, impish look in his eyes again.

I blew out a sigh and pulled out my phone. "Let me look up who the congressman was."

CHAPTER 8

Ricky and I debated for a moment whether to start with the bars on Connecticut Avenue or with the congressman, who Google, *Politico*, the *Washington Post*, and TMZ all reliably informed me was Rep. Gerald "Jerry" Richfield III of Massachusetts. We were close to Connecticut Avenue and across town from Capitol Hill, but it was a bit early for bars to be open. I wanted to change out of yesterday's clothes more than anything, and my hotel was on the way to Capitol Hill. I also lobbed in one more desperate bid for Georgetown, which Ricky roundly ignored. Finally, Ricky fished a quarter out of the ashtray, we flipped it, and Connecticut Avenue won.

Ricky fired up the Corvair and, whistling, pulled away from the precinct, and I searched on my phone for a recent photo of Elise to show at the bars, one that wasn't a screen grab of her looking wild-eyed as she confronted Richfield during her testimony. She had made a big splash by opening up a fresh sex scandal on the House floor yesterday morning; so far, her death seemed to have escaped notice. I wondered if Moonshot was somehow hushing it up.

Ricky glanced over at my phone at a red light. "Why are you Googling her? Go to social media. She'll have lots of photos to choose from, I guarantee it."

"Duh. I should have thought of that."

"Twenty-four, you said? You sure you didn't mean ninety? Heck, even then, my eighty-seven-year-old grandmother is on Facebook."

I turned my screen away so he couldn't see that I had to wait for the Instagram app to update before I could open it, having never touched it since creating an account on a whim months ago, then quickly failing to see the point in going any further. Once in, I searched for "Elise Perkins," scrolling through dozens of results and squinting at the tiny profile pictures to try to find her familiar face. No luck. I tried one with a profile picture of some flowers, who turned out to be an avid gardener in England, then one with a profile picture of a plate of tacos. Bingo.

There were hundreds of photos. The most recent had been posted Tuesday morning, before she went to the airport, or maybe while she was there waiting to get onto the plane where we had our last fleeting reunion. She was in the fluffy blue sweater that I remembered, making a kissy face to the camera to show her freshly applied lipstick, the caption reading, "Ready to take on TSA, Congress, and all the other haters!"

Farther down, Elise was at parties, brunches with her sister, playing with an adorable nephew. She was in oversized sunglasses behind the wheel of her car, at concerts, going on the Napa Valley Wine Train with a bachelorette party. She posted a new photo of tacos almost every Tuesday. She was a vibrant, active, healthy young woman. She had been my friend once, and it was obvious that she still had a wide network of friends and close family members. She had been loved.

Now she was dead, and suddenly I was angry because none of who she had been seemed to matter to anyone here. They regarded her only as a stranger with a possible alcohol problem who had embarrassed herself and a lot of people more important than her, then died in a freak accident, which everyone would prefer to sweep under the rug lest she cause more embarrassment.

Maybe it had been an accident. It all seemed too strange to me, but even if it had, I wanted to know more. I wanted to know for sure.

As Ricky pulled up to the curb along Connecticut Avenue in Cleveland Park, I selected and bookmarked a photo she had posted the week before, holding her nephew on her lap, happy smiles on both their faces. It was a good representation of how I remembered her normal expression, so I figured if anyone had seen her, they would recognize this version of her.

"Got one?" Ricky asked, turning off the car.

"Yep. Any idea where we should start?"

"This block is the most likely spot. There are several bars and restaurants with bars here, plus it's only a block from where . . . you know. So I think we should start at one end and work our way down."

The first bar, near the end of the block, was an Irish pub. It was quiet inside, a few patrons enjoying sandwiches or fish and chips with tall glasses of Guinness for lunch. The bartender hadn't been working the previous evening, but he had heard about the accident. He flagged over his manager, who had worked the previous night; she said Elise hadn't been there, and she didn't know where she had been. We thanked them and moved on.

The restaurant next door, some kind of Tex-Mex fusion place, wasn't open yet. I thought of Elise's fondness for tacos; if we couldn't track her movements anywhere else, this place might be worth coming back to. A sushi restaurant a few doors down was open. This time the bartender on duty had also been there last night and knew about the accident, which had apparently been the talk of the street last night, but she hadn't served Elise, either.

We were halfway down the block. As we stepped out of the

sushi bar, I scanned across the street. A library, a post office, a deli, a tanning salon, a movie theater. Nowhere to get a drink. If we were going to get lucky, it was going to be in one of the places left on this side of the street.

The next possibility was a barbecue restaurant with a well-stocked bar running the length of one side of the dining room. There was nobody manning the bar, and when we flagged down a server, a generously tattooed young woman with a name tag that said KAITLYN, she told us that there wasn't a bartender on duty until 5:00 p.m. The dining room was nearly empty, and she didn't seem to be in a hurry, so I asked if I could have a minute, and she agreed.

"Were you working here last night?" I asked, pulling out my phone with the photo of Elise. "Did you see this woman?"

She barely glanced at the picture and sighed. "Yeah, I was actually working the bar last night, and I saw her. I didn't over-serve her, though, I swear. I already told the cops that last night. Are you cops, too?"

"No, we're not cops," Ricky assured her. "We're investigative reporters."

I looked at him, realization dawning. "We probably should have led with that, huh." He shushed me, and I turned back to the server. "Don't worry, we'll protect your identity. We might not even have to name the restaurant, maybe." I mentally kicked myself for what a poor performance I was giving as an investigative reporter, but Kaitlyn seemed unfazed.

"Yeah, okay. Like I said, though, I didn't overserve her. She had, like, two whiskeys on the rocks. I didn't talk to her much, either, basically just took her orders."

"Could you tell us anything about the woman with her?"

"Not much, no. I guess she was about the same age, maybe a little older. Average height, seemed fairly thin. Dark hair . . . It gets kinda dark in here at night, so it could have been dark brown or black, I don't know. I don't remember anything she was wearing, so it must have been normal stuff, you know? Normal makeup. Maybe a lot of mascara. She kind of had a little bit of a New York accent."

Ricky knit his brows. "What kind of New York accent? Can you be more specific?"

"She sounded a little like . . . What's that one lady? She was in that old movie, what was it called, *Do the Right Thing* . . ."

"Rosie Perez?" he asked.

"Yeah, her! Like, kind of like that, but the accent wasn't as strong."

"Did you hear anything they were talking about?" I asked.

"No, sorry. I only took their orders. The other lady, the New York one, she had a white wine. One. They weren't here all that long."

Ricky looked at the dining room around us. "Do a lot of people only come in for drinks? Seems like more of a family-style place where you'd come for a meal."

Kaitlyn shrugged disinterestedly. "I dunno. Sometimes, I guess."

I didn't think we'd get much more out of her, but one last idea hit me. "Is there any way to see if she paid with a credit card? Would that give us a record of her name?"

"The cops already asked about that. She paid cash. Left a nice tip, too."

This last remark seemed meant to point out to us how much of her time we were taking, so I asked if we could get a table and order lunch. This piqued her interest far more than our line of questioning had.

We ordered sandwiches, pulled pork for Ricky and brisket for me, and as we waited for them to arrive, I said, "Well, that didn't accomplish much. We got a vague description of a woman who might have some kind of Brooklyn Puerto Rican accent but otherwise leaves no impression. Another Moonshot employee maybe? I thought they were all at that event, but who else would Elise have known here?"

"She could have been a distant relative or a friend from college or, I don't know, a real estate agent helping Elise buy a private island to hide on," Ricky agreed. "What other threads do we have to follow?"

I wished I had my notepad. I flagged Kaitlyn down and asked to borrow a pen, then pulled a napkin out of the table-top dispenser and began to make a list.

"We have the mystery woman. Not much there, but likely the last person to see her alive. Possibly a Moonshot coworker. There's the congressman, Richfield, with whom she apparently had an affair. No idea how that could have happened, but she seemed to blow it up in both their faces. Then, not really connected but weird, there's this thing about hackers targeting Moonshots and messing with the self-driving software, which *was* Elise's department."

"Those protesters, too. Relevant to our Moonshot story, at least," Ricky said. "Here's a wild thought: what if Kelso King, or someone else from Moonshot, had her bumped off? To shut her up about the flaws in their software?"

"But why would they do it with one of their own cars, in a way that draws attention to those very same flaws?"

He thought about this. "Someone with motives at cross-purposes? She knew too much, but they also wanted to, like, tank the company's stock or something?"

I was dubious but added a question to my list: *Moonshot stock manipulation?*

"Here's another thing that's bugging me," I said, tucking into my freshly arrived sandwich. "Officer Sanchez this morning said that twenty minutes passed between when Elise and the mystery woman left here and when she was hit by the car. I know we're not twenty minutes away from where it happened. So what was she—or they, if she was still with the other woman—doing during that time? And why didn't anybody see them after that?"

"I don't know if you're up for it," Ricky said, "but after we finish, we could walk down to where it happened. Take a look around."

I chewed thoughtfully. "Yeah, I think we should. I really have no conception of what that spot was like. I kind of wasn't seeing anything, you know?"

We left Kaitlyn a generous tip, and I pocketed my napkin notes as we got up to leave. We turned out of the restaurant and retraced our steps back down the block, crossing the next cross street to locate the spot where Elise had been struck.

It was amazing to me how little of the landscape I recognized today. Everything was calm and quiet, with little sign of the previous evening's trauma, although I eyed every shard of glass in the gutter warily. I knew we weren't responsible for what had happened, but I still felt guilty.

I was surprised to find that this block of Connecticut Avenue included another bridge, marking the border between the Cleveland Park and Woodley Park neighborhoods. One large apartment building stood between the intersection and the bridge; Elise had to have left the sidewalk and entered the roadway somewhere in front of this building.

We stood on the sidewalk for a moment, looking around. It was cool and shady, and if not for what I knew had happened here, it would have felt like somewhere I might like to live. There was a verge between the sidewalk and the road, from which several large trees grew to provide a leafy canopy. There were a couple of old-fashioned streetlamps, but I could see that, compared to the commercial block we had scoured earlier, this spot would be much darker at night, with no other buildings to cast light but this one, and the trees blocking out its upper stories. There were also far fewer pedestrians here, even now, in the middle of the day, and I imagined that if you timed it right at night, the area could feel almost deserted.

"What are you thinking?" Ricky asked.

"I'm thinking it could have been very dark and private here

last night. What if the other woman, or someone else, was here with Elise and pushed her into the road in front of us?"

"Playing devil's advocate," he said, "do you think it's possible she really was drunk—or maybe there was some other cause—and she accidentally stepped out into the street in front of us?"

"It's possible," I admitted. "But she'd have to have stepped awfully far—it's not right off the sidewalk, but also through this planter past the trees. Another question is: was she actually standing in the road when the car hit her? Was she moving? Or did she hit us? That is, was she pushed or thrown or something onto the car as it passed?"

"I don't know. I wasn't looking in the right direction. It's so frustrating!"

I was frustrated, too, but tried to mentally work methodically through the avenues of information open to us. "What about the car? What kind of sensors or cameras does it use to detect road hazards? Could it have recorded anything that could tell us about the position of her body in the road before we hit her?"

"That's a good question—maybe one for your boy Joey. You know you're going to have to pay him a visit, right? And it would probably be best if I wasn't there."

I gritted my teeth. The thought had occurred to me, too, but I wasn't ready to face it yet. "What about Representative Richfield? Any idea how we might get to him?"

"Hmm. He was from Massachusetts, right? It's a long shot, but . . ." Ricky pulled out his phone and began searching through his social media apps.

He began to laugh. "Remember what you said about how maybe I had dated a staffer and could get us in? Well, guess what, buttercup."

"I don't know why I took your call," Representative Richfield's aide sniffed disdainfully as he met us at the security checkpoint inside the entrance to the Rayburn House Office

Building. "And I don't know why I agreed to let you come here."

"You missed me, obviously," Ricky said. "Oliver, this is Derek Jacobs. Derek, my colleague and friend Oliver Popp."

Derek looked me over with an expression that I was afraid meant he thought I smelled like I had crawled out of a dumpster, even though I had freshened up at my hotel moments before, then turned on his heel to lead us up to Richfield's suite of offices. I shot Ricky a look that said, "What did I do?" and he shook his head, smiled, and patted my shoulder.

Although, like all buildings within the complex surrounding the Capitol, the exterior of the Rayburn Building was neoclassical, it was one of the newest congressional office buildings, completed in the 1960s, and the interior was an odd mixture of traditional and mid-century modern. The heels of Derek's Weejuns echoed off the terrazzo floors in the hallways as fluorescent lights buzzed overhead, but when we reached Richfield's suite, we entered through impressive, heavy-looking cherry paneled doors.

Derek settled in behind a desk in the anteroom and grunted toward two chairs in a grudging invitation for us to sit. I gathered by his placement near the door that Derek wasn't a very senior person in this office. The door to the offices beyond was half-open, and I wondered how many levels of bureaucracy stood between us and Representative Richfield.

"So what can I do for you fine representatives of the press?" Derek smirked. "What was it? *Motor Mania?*"

"Well, we're doing research for a story on Moonshot Motors, and Representative Richfield's questions about hacking at the hearing yesterday morning caught our attention. We were hoping he would speak to us about that," I said, hoping I could win over Derek and however many of his bosses as necessary by being substantive rather than sensational.

"Here," Derek said, pulling a packet of stapled papers out

of a folder on his desk and tossing it at me. "Here's a briefing paper we put together with the research the questions were based on. Most of it came from this nutjob lady who came in here and wouldn't leave me alone, going on about this support group or something she's in that's scared of how dangerous the self-driving cars are."

"LOCOMOTO?" I ventured.

"Yeah, I think that was it. She was a fruitcake. Go talk to her. Is that all? Come, I'll see you out."

"I really was hoping—"

"Look, that was one of the better tries we've heard over the past couple of days, but I know if you get to Richfield, you'll have . . . other . . . questions you'll want to ask. And we're not going there. So—"

"*Derek*," Ricky said, the note of warning in his voice catching me by surprise. It caught Derek, too. He went still, pursing his lips, his eyes darting from us to the open door to the main offices to the door out to the hallway. I wondered if maybe the suite wasn't as big as I had imagined, and who was on the other side of that door and how much they could hear—and how much they knew.

I raised my volume, playing my hunch. "I wonder if Representative Richfield is aware that there was yet another accident involving a self-driving Moonshot, right here in Washington, last night. The young woman who was testifying yesterday is dead. She was a friend of mine, so my interest is personal as well as professional."

There was a clinking clatter in the next room, as if something had been dropped, and a second later the door opened wider. Representative Richfield stepped into view, hovering tentatively in the doorway. He was an attractive man, probably in his early forties, with a thick head of chestnut-brown hair, which he took obvious pride in. He was the type of man clearly accustomed to being gym toned and shined to a polish, but today he looked rough and unshaven, with bags under his eyes, his shirt unbuttoned at the neck and his sleeves rolled up.

"You knew Elise?" he asked cautiously.

I turned to him. "Yes, sir, I did, but not the way you did. I'm sorry for your loss."

His shoulders sagged. He gave us a feeble wave of summons. "Get in here."

The office beyond the anteroom wasn't his private office, but it was unoccupied, and it appeared that he had been camping out at an aide's desk when he overheard us. The overhead lights were off, the room lit only by what filtered through the sheer curtains on the windows and the backlit computer screens on the desks. He had apparently knocked over a cup of pens at the mention of Elise. He made no motion to clean them up now. Instead, he gestured toward a coffeepot in silent offering as he led us through to his own office.

"The police were here right before you came," he said as he walked, his back still to us. "I sent everyone out, except Derek. He was supposed to see that I wasn't disturbed," he said, his voice rising on the last sentence for Derek's benefit. Upon reaching his desk, he slumped into the high-backed leather chair, and we took the compact armchairs facing him.

Richfield seemed lost in thought for a moment; then he leaned forward and placed his elbows on his desk, jabbing a finger at us. "Everything I tell you right now is on deep background, capisce? You got none of this from me. I'm too tired to pussyfoot around."

I nodded in agreement and pulled out my notepad, noticed him glaring at it, and put it back into my pocket. Instead, I sat back in the chair and folded my hands in front of me.

"Let's cut to the chase. Like I said, I have a personal interest in this, too. So this has nothing to do with any story I'm working on—I just want to know. How did you meet Elise?"

He sighed. "She came on as a volunteer on one of my campaigns when she was a college student, maybe five, six years ago? MIT is in my district. She was active with the College Democrats, but she was also studying to be an engineer or a computer scientist or whatever. It wasn't like she was some politically ambitious Harvard poli-sci major, where I had to worry about her coming back to bite me in the butt later, you know? I figured she was safe; we'd have our fun, with no real professional ramifications."

"That seems awfully cynical."

He gave me a heavy-lidded stare. "You don't know much about politics, do you? Anyway, I spent last night here, hiding from my wife, so clearly I didn't keep it as casual as I intended. We . . . kept seeing each other pretty heavily the rest of the time she was in college. After she graduated and went back to California, things cooled off a bit, but she came to visit me a few times over the last few years."

"We saw you with her at our hotel bar the other night. Another reunion?"

"Kind of. We only had one drink. She wanted me to tip her off about what the committee would be asking the next day, which I couldn't tell her, and I wanted to make it clear that I couldn't see her anymore. She wasn't very happy with me by the time I left—as everyone saw yesterday."

I thought about his story for a moment. A question was bubbling up to the surface, and I was trying to figure out how to phrase it tactfully when Ricky beat me to the punch, taking a much more direct route. "Do you have a picture of your wife handy?"

Richfield looked confused but reached across the desk and turned a framed photo around to face us. His wife was blond and blue-eyed. Not someone I thought too likely to have a Spanish-inflected Brooklyn accent, but to be sure, I asked, "Where is she from, originally?"

"She's from Boston. Why the sudden interest in my wife?"

Ricky forged ahead. "You said you were here all night. Did you leave at any point?"

"What? No, I didn't leave," he said, his confusion turning to agitation.

"Can anyone verify that?" Ricky asked, pushing his luck a little too far for my comfort.

"All right, get out of here," Richfield growled, standing up, with his palms planted on the desk. It occurred to me that he probably wasn't used to his authority being questioned, and he clearly didn't like this affront to his power.

"Thank you for your time, Representative," I said meekly as I backed out of the room on Ricky's heels. We passed through the darkened inner office, and Ricky gave Derek a finger wave as we hustled through the anteroom, to which Derek responded with an eye roll.

As we waited for the elevator, I finally asked Ricky something that had been nagging at me. "What did you have on Derek? He almost seemed afraid of you for a minute there."

"Not much, really. We went out once or twice, fooled around a little, you know. He was really boring, and really full of himself—all these Capitol Hill nobodies are. But, see, while he gets his jollies on the side with boys his own age, he also has a sugar daddy, who I don't think he'd want his boss to know about."

"That's a little closed-minded. I mean, it's not like Richfield's a saint, either."

"It has nothing to do with morality, and more to do with the fact that the sugar daddy is a prominent member of the loyal opposition, and little Derek isn't always as discreet about not taking his work home with him as he should be."

CHAPTER 9

Joey had accepted my invitation for a predinner drink in the hotel bar a little too eagerly. When I had made it clear that it was to be a professional meeting, he had laughed and made a joke that he would be professional this time, as long as next time was personal. I had gritted my teeth and felt a constriction in my chest at this, but Ricky, listening in, had stifled a giggle and suggested that I change back into his T-shirt from this morning for the meeting.

I left Ricky in my room with instructions to do some research on LOCOMOTO—to see if he could learn more about who was involved, who was funding them, and more about their patron saint Dr. van Veldt's involvement with Moonshot's self-driving technology. Now I was sitting at a table in the bar, fidgeting with the straw in my glass of Sprite to keep my hands from pulling at the T-shirt, which I couldn't believe I had agreed to put back on, and waiting for Joey to appear.

He bounded in, looking trim in a handsome navy blue sweater but wearing entirely too much scent, apologized for keeping me waiting, and tried to do an air-kiss thing by my ear, which I flinched away from, nearly knocking over my drink. He didn't seem to notice, settling into his seat across from me with a smile and signaling the bartender for a glass of white wine.

"Okay," he said, folding his elbows under him on the table and leaning in. "What can I do for you?"

I could swear he winked as he said this, but I decided to play it straight. "First of all, I'd like to offer my condolences to you on the loss of your friend, and to ask if Moonshot has an official statement on the death of Elise Perkins."

He sat back and sighed. "Poor Elise. I mean, we weren't super close or anything, but we hung out at happy hours and holiday parties and stuff. She was always good for spilling some tea and having a laugh, but between us, girl was kind of a mess. She did drink a lot."

"Is that the company's official statement?"

"Of course not! Let me see, I have it here." He pulled up a memo on his phone and read: "'The Moonshot Motors family mourns the sudden loss of our valued colleague Elise Perkins. Out of respect for the privacy of her family and loved ones, we have no further comment at this time.'"

"But is it the company's position that alcohol was a factor in Elise's death? That would shift some blame, or at least attention, away from the car."

His brow furrowed, and he consulted his phone. "I guess we have no position on that?"

"What about the car? Why didn't it stop before it hit her? Has any data been retrieved from the car to explain why it didn't stop or how the impact happened?"

"Well, the police are being a big pain there. They impounded the car and won't release it to us so that we can inspect it. In fact, I think they're turning it over to NHTSA, so we'll probably never get a chance. Of course, we can always—" He stopped himself short.

"Can always what? Do you have the ability to access data from the car remotely? Have you?"

"Me? No . . ." He looked uncomfortable, his eyes scanning the room around us.

"Not you personally, the company."

"I don't—No comment. Jeez, I thought we were friends here."

"We're still friends," I lied, forcing myself to smile, feeling like a crocodile grinning as I bit his head off. "We're both just doing our jobs." He took a steadying sip of his wine, and I pressed on. "What about a response to the allegations raised by Representative Richfield yesterday about Moonshot's over-the-air updates being vulnerable to hackers?"

He gave me a forlorn look. "I told you, Oliver, I don't know anything about that stuff."

"Yeah, but you're doing PR for this company. Shouldn't you be prepared to answer questions like this?"

His shoulders slumped, and his voice dropped. "Look, I ask for statements and talking points all the time. Our department's a joke. Mr. King doesn't let us say anything, because he wants his to be the only voice in the room. So we wait around until he makes a grand pronouncement on whatever and then parrot what he says. But this hearing, and now the accident, has him so distracted that he's not saying anything. I don't know what to tell you. I've got nothing."

I thought about this for a moment, then leveled my gaze across the table at Joey. "So take me to King. Let me get his answers." He hesitated, and I decided I'd better shoot my shot and pray he never called my bluff. I cocked an eyebrow suggestively and added, "I'd make it worth your while."

"Let me see what I can do," he said, returning my raised eyebrow and picking his phone up from the table, beginning to tap out a text message. I sipped my Sprite while I waited, and a moment later he looked up. "Okay, come with me."

Joey signaled the bartender to charge the drinks to his room, then led me to the elevator, where he punched the button for the top floor. As we ascended, he pulled his wallet out of his pocket and fished out a room key. We exited the elevator and walked to the end of the hallway, where a set of double doors marked the entrance to the presidential suite. He lightly knocked on the door, then, without waiting for a response, keyed us in with another wink at me. I suppressed the urge to roll my eyes.

The suite was impressively palatial. We had entered into a sitting room, which included a full bar, multiple seating areas of couches and chairs upholstered in soft creams and grays, a baby grand piano in one corner, and a full wall of windows showcasing a view that encompassed the Capitol and, from the right angles, the Washington Monument farther down the Mall.

In addition to the waning daylight from the windows, there was a glittering chandelier lighting one end of the room, over a dining set positioned next to the bar, and the rest of the room was pooled in golden light from table lamps illuminating two of the seating areas. In one, Mimi sat curled in an armchair, idly scrolling on a big MacBook on her lap. She was enveloped in a giant, fluffy white bathrobe, her hair wrapped in a towel atop her head, although she was still in full face. She didn't look up as we entered. Kelso King was seated on a couch next to the other lamp, stacks of file folders spread around him. He closed the one on his lap as he heard the click of the door, and set it down beside him as he stood, plastering a smile of dubious authenticity on his face.

"Well, Mr. Harris, good evenin'," he drawled, clapping Joey on the back. "And you must be Mr. Popp. What a pleasure to meet you." He extended a giant hand to pump mine enthusiastically.

I had seen him at the event last night, of course, but up close he seemed much taller and quite a bit older than he did from a distance. The color of his face suggested liberal use of bronzer, but the fine lines suggested that he'd also had plenty of bronzing from the sun in his day. Without his trademark Stetson, it was evident that his sandy hair, while carefully trimmed to conceal the fact as much as possible, was thinning on top. His teeth were as dazzlingly straight and white as they had appeared when I had noticed them on the cover of the in-flight magazine, but in person you could see how the veneers created a slight overbite, which probably hadn't been there before. His watery blue eyes regarded me with a mixture of curiosity and leeriness.

He turned to Mimi, raising his voice unnecessarily to shout across the room at her, "Mimi, darlin', come say hello to Mr. Popp." She shut the laptop and tossed it onto the couch next to her and shuffled over in her hotel slippers, painting on an artificial smile of her own as she crossed over to us, giving Joey a finger wave and locking her eyes on me. They were a strikingly variegated blue-green and, like everything about her, were almost certainly not her original equipment.

Her voice was as startling as I remembered from the first time I had heard it, an affected schoolgirl lilt unlike anything I'd ever heard before. "Mr. Popp—what an adorable name! I'm Mimi. Do you like *my* name?"

"It's very nice," I said politely, trying to hide my confusion at this bizarre introduction. "Is it your only name?"

She tittered, a hand over her mouth, but did not answer.

Joey said in a low tone, "Oliver—Mr. Popp here—was with us last night, and he was in the car that . . . you know . . ."

King regarded me solemnly. Mimi looked momentarily confused. "The car that . . . ? Oh!" She reached out and clutched my arm with one hand, raising the other to her heart. "That poor girl. I'm sorry about your friend, Oliver."

"Thank you," I said. I turned to King. "I'm hoping you might be able to answer a couple of questions that Mr. Harris couldn't about the accident."

"Well, now, let's pull up a seat and chat," he said, indicating the armchairs facing the couch. Mimi padded away toward the bedroom, saying she needed to rest before getting dressed for dinner. "Don't forget, we have that eight o'clock reservation," King called after her. Turning back to me, he stabbed the air with a finger in the direction of Mimi's receding figure.

"You might not think it to look at her, 'cause she's so pretty and feminine and all, but that woman is a certifiable genius," he confided. I wasn't sure what one had to do with the other, but I let him continue. "Hand to god, if I dropped dead today, I'd want her to replace me as the CEO of all my companies. She's much more up on what's new than I am, believe it or not. I mean, I do the Twitter—that, I get—but otherwise, I'm real old-fashioned. Everybody thinks I'm a real techie, but I like pens and paper." He indicated the stacks of folders surrounding him. "But even more important is what's in her *soul*. She's an empath. You know what that is?"

I had a vague idea—mostly that people who called themselves empaths were generally full of baloney—but I shook my head.

"It means she can actually feel what you're feeling. Not just, you know, look at you and tell how you're feeling—no, she actually *feels* it. She's very spiritually aware, too. Like, right now, you didn't say Ms. Perkins was a friend of yours, but she was, wasn't she?"

"Yes, she was," I conceded.

"See, and Mimi picked up on that from your energy! Me, I would have thought you were as stony-faced as anybody, not a clue. But she could tell that you were feeling grief and loss inside. That's a remarkable gift. I trust her completely when it comes to making the big, important decisions my job requires."

"Does she have an official role within your company?"

"I keep pestering her to become my official right-hand man, but she won't do it. She says she prefers to act as my personal spiritual advisor and consigliere behind the scenes. But she's my heir apparent, I tell you."

Something about the combination of King's Texas accent

and all this New Age gibberish struck me as a bit comical—not to mention his pronunciation of *consigliere*—and I thought it best to bring things back to the purpose for my being here.

"Mr. King, I'm wondering what your position is on the circumstances of Ms. Perkins's death. Do you believe it was an accident? Do you believe that alcohol was a factor? Do you feel that your company bears any responsibility, since the car failed to stop before hitting her?"

He regarded me thoughtfully. "Candidly—with all due respect to your friendship with Ms. Perkins, and off the record, you understand—my position is that no matter how you slice it, this accident puts us in a hell of a pickle. I mean, it was our car, but also one of our people. If she's stumbling around drunk, that don't reflect too positively on us, and the car not stopping is a problem, for sure. There don't seem to be any way for us to come out of this looking good."

"I've noticed that there has been very little coverage of the incident so far. Pretty lucky for you, then, isn't it?"

He gave a small smile. "Yep, I'd say so." By his tone, I knew that we understood each other, although how he had managed to suppress the story would have to be a question for another time.

"What about the car? Have you been able to pull any data about what the car did or didn't do in the moments before and during the collision with Ms. Perkins?"

"Officially, the data recorders and camera footage for that car are in the possession of the police, and now, I suppose, NHTSA," he said.

"Unofficially?"

He didn't answer, but the small smile returned, and he cut his eyes to the folders next to him on the couch.

"Is there anything you'd like to share? It could be an anonymous leak."

"No, sir, you'll get no leaks from me. Maybe the NHTSA

folks will oblige, although I'm not sure how much they'll have to work with." He chuckled at this obscure comment.

I moved on. "Do you have a response to Representative Richfield's allegations that Moonshot's OTA updates are vulnerable to hacking?"

He looked pained. "That's another kettle of fish, ain't it. I mean, we're damned if they are: why weren't we more careful about encryption, server security, and so on? And we're damned if they're not: if not hacking, how can you explain why the system keeps screwing up?" He looked me dead in the eyes. "And it *is* screwing up, Mr. Popp. If it was drunk little Ms. Perkins telling me this, I might not totally buy it, but I've got teams of people working for me, and teams of people I've brought in from the outside, all swearing up and down that the basic system is sound. I want to be clear about that. I'm not shipping cars with a fundamentally unsafe technology. Something's going wrong once the cars are out in the world."

King put his palms up. "So, it would seem I gotta own that we haven't made our systems as secure as we should have, and try to make it right with the universe. You can believe we're trying to tighten everything down now." He indicated the folders again. "I got reports on top of reports here about how we're gonna eliminate our vulnerabilities. It makes me sick that we messed this up bad enough to get caught up in these stupid hearings, and now we're gonna be drowning in red tape."

I wondered if he lost any sleep, too, over the many people whose lives these security failures had endangered, or worse, or if it was only getting caught and being subjected to regulation that bothered him. I wondered what Mimi's spiritual counsel on the matter would be.

"Sir, I appreciate how forthcoming you've been with me," I said, "but it would really be helpful, to both of us and to my readers, if you had some substantive data you could share with me. Anything from the data recorders of the car in the accident, proof of hacking, or concrete examples of how you'll safeguard against hacking in the future?"

King stared at me for a long moment. I wondered if he regretted having spoken so freely. He liked to present himself to the world as a man who shot from the hip, but I had to think he was more strategic than that. Finally, he said, "No, I guess your readers will have to take my word for it. And that's the last comment you'll get from anybody at Moonshot for this story." Without breaking eye contact with me, he pointed to Joey. "You got that, Mr. Harris?"

He rose and once again thrust his giant paw in my direction. "It's been a pleasure, Mr. Popp. You have a good evening, you hear?"

I returned to my room to find Ricky sitting on my bed, my laptop on his lap, a notepad and his phone on one side of him and a pizza box on the other.

"You're just in time—I was about to give up on you. Room service brought up this pizza a little while ago, and I was getting ready to eat the whole thing myself."

I motioned for him to scoot over, then kicked off my shoes and joined him, flipping open the box between us to grab a slice. "Joey took me up to see Kelso King. That was . . . an experience."

"Here I was, thinking Joey had taken you up to see his room, and who knows what else. I feel like I should tell you—as a friend, of course—you could do better."

I knew he wanted me to ask so that he could position himself as the superior alternative, but for once I wasn't biting. "What did you find out about LOCOMOTO?"

He set down his slice of pizza, wiped his hands on a napkin, and picked up the hotel notepad where he had been scrawling notes. "Nothing that exciting, I'm afraid. They don't seem to be a fundraising powerhouse, and what money they do have seems to have come mostly from their members—the grass-roots, if you will. That Melba lady seems to be the leader of the local group, but they do have chapters around the country and a Facebook following of over twenty thousand. They talk about this van Veldt lady like she's Mother Teresa or something, but she doesn't seem that actively involved—like, she's not posting on their Facebook page or anything."

"Any idea what her connection to Moonshot is?"

"Not exactly, no, but there is one interesting thing. I tracked her down to the computer science department at none other than . . . MIT. Isn't that where you said Elise had gone?"

"Yeah," I said, chewing dubiously, "but tons of engineers and computer scientists and people that a company like Moonshot would want to recruit go through MIT."

"Well, anyway, I tried to call her at the number I found in their online directory, but she didn't answer, so I left a message and sent her an email. I also emailed a guy I know who works at NHTSA, to see if he can connect us with any intel on the car."

"A guy you *know*?" I asked dubiously.

"Yeah, I know people. Some platonically, even. This guy happens to have been one of my roommates in college."

We ate our pizza in companionable silence for a moment. "So, what'd you get from King?" Ricky finally asked.

"He's a weird character. Slippery. One minute he's being totally open with his opinions about things, but as soon as you ask him for something verifiable to support those opinions, he clams up and won't share. He all but admitted there was something wrong with the car that hit Elise, but wouldn't say what—and it sounds like they might even be destroying evidence before the authorities can find out what went wrong, so it'll be interesting to see what your friend at NHTSA has to say about what they find."

Ricky looked at me in shock, his cynical façade momentarily broken. "Why would they destroy evidence?"

"I don't know. To cover up the fact that their cars are vulnerable to hacking, maybe? He admitted that, too, by the way."

"We should see if we can find out whether the police were able to get anything from the car before they turned it over to NHTSA."

"Yeah, let's put that on the list for tomorrow morning," I agreed. "But if they weren't able to retrieve any data, I have a feeling I know where we could find it."

"King has it?"

"He didn't say so directly, but I'm pretty sure it's in his room. He had a bunch of files up there that seemed to be related to the hacking and to the accident data."

We again lapsed into meditative chewing. After a minute I noticed that Ricky was chewing without swallowing for an unnaturally long time, a faraway look in his eyes. "I can smell your clutch burning from here," I said. "What are you thinking?"

"Let me see if I have this straight. He has evidence of what happened, but he wouldn't share any of it with you, and he implied that the authorities wouldn't be able to get it, either?"

"Yeah, that's what I said."

"That's rotten. I wish there was a way to get our hands on those files. A way to get into his room when he's not there or something."

My eyes went wide as he said this, and a horrible thought registered in my mind. "There may be a way, but I really don't want to say what it is," I said slowly.

He stared at me expectantly. "Well?"

I swallowed hard. "Joey . . . has . . . a key to King's room. He keeps it in his wallet."

His eyes lit up. He jumped around to sit cross-legged, facing me, knocking aside the now-empty pizza box. "Yes! You swipe the key from Joey, we watch the room until we know nobody's home, and we go in and look for those files!"

"Ugh. I know when they'll be gone, too. They have an eight o'clock dinner reservation." Why was I giving him more information? *Stupid, Oliver!*

"Then we gotta get moving. Let's get you in to get that key from Joey."

"Why am *I* swiping the key?" I croaked. "Haven't I had to spend enough time with Joey today? You said I could do better."

"You can do better, but that doesn't mean you can't use him. I'd love to help, but I've forgotten all my pickpocket lessons, so you'll have to use your seductive wiles to get the key."

"I don't think I have any of those."

"Of course you do," he said, giving me a playful shot to the knee. "He wanted a personal get-together with you, didn't he?"

"Oh god," I wailed, flopping backward into the pillows and throwing an arm over my face. "I might also have told him I'd make it 'worth his while' if he took me to see King! Why did I use such a stupid phrase?"

"You did not! You tricky little tramp. Well, there you go. You're going to make our Joey very happy, and then we'll get those files. Everybody wins."

"How happy do I have to make him?"

"Not *that* happy. Happy enough that you can get to his wallet and steal that key, that's all. I'd be devastated if you made him too happy."

I peeked out at Ricky from under my arm. He looked entirely too excited about this cockeyed plan. Excited, and a little smug.

"You're forcing me into this," I warned him. "You'd better be prepared to live with the consequences, even if that means I have to make Joey *very, very* happy."

CHAPTER 10

I briefly held out hope that Joey would take King's instructions close to heart and have nothing more to do with me, professionally or personally. I explained this wrinkle to Ricky, but he waved it away, unconcerned.

"Give me your phone," he demanded, snatching it from me. He tapped out a text, leered at me from across the bed for a few seconds, then received a buzz in response. He looked at the message. "He'll be ready for you in twenty minutes."

"Jeez, what did you say?"

"I didn't say anything, you did. Don't be surprised if he answers the door in the nude. I think he wants the twenty minutes to . . . you know."

"No, I don't know. To what?"

Ricky stared at me, deadpan, for a long moment.

"To what?" I repeated.

"To clean up," Ricky said, more suggestively than I would have said something so prosaic.

"Is that all," I said.

Ricky started laughing. "To douche, Oliver! Jeez!"

"*Oh, my god!*"

I was still half shouting, half crying protestations and swatting at Ricky when he shoved me out the door several minutes later. "Quit whining, you'll be fine. Good luck!"

I took my time walking down the hall and took the stairs down to the third floor, trying to gather my composure. What had I gotten myself into? Would he really answer the door naked? No, of course not—right? It would make it easier to get the wallet out of his pocket if he wasn't wearing the pants. . . . I arrived at his room, took one last ragged breath, smoothed the front of Ricky's infernally well-fitting T-shirt, and knocked.

Joey answered, mercifully still fully dressed. His smile was tentative. "Come in, come in. I'm so glad you asked to come over. I didn't expect it so soon, and I was afraid you wouldn't call at all—that you'd be upset with me after that interview with Mr. King."

"Uh, no," I stammered as I followed him to the sitting area of his room, where the TV was tuned to one of *The Real Housewives* shows. "I know that wasn't personal. No reason we can't still be friends."

"I agree," he purred, sitting down on the sofa and patting the cushion next to him. Now that the reassurances were out of the way, his confidence in our chemistry was back.

I sat warily and was immediately distracted by the television. Long, perfectly lacquered fingernails were being pointed back and forth between women with hair extensions in clashing shades of blond and plumped lips in complementary shades of pink.

"Which one is this?" I mumbled, transfixed, then glanced toward Joey. He was sitting in the corner of the couch, his knee up on the seat, his elbow propped along the back, his chin in his hand, his face angled toward me and grinning hungrily. He reached across and put his other hand on my leg, then slowly drew it upward and reached farther inward. My stomach lurched as he neared the danger zone.

"Uh . . . yeah, ha ha," I babbled, squirming away to assume a position mirroring his, my back in the opposite corner of the couch, my crotch safely out of reach.

He was unfazed, still giving me what I guess he thought was

a seductive look. "You're so shy, aren't you, Oliver. Let's get more comfortable. I'll be right back."

He stood and walked toward the bedroom area beyond the bathroom, giving me a glance over his shoulder as he went. Did he really excuse himself to slip into something more comfortable? I began to worry I was going to barf.

Maybe he had taken his wallet out of his pocket and left it somewhere here, where I could grab the key and slip out before he came back! People do that, right? Take the stuff out of their pockets and put it on a table by the door when they come in? I latched on to this thought and quickly scanned the coffee table and the countertop by the door, over the mini fridge. No such luck.

A moment later Joey padded back into view, wearing a short terry-cloth robe and, I shuddered to realize from all the bare skin otherwise on display, possibly nothing else. His arms and legs and what was visible of his chest were surprisingly hairy, and I blanched at the thought of him rubbing his lotions through all that hair. My second thought was of his now-absent pants. Where had he put them?

He beckoned me toward the bedroom area. I gritted my teeth and followed him. He reached back to take my hand, and I reluctantly, gingerly gave it to him, trying to keep the grip between his soft fingers and mine as loose as possible. As we passed into the bedroom, I quickly checked the desktop—no wallet—then glanced at the floor between the bed and the wall. Bingo. There were his clothes, crumpled on the floor next to the bed.

Joey stopped short in front of the bed, pulling me into him and bringing our faces close together. *This is it, Oliver. He's going to kiss you. Your first real kiss, and it's a total sham. You're taking advantage of this probably perfectly nice guy who likes you and can't help that he has a problem with moisturizers.* I was starting to hate myself.

But he didn't kiss me. He hovered close for a moment as

though he was going to, his lips parted and his eyes nearly closed; then he grinned and pushed me backward onto the bed.

"Oof!" I considered trying to gracefully turn my bounce into a nice, clean roll right off the bed onto the floor, on top of his clothes, but he was too quick, putting a knee between my legs and assuming a crawling position above me.

He raised a hand and clawed at the air. "Rawr!" he purred, then dove for my neck.

"Oh! Ah! Uh," I gasped, then couldn't stop myself from giggling as his beard tickled my neck, though underneath the laughter was a considerable amount of alarm, especially as I felt his teeth brush my skin. Crud, now he'd think I was into this. I needed an escape route, and quick.

He had me pinned, but I could turn my head and look over the side of the bed. The pants were there, under his shirt—no sign of his underwear, thank god, so he must still have it on—and I could almost reach. . . .

"Woof!" I yelped as Joey's hand suddenly clamped down around the crotch of my pants. I jumped reflexively, he tumbled to one side, and, arms and legs flailing, I flew over the side of the bed and landed squarely on top of his clothes.

Not a planned maneuver, nor a graceful one, but the one I needed to make, and at the right time, before he got any further. He peered over the edge of the bed at me. The disarray of my limbs concealed from his view the fact that my hand was in his pocket, wrapping around his wallet.

"Are you okay?"

I wriggled a little to make sure he couldn't see what I was doing and, perhaps subconsciously, to make sure I really hadn't broken my coccyx or something. "A little winded. Give me a sec."

He disappeared back onto the bed, and I whipped the wallet up to where I could see inside, and pulled out two identical room keys. Two? One must be for his own room. I didn't have time to see if the room numbers were written on the cards; he would have to get locked out of his room the next time he left. I grabbed both and stuffed them into my own pocket.

"Come up here, and I'll kiss it all better," he cooed. "I'll kiss *ev-er-y-thing.*"

Yikes. Time to boogie. "Ouch. I, um, really hit my head. I think I might have a concussion."

He appeared over the edge of the bed again. "A concussion? Are you serious? Let me see your eyes."

"Ooh, yeah, ouch," I moaned, lolling my head around so that he couldn't get a good look at my presumably perfectly normal pupils. "I think I smell toast. Do you smell that? That's weird, right? I think I need to lie down."

I scrambled to my feet as he gave me a confused look from the bed. "Toast? Isn't that a stroke? Oliver, are you okay?"

"Yeah, sorry, I should go. I'm getting really sleepy, so I should go sleep, right? I'm sure I'll be fine. Sorry," I said as I shuffled quickly to the door.

"No, if you have a concussion, don't go to sleep! Come back," I heard him call as I dashed into the hall, leaving only my dignity behind.

Ricky was on the couch when I returned to my room, and one of *The Real Housewives* leered at me from the TV.

"Please turn that off. I don't ever want to see one of those shows again. If it means giving up homosexuality, I'm prepared to do it," I said, slumping onto the couch.

He grinned at me as he clicked the OFF button on the remote. "You had fun, huh? Wait, is that a *hickey?* Oliver, he gave you a hickey! What is he, twelve? Are *you* twelve?" He dissolved into laughter. I pulled the throw pillow out from under my side and whacked him with it.

"Did you get the key?" he asked once he could speak again.

"Yeah, I got it. I had to take his room key, too, because I

couldn't tell them apart." I pulled both cards out of my pocket, and flipped them over to see that there were no room numbers on either. We'd have to try both.

"You sure you didn't take it so you could go back for round two? What else did you two get up to besides necking?"

"You know, heavy petting, going steady, car dates at the malt shop . . . Jeez, no, I don't want to go back! That was humiliating! And not . . . not how—" I couldn't bring myself to admit to Ricky that, as little and as clumsy as it had been, I had gone further with Joey than I had ever gone with anyone before. And I felt pretty gross about it. And I was a little upset—no, more than a little—that Ricky had pushed me into it so cavalierly. I knew he didn't know how different it was for me than it would have been for him, but I thought he liked me, maybe even cared about me.

Now I was brooding, and Ricky noticed.

"Hey, are you okay?"

"It's fine." I wanted to be alone. I stood and headed for the bedroom area. "You can turn your show back on," I said over my shoulder as I left.

I stretched out on the bed, my back toward the sitting area, my face buried in the pillows. The TV didn't come back on, and a moment later I heard Ricky's voice behind me. Not too close. Keeping a respectful distance.

"Do you want to talk about it?"

"No."

"Did he hurt you?"

"No!"

"If we're still going to go up there, we should probably do it in about half an hour. Do you still want to go?"

"Sure. Might as well."

"Okay. I'll be over here if you need anything." Then, after a pause: "I'm sorry."

I listened to his retreat back to the couch and felt the sting of tears in the corners of my eyes. If someone had told me yesterday that today I'd be making out with a nice guy who liked me, I'd have pictured something, and someone, very different than what had happened in Joey's room and how I had gotten to that point. Now I wasn't sure how nice Ricky was.

I mean, I *had* told him I thought we should stick to being friends. And we *had* joked around about seducing Joey to get information we wanted. I had thought it was only banter, but as always seemed to be happening with Ricky, it had gotten away from me.

Then I heard my aunt Julie's voice in my head, telling me to be young and dumb and to have fun. I had been so certain I wouldn't take that advice, but Ricky had gotten me to do some dumb stuff, that was for sure. And digging around in a mysterious death, chasing an investigative report into a shady company that seemed to have lost control of its products . . . What had happened to my itinerary and my nice, simple travel article on Washington, DC? I definitely felt young and out of my depth. And despite it all, I had been having fun, mostly because of Ricky. He had made me feel like I was witty and observant and decisive and maybe even a little sexy. It was even fun sometimes to let him carry me away—sometimes. Maybe all I needed was to try to get a better handle on that part of things.

I sat up on the edge of the bed, ready to face Ricky again, and trying to ignore how aware I was of the irony of what I had just resolved to do as we set out to break into someone else's hotel room.

I was still feeling a little frosty toward Ricky, so we didn't talk as we rode the elevator to the top floor, but I realized once we got there that we hadn't really planned the logistics of this escapade. I grabbed his arm and pulled him to the side of the hallway outside the elevator.

"What's our plan? Do we waltz right in? What if somebody's in there? Do we turn on lights, or is there some reason we should skulk around in the dark?"

"Skulking around in the dark would be good for dramatic effect, but I don't think it's necessary," he mused. "I think we walk up to the door, knock in case there's somebody in there, and assuming there isn't, we key ourselves in. Look like we're supposed to be here. Casual."

"Casual. Okay, we're casual."

Saying it made me suddenly hyperconscious of my body, and my first few steps down the hallway were stiff-legged and lopsided before I remembered how to walk like a human.

Reaching the double doors, Ricky rapped authoritatively three times, then waited, counting under his breath. There was no movement inside. "Fifteen Mississippi," he finished. "Okay, I think it's safe to say nobody's home. Try the keys."

I fumbled the keys out of my pocket, my sweaty palm sticking to both the plastic cards and the fabric lining, pulling everything out in a tangled mess. I pulled them apart with shaky hands before inserting the first one into the slot in the door. The diode turned green, we heard the beep, and we were in.

I tried to lock into my memory which key had done the trick, holding one in each hand. "Should I keep these separate, now that we know which is which?"

"What, are you going to try to give Joey his key back? What would you say, 'Sorry, when you thought I was feeling you up, I was actually picking your pocket and I stole your key'? No, man, we use it, then we lose it—both of them."

"That wasn't how it happened," I muttered darkly, following him inside and closing the door before reaching for the light switch.

The two switches by the door activated a bank of canned lights along the perimeter of the room and the chandelier over the dining set. Ricky gave a low whistle. "Fancy digs."

Aside from Mimi's computer and the stacks of folders on

the couch, there had been little sign of personal effects in this room when I had been here several hours ago. King and Mimi were apparently tidy guests, although for all I knew, the bedroom was strewn with their clothes and toiletries. If anything, the room felt even less personal now; even the computer and folders were nowhere to be seen.

"What exactly are we looking for?" Ricky asked.

"King had a bunch of manila folders on the couch when I was here. Whatever he had from the accident log was in one, and others had reports about the hacking, I think."

"Well, they're not there now," Ricky pointed out, scanning the room. "I don't see any folders anywhere. Maybe the drawers on that table, or the desk over there? You take the table."

I eyed the side table by the door dubiously. It had two shallow drawers, wide enough but almost certainly not deep enough to hold the number of folders I had seen. The first drawer contained a Gideon Bible and a folder with a room service menu and information on other hotel amenities. The second drawer was empty, other than a hairpin and a hotel-branded pen rolling around at the back.

"Nothing here—" I said, then stopped myself. Someone was out in the hall. It was only 8:35 p.m., so the odds that it was King or Mimi returning from their dinner reservation already were low, but it occurred to me that the odds that multiple staff lackeys had keys to the suite and could be dispatched here at any time were considerably less low. I held up a hand to my lips and waited, not breathing again until I heard the elevator doors open and close down the hall. "Whew. All clear. Anything in the desk?"

"Not a thing." Ricky stood up, hands on his hips, again casting his eye around the room. We both craned our necks to look at the lower shelves of the two coffee tables, both of which were bare. He gritted his teeth. "Bedroom?"

"I guess we have to."

A wall of glistening white granite with a double-sided fire-place separated the sitting room from the bedroom. Passing through the doorway, we entered another immense space, with still more couches and armchairs as well as the biggest bed I had ever seen. Closets took up the entirety of one wall of the room, while the other end, fronting the room-width, floor-to-ceiling windows, was occupied by an exhibitionist's dream bathroom, separated from the bedroom only by a glass partition.

There weren't exactly clothes strewn everywhere, but the room did feel less unoccupied than the sitting room. Half the bed was still neatly made from this morning's service, but half was rumpled, presumably from Mimi's nap this afternoon. Several pairs of women's shoes were arrayed in front of one of the armchairs, and a few coats, shirts, and pairs of pants were draped over the back of the couch. The bathroom vanity was barely visible under a mountain of makeup and skin care products, and an open valise on the bathroom floor was overflowing with bottles of pills and supplements.

There weren't many places to stash the folders other than the closets, so I started there. Ricky went to the bed to check the nightstands. I heard him quickly open and close the drawer on King's side of the bed, then open the drawer on Mimi's side.

"Psst, Oliver," he hissed, stifling a giggle.

I turned to look. He was holding up a pair of handcuffs and a small plastic baggie of white powder.

"Is that cocaine?" I gasped.

Ricky peered more closely at the baggie. "I assume so. Believe it or not, I wouldn't know. The limits of my depravity might surprise you," he said, then gingerly put the items back, closed the drawer, and came over to join me at the closet.

I had started at one end, so he took the other. Our inspection was complicated by the fact that not only was the closet massive but also behind each door was a bank of drawers of various sizes below the space for hanging clothes. Many were empty, but those that weren't had King and Mimi's clothes in them. This felt too invasive.

I finished my second door, meeting Ricky in the middle, where he was hesitating over an open drawer. It was the largest in the bay, the most plausible hiding place for the number of folders I had seen, and all that was visible at the top was a mess of underwear. Mostly Mimi's, from the look of it, although there were a few men's pairs as well, and who was to say King didn't like the feel of something silky under his urban cowboy duds?

"What are you waiting for?" I asked. "I'm pretty sure it was you who told me I had to be ready to get my hands dirty in pretty much this exact scenario."

"Yeah, but I was talking about *you* going through *my* underwear. You know, sexy fun. This is creepy."

I sighed and pushed him out of the way, plunging my hand in to push the underwear aside. Underneath was a big wooden box. I doubted it was big enough for the folders, but to be sure, I undid the clasp and lifted the lid. Inside, nestled in green velvet, was a big, gleaming, chrome and walnut revolver.

"Jeez, King takes the Texan thing a little too seriously, doesn't he," Ricky said.

"What a wackadoo," I agreed, snapping the box closed and pushing the underwear back in place on top. "Looks like the bedroom is a bust, too. Where could that stuff be?"

Ricky voiced what I was beginning to worry. "Maybe it's not here. Maybe he handed it off to someone else, and it's in their room."

"In that case, maybe it's time for us to leave," I sighed.

Passing back into the sitting room, I gave the room a final once-over. "What about . . . ?" I muttered, opening the piano bench in a desperate final bid. Of course they weren't in there; it wouldn't have been big enough to hold them all anyway.

As I headed for the door, Ricky broke toward the big wet bar beyond it. Rounding the bar, he stifled an exclamation, instead pointing down to the counter behind the bar. I was about to join him when I heard the elevator doors open down the hall.

"Someone's coming!" I hissed.

A man coughed once; then I heard heavy, uneven footsteps, then another hacking cough. He paused right in front of the door to the suite. Ricky ducked down behind the bar, and I flattened myself against the wall, behind where the door would open.

What were we going to do? Why hadn't I turned off the lights? There was no way these pathetic hiding places would work—was there?

The key slotted into the door. The beep. The handle unlatching, turning.

I shot a glance to the side table on the other side of the door. Should I have grabbed that big vase? I could whack whoever this was over the head—but no, that was stupid. That only worked in cartoons, right?

The door hung open for a terribly long time. In the shadow cast from the hallway lights, I could see the silhouette of a person leaning against the doorframe. He was gasping, a deep, phlegmy rattle from deep in his chest. My clammy back and palms were beginning to stick to the wall, and my heart was doing its best to make a speedy escape from my body via my esophagus.

Finally, he left the safety of the doorframe to take a staggering step into the room. He stumbled forward, wheezing, turned to close the door, and saw me. His eyes bugged out, and he gasped, "You—wha—"

Then, on a choking gurgle, Kelso King pitched to the floor.

CHAPTER 11

"Ricky!" I screamed, staring in horror at King's convulsing form on the floor. "What do we do?"

He had popped up from his hiding place behind the bar at King's collapse, and ran around and knelt at his side.

"Call 911," Ricky said, reasonably calmly considering the circumstances. He remained close but made no move to touch King. "He needs an ambulance."

"Shouldn't we be doing CPR or something? What's happening?" I fumbled for the phone on the side table next to the door, my hands too shaky to pick up the handset on the first try.

"He's having a seizure. We need to make sure he doesn't hurt himself. Otherwise, I'm not sure there's anything we can do. Besides, I'm not trained in CPR, are you?"

I shook my head as the 911 dispatcher answered. I hurriedly gave as many details as I could, growing increasingly panicked as the number of questions I couldn't answer piled up. Was I aware of any allergies? Had he had anything to eat or drink? Had he been using any prescription or recreational drugs? By the time I was assured an ambulance was on the way, I was a wreck.

"You'd better call down to the front desk, too, so they'll know where to direct the EMTs," Ricky said as I put down the phone.

"What if they ask who I am or what I'm doing here?"

"It's an emergency! When they hear an ambulance is coming, they won't care about any of that!"

I picked the phone back up. Already I could hear a faint siren down on the street outside, coming closer.

"Good evening, front desk," came the calm, singsong answer.

"Uh, yes, hello. In a moment an ambulance will be arriving . . ."

"Oh, my goodness!" Her cadence betrayed no increase in alarm.

"Yes," I replied, taken aback, but also oddly soothed by this stilted two-person performance of a perfectly normal conversation. "Yes, so if you would please direct them to the presidential suite?"

"Is something the matter with Mr. King? Or Miss Mimi? Who am I speaking to?"

"Ah, yes, Mr. King seems to be having a medical emergency of some kind . . ." I was doing my best to be evasive.

Already I could hear the siren getting louder through the phone as it pulled up to the entrance to the hotel, and presently there was a commotion as the EMTs passed into the lobby. On the other end, the clerk called out, muffled by a hand over the handset, "Top floor, presidential suite."

Returning to the phone, she said, "I've sent the EMTs up to you. I'll send the manager up as well to assist. Is there anything else I can do?"

"No, thank you, you've been incredibly helpful," I said, pulling the phone cord far enough to poke my head through the open door and watch down the hall for the elevator to open.

Turning back to look inside, I found Ricky staring at me from his crouch next to King, an odd look on his face. "Did you have a nice chat?"

As I shrugged in response and set down the receiver, the elevator doors dinged open behind me, and a rush of activity tumbled out and started down the hall toward us.

"Damn, I was hoping we'd have time to leave before they got here," Ricky hissed.

"What, we were going to leave him like this?"

"For, like, two seconds! They wouldn't have found him any worse off—"

He cut himself off as the EMTs swarmed the door.

We were pushed aside—farther into the room, thwarting what I imagined was Ricky's plan to slink down the hall and disappear—as the professionals got to work. Again we were peppered with questions, very few of which we could answer. Within a moment a small contingent of hotel staff had joined the hubbub, doing little as far as I could tell to actually help anyone but enjoying being part of the action.

"Is he alive?" I whispered to Ricky, fidgeting, as we stood next to the cluster of couch and armchairs where I had interviewed King earlier that afternoon.

"He was, although he seemed to be losing consciousness as the seizure passed," he whispered back. "Maybe he's epileptic or something?"

"I don't know, didn't it seem like he was struggling to breathe? Is that common with epilepsy?"

"I have no idea," he admitted.

A man in a navy blazer slipped up next to us, and I wondered for a second why he looked so familiar before I placed him as the hotel manager who had welcomed me when I checked in on Tuesday. His brow was furrowed, his voice low.

"May I ask how you gentlemen came to find Mr. King here?"

"We . . . were passing in the hallway?" I attempted, though I was sure the deep flush of shame and terror I felt rising in my cheeks would betray the lie.

"Passing in the hallway? Going where?" Yeah, he wasn't buying it.

Ricky jumped in. "We were on our way to visit Mr. King, actually. My colleague here met with him earlier this afternoon, and he invited us to come back tonight."

The manager had his phone in his hand, and he punched open an app that connected him to the hotel's security camera footage.

"Your version is more convincing than his," he told Ricky, pointing vaguely in my direction but still looking at his phone, bringing up the footage he had been looking for. "But it's curious that I have footage of you entering this room several minutes before Mr. King . . ."

I could sense more bluster working its way from Ricky's brain to his mouth, but I was suddenly much too tired. I needed to put an end to this caper. "Look, we didn't take anything. You can search us. You can search our phones. It was nothing."

King had been loaded onto a stretcher, and the EMTs began maneuvering him out into the hall.

"We did save his life, maybe," Ricky pointed out to the manager, waving feebly at the retreating stretcher.

"Empty your pockets," said the manager through clenched teeth, his face red and the veins in his neck bulging under his shirt collar. "Unlock your phones. I'm going to pat you down. Then I'm going to search this room from top to bottom to make sure you didn't plant anything. Afterward—assuming you're not lying and I don't find anything—I won't turn you in to the police, but you will leave this hotel. You will include in your article that this is the finest hotel in the whole godforsaken world, but you will write nothing of this incident, and your card will be charged for the full room fee and all incidentals, and if I can figure out how to tack on some extra pay-per-view, I will. Do you understand me?"

I nodded, my body slumped, as I reached to pull my pockets inside out.

"The cocaine was already here, I swear. We didn't plant anything," Ricky said, doing the same. The manager raised an eyebrow but didn't say anything.

After a humiliating search of our persons and our phones' camera rolls and recording apps, we shuffled nervously for several minutes while the manager conducted an efficient but thorough search of the suite. I tried not to scratch too hard as an anxiety itch convention broke out on both of my arms.

"I don't think I can put exactly what he said about the hotel in my article," I whispered forlornly to Ricky as we waited, and I scratched. "What am I going to tell Drea about this? Where will I go? I'm gonna lose my job, aren't I? I don't need to worry about the article, because I'm going to lose my job."

"You'll come back to my place, and you're not going to lose your job. Drea's cool—she'll probably be proud of you for raising a little hell. Or just blame me."

"Ricky, we were trying to"—I lowered my voice so far that I was basically mouthing the next word—"*steal* information that a source declined to share. That's not okay! That's a serious no-no! Why were we doing that?"

"Youthful indiscretion?" He shrugged as nonchalantly as he could muster.

"You're not that young," I muttered, giving him a dark look, as the manager returned.

"Okay, Mr. Popp, let's go gather your things, shall we?"

The manager instructed Ricky to stay in the hall and followed me around my room as I packed, making sure I didn't slip anything into my bag that wasn't mine and ensuring that I did the deed as quickly as possible. As I passed into the hallway, I handed him first my key card, then Joey's, wishing I really could die of embarrassment but simply saying, with as much dignity as I could muster, "Could you please return this to Mr. Harris in room three-fourteen?"

"I will, thank you," the manager replied icily. "Good evening, Mr. Popp. Please don't ever come here again."

I was silent for the entire ride across town to Ricky's apartment. I was trying to sort through my jumbled thoughts, to make sense of the wild day I had just had, but if he wanted to think I was giving him the silent treatment, I wasn't about to disabuse him of the notion. When we reached the apartment, he meekly told me he'd take the armchair hide-a-bed again as I stalked into the bedroom without a word and closed the door behind me.

It was late, and I was exhausted. What had this day been? Where had it all started? Here, that was where. I had awakened in this very bed, then spent the day completely ignoring my itinerary and ping-ponging across town, playing detective with Ricky, only for it all to end in disaster right back where I had started, which had not been where I was supposed to be in the first place.

I was embarrassed and ashamed. I had fully expected the hotel manager to call the police and have us arrested, so there was a tinge of relief, too, but even that was colored by distress. What would have happened then? I couldn't go to jail. I would have shut down or had a panic attack or something, and they wouldn't have known what to do with me, or cared, and it would have gotten worse and worse. As it was, even without going to jail, I had been touched, groped, given a hickey, patted down, busted, and had my privacy revoked. And I had no idea what had happened to working on my article or if I'd be able to get back on track. Add my feature writing career to the list of the day's victims. I was beginning to wonder how long it had been since my last good, angry cry, and whether I wasn't due for another one.

It was all Ricky's fault. What was it that drove me to always go along with him, that kept us always escalating each other until we were on the brink of disaster? I had never been susceptible to peer pressure before. I had always known my own mind, stuck resolutely to my own path. Why couldn't I do the same with him?

Because you like him, a voice in my head piped up, unwelcome. *And you want him to like you.* Well, today should be enough to put an end to that, I resolved. The price was too high.

I sat back against the wall, my legs outstretched on the bed, and rolled my head back and closed my eyes to try to shut out the day, or at least to conjure up some cleansing tears. After a moment, I was aware of a vibration in my pocket. My phone. I pulled it out, and it took a second for the picture on the screen to register. Mom. My mom was calling. I took a deep breath and accepted the call.

"Hi, Mom."

"Oliver! I hope it's not too late. I wanted to see how everything's going!"

Her voice was so warm and welcome and excited, and I had no idea how to respond to her. I was worried the tears would choose this moment to come at last. Instead, I forced myself not to mumble as I replied, "I guess it's going okay."

"Just okay? What's wrong?"

"Mama, I want to come home." My voice broke, and a tear—only one, thank god—ran down my cheek.

"Honey, what happened? Are you overwhelmed?"

"I don't know, maybe," I sniffled. "Nothing's going the way I planned." That was the simple answer. I wasn't sure I had the energy to go into the whole story, to tell her about Elise and Moonshot and how everything had veered so wildly off track.

"Well, you have two days left. I bet things will turn around. And it's only two days, and then you'll be home. I know you can do that."

I didn't know what to say. I couldn't imagine what the next two days would hold, but I was pretty sure it wasn't a quiet return to my itinerary.

"What about—what was his name? Ricky? How are you getting along with him? Is he nice?"

"No . . . I mean, yes, his name is Ricky. I don't know. I guess he's—" I struggled to shake out my current feelings in language that I would use in front of my mother. "He's okay, but he's kind of a handful."

"Aw, that's too bad. I hoped you'd make a friend. And I think Drea hoped—" She stopped herself short.

"Drea hoped what? Are you messaging my boss on Facebook again?"

"No, I'm not *messaging your boss*," my mom said guiltily. "I'm messaging my good Facebook friend Drea, who happens to be your boss and who thought you and Ricky would . . . work well together."

"What does 'work well together' mean in this context?" I asked suspiciously. "No, you know what, I don't care. No matter what context, I don't think we're working well together. He's a good photographer, and I guess he's nice . . ." My chest ached as I had a sudden vision of Ricky's arms around me as I sat on the sidewalk last night, of his eyes shining at me from the back seat of the darkened car before the accident, watching me softly over the breakfast he'd made me, studying me, seeing me. "But . . ."

"But what? That doesn't sound so bad."

"But he makes me crazy!"

"Hmm."

"Don't you 'hmm' me. It's a real problem."

"I see," she said crisply. "Well, tell me something good. Tell me where you've gone so far."

I thought back. "We had a good dinner the first night, then

too much food the next morning, but Ricky also took me to a pet shop that had these really cute kittens . . . and then we went to Hillwood last night, which is a really amazing museum I'd never heard of before. And, um . . ." I still didn't want to get into too much detail about Elise or the Moonshot mess, but I had to decide what I could recoup from today's misadventures. "I guess we also saw a congressional office building and the presidential suite of the hotel."

"That all sounds great—some traditional DC stuff and some more offbeat activities. I'm not seeing the problem here." My mom had taken on the matter-of-fact tone she liked to use when she thought I was spiraling and needed a reality check.

What was the problem here? Elise was dead, and I wanted to know why. That was a big problem, which made my struggle to stick to my itinerary seem downright understandable as well as extremely petty in comparison. Maybe it had been worth it to dedicate today to that problem, and I had just proven to myself that the day wasn't necessarily even a loss as far as my article was concerned. "And he said he likes me . . ." I mumbled. Wait, did I say that aloud?

"Hmm," my mom said again, with a triumphant air this time.

We chatted for a minute more, until my energy started to really flag, then said good night. A moment after I had hung up, Ricky rapped tentatively on the door.

"Oliver, can I come in for a minute? I'd like to grab some clothes."

"Yeah," I called wearily, leaning back to the wall and closing my eyes again.

He opened the door and hovered there a minute, long enough that I opened my eyes to see what he was doing. "You can come in," I reminded him.

He crossed to the armoire, opened the doors, then sat on the corner at the foot of the bed and began taking off his shoes.

He stood again, picked them up, and set them neatly at the bottom of the armoire. Straightening up, he peeled off his jacket and put it on a hanger. He took off his socks, tossed them into a hamper in the armoire, then, before I realized what was happening, he had unbuttoned and was removing his jeans.

I tried not to stare at the display before me: the firm, shapely muscles in his calves and thighs working and flexing as he lifted his legs out of the pants one at a time, his incredible butt rippling with every movement from smooth to firm and back under a pair of black briefs. If this was how he intended to get back into my good graces . . . Well, he didn't need to try this hard, but I wasn't complaining.

Stay strong, Oliver, said the voice in my head. *That's just your virginity talking.*

Yeah, well, so what if it is? challenged the voice of my virginity. *I'm sick of this dump. I want out. Go ahead, jump those fine bones and set me free.*

I tamped down my internal dialogue as Ricky, now down to his T-shirt and underwear, sat gingerly on the edge of the bed, folding his jeans and looking over his shoulder toward me, but not turning far enough to make eye contact.

"I'm sorry about today. I know things got out of hand."

I took advantage of his inability to make eye contact to regard him fully, taking in his profile with a mixture of curiosity, diminishing annoyance, and a creeping hint of affection. "Yeah, what happened?"

"I don't know," he sighed. "I think I was excited to have a friend and got carried away. And I wanted to feel in control, you know? Like, last night we gave up control to that stupid car, and something horrible happened. Maybe I wanted to feel like I could take back control and make it right."

I was surprised. If the question had been put to me and I'd had to rationalize the day, my answer would probably have been shockingly similar, I realized.

He turned to look more fully at me. "Are you sure you didn't get hurt when you were with Joey?"

I looked down at my lap. "I didn't get hurt. And whatever happened was my fault, I guess. I told him I wanted to come, and that I wanted to . . . whatever."

"No, *I* told him you wanted to come," Ricky said, his eyes now cast down to the floor by his feet. "I'm sorry. I shouldn't have done any of that."

"I went along with it."

He turned back to look at me again and shyly reached a finger up to brush my neck. "I wish it had been me giving you that."

"Ugh, what are you, twelve?" I said with a half smile. "Were you aware that this whole trip was a setup?"

"I mean, I maybe wasn't *not* aware."

"So everybody—including my mother, by the way—was in on this except me?"

"Look, it wasn't just a setup. Drea really thinks you deserve a shot at this kind of work. And I needed the work, too. But I was really excited to meet you. I've been . . . lonely. And you were exactly what Drea said you'd be, and I was having so much fun, and—and I'm sorry. I know this is really important to you, and I've been taking us away from your plans the whole time."

"I've gone along with it," I said, shrugging my shoulders against the wall and filing away a mental note to ask what Drea had said about me. "And seeing what happened to Elise, that wasn't in our plans, and it definitely wasn't your fault. I'm every bit as responsible for today as you are, and I'm sorry if I made you feel otherwise. And I'm sorry the setup was a bust."

Ricky looked back at me gratefully. "Look, tomorrow we'll go back to the original plans, okay? I promise."

"Unless something comes up," I shot back, raising an eyebrow. "Then I promise to be flexible."

He got up, gave me another little show as he headed to the door, then turned once more to say over his shoulder, "I'm not responding to your double entendres, other than to point out that you said it, not me. And I appreciate your willingness to be a little loosey-goosey if needed. Good night, Oliver."

I flushed crimson and sank down, pulling the covers over my head as I went.

CHAPTER 12

As agreed, we set out the next morning to try to salvage a bit of my original itinerary. Georgetown had been thoroughly blown off, much to Ricky's satisfaction, but we could still make it to the National Building Museum this morning as planned.

After one last inventory of the eventfulness of yesterday, I had finally gone to bed the night before determined to put death out of my mind, to try to start over with a clean slate. Then I had tossed and turned for hours, wondering what had happened to Kelso King. Was he all right? Was he alive? Had someone tried to kill him? Did this mean someone had killed Elise? Or were the two incidents not related at all?

There were too many questions, all of them orbiting around Moonshot Motors and their seemingly cursed self-driving cars, which I was beginning to wish I had never heard of. None of this made sense, and other than the Moonshot connection, none of these occurrences seemed definitively linked. I was confused and frustrated and felt helpless. And I wasn't sure how I kept ending up in the middle of it when it had nothing to do with my reason for being here.

As we walked from Ricky's apartment to the Metro station, passing down tree-lined streets of cozy row houses, their front porches rambling together in a multicolored chain of welcome,

I took stock of the beautiful spring morning around me. Sunlight filtered down through the leaves, dappling the sidewalk at our feet. A sweet, almost warm breeze wrapped around us. I wondered with a start whether all the days here so far had been this beautiful, and realized that they had, and I was sorry I hadn't been paying closer attention. April was clearly Washington's month.

Glancing toward Ricky, I wished things had gone differently so that I could slip my arm through his, but contented myself with having made peace with him after yesterday. I couldn't deny that I felt relieved to be going back to the safety of my plans, but a little part of me hoped that Ricky's inner chaos monster would come out to egg us into more mayhem today. I couldn't quite reconcile this secret wish with my desire to write the article that had originally seemed so clearly defined by my itinerary—but what if giving in to chaos led to something better? Something better in the article, and in—

I snapped myself back to reality, back to Ricky's peaceful, sun-kissed neighborhood. "What is this part of town called? Anything article-worthy here?"

"This is Mount Pleasant," Ricky answered languidly, in full morning mellow mode. "And, no, it's not for your article. No tourists. This is home. We get to keep this spot for us."

I blushed a little at the intimacy of his phrasing, but I thought I knew what he meant. I was part of "us" only as long as I was crashing at his apartment, and the "us" was much more than the two of us, no matter how much I wanted to hear it otherwise. The real people of Washington needed places to go that were theirs alone, and this tranquil enclave struck me as just such a spot.

"How long have you lived here?"

"Almost ten years. I moved into my apartment toward the end of college, with my first serious boyfriend, if you must know. Howard's not too far that way," he said, waving vaguely ahead of us.

"How long have you lived there alone?"

"He moved out not long after we graduated. I had another boyfriend after that who lived with me for about a year, but by then it was *my* place, you know? So when he left, there was no question of me not staying. I like it here." He shrugged. "It's a little quiet—lots of families, mostly working people, some retired folks—but I like that. It feels loved. And living right off the park, I see lots of critters in the alley outside my apartment: raccoons, foxes, deer. It's kind of cool to see that in the middle of the city."

"Do you like living alone?"

"I don't mind it, I'll say that. Maybe you've noticed I'm a bit of a neat freak, so it's nice not to have to worry about me and somebody else driving each other up the wall. But when I'm between gigs and it's just me rattling around alone in the dark down there, it can get lonely. Are you worried about being alone when you move into your apartment?"

I was surprised he remembered. "No, I don't think so. To tell you the truth, my mom and I live in a duplex, and the apartment is the other half of the house. So I'll still be close to my mom. I've never actually been alone, but I think I'll like it."

"Sounds like a pretty good deal," he agreed. "Your own place, but with all the comforts of home and family upstairs anytime you want. I wouldn't mind something like that."

I gave him a sidelong look. "So why don't you live closer to your mom? You said she's just over in Virginia, right?"

"Not just over, like not right across the river. She lives halfway between here and Richmond, in a cute little college town where I grew up feeling absolutely stuck. There's nowhere that I, as a multiracial, gay, single young man—don't you look at me like that, *not old*, then—feel welcome, other than her house. She's pals with the editor in chief of the local newspaper who has tried to lure me with a staff job there, I don't know how many times. But, no, I'm a city boy."

"I think I get that. I don't even go out that much, but I couldn't imagine living somewhere small, where anything I needed was more than a short walk or bus ride away. My aunts—they're the ones who live in the other half of our house now—they're moving to Sacramento, and even that feels too suburban to me."

"I've never been to Sacramento," Ricky said. "But it seems like it would be a weird place. Like, it's kind of in the middle of the state, isn't it, where there's not much else around?"

"Kind of," I agreed. "What about the Bay Area? Have you been there?"

"Sure, I did my pilgrimage to San Francisco as a baby gay when Drea first moved out there after college. But I'd love to see Oakland through a native's eyes. I bet you could show me something totally different."

"Maybe I could," I said, suddenly feeling that old familiar chest pain—could it really be *heartache?*—at the idea of Ricky existing in my day-to-day world, not merely in this travel bubble where he lived. But I was saved from having to reply any further by our arrival at the Columbia Heights Metro station.

The National Building Museum was housed in an enormous redbrick edifice that was built in the late nineteenth century as the main offices of the United States Pension Bureau. A terracotta frieze ran in a continuous band around the building, above the first-floor doorways and windows, depicting scenes of the Civil War soldiers, sailors, and medics who were the Pension Bureau's primary clientele when it was built.

As we walked up to the building's entrance, Ricky pointed up to the frieze, showing me the Black teamster, meant to represent a slave freed by the war, which had been placed above this entrance at the specific request of the architect. "My dad always points that out," he said as we passed through the doors.

"He loves this place—the museum, I mean—but the history of the building is interesting, too. We come here every time he visits."

Entering the main hall of the building, I was stunned for a moment. From the dark, compact hallway we had entered, we suddenly emerged into a vast, soaring space, the roof at least six stories above us. The gables of the roof formed a cross, with the beams framing either side of the central section, supported by two rows of the largest columns I had ever seen. The museum's galleries, once the offices of the Pension Bureau's employees, ringed the outer perimeter of this central hall, entered through colonnaded mezzanines. A mosaic of the presidential seal was inlaid into the floor at one end of the hall—"For the inaugural balls," Ricky explained. A shallow tile fountain, ringed by potted plants and benches, sat in the center of the massive room. Children's undermodulated voices careened off the columns and rose to the clerestory windows above as they ran joyful rings of never-ending hide-and-seek and tag around their enormous bases.

We had an appointment to meet with a curator to get a preview of an exhibition that would be opening as our article went to print, but we had arrived early and went into the gift shop to kill a little time. Ricky went to a display of T-shirts to buy a birthday gift for his dad. I was idly picking up and putting down books and trinkets, wondering vaguely if I should bring my mom a souvenir, when I heard an unmistakable voice echoing out in the hall.

"Ooh, yes, Marisol, let's do it right here! This one is perfect. I can give it a big huggy-poo, and you can get all the pieces in the shot."

I moved cautiously to the gift shop door and peered out into the hall, where I saw the blond form of Mimi, clad in a boho peasant dress that looked simple but probably cost more than my life was worth, wrapping her arms around one of the giant columns, one of her ankle-booted feet kicked up behind her. A young woman with long dark hair and terrible posture in a vintage-style baby-doll dress was taking photos of her with an expensive-looking camera, and as she hugged and cooed, working her puffy lips into a pout, Mimi was modeling the hand on the side of the column facing the camera to show off a display case's worth of rings and bracelets.

Ricky came up beside me. "What the . . . Who is that woman, and what on earth is she doing?"

"Shhh, I don't want her to see me," I said under my breath, realizing that Ricky hadn't yet had the singular experience of meeting Mimi. Had King told her that we had broken into their suite last night? Was he even conscious, or alive? What was she doing here? Shouldn't she be at his side?

"You know that kook?" Ricky asked in wonderment.

"I guess our pal Kelso King must be doing okay, because that is his girlfriend, Mimi, and it appears that she's decided to go to work today. She's an influencer, you know, and it looks like today she's influencing everybody to buy jewelry."

"Wait, that's King's girlfriend?" Ricky asked, ducking behind me to hide from her. My hero. "Do you think she knows about—what we—last night?"

"I have no idea, but I don't really want to find out. Jeez, why can't I shake these Moonshot people?"

At that moment, a docent waved to us from outside the gift shop to let us know the curator was ready. Sticking to the colonnade and trying to hug the far wall to hide in the shadows, we followed the docent to a stairwell, then up to a gallery on the second floor. I could still hear Mimi's peculiar falsetto occasionally piercing through the low hum of voices below us but breathed easier knowing we were out of sight.

The exhibition on display now in this gallery, on the work of industrial architect Albert Kahn, was in its final weeks. By the time our article went to press, it would be gone, and in its place would be a new exhibition on how parking lots and garages had reshaped America's urban landscapes—ironic, since Kahn had designed the factories that built many of the cars that necessitated all that parking. The curator walked us through the space, explaining the topic and showing us renderings of how the gallery would be transformed, handing us a press packet and pointing out the link to where we could access photos and renderings that we could use to accompany our article. He painted his picture with such enthusiasm that the exhibition started to sound more interesting than I had originally thought, but as soon as we left him after about twenty minutes, the feeling passed.

"Parking lots?" I said to Ricky as we descended the stairs.

"Yeah, I don't think my dad will be rushing up here from North Carolina for that one."

I had paused at the top of the stairs for a moment to listen for Mimi's voice but hadn't picked anything out. As we stepped onto the ground floor, I listened again but still heard nary a squeak. I thought the coast was clear when, as we began to cut across the main hall toward another gallery, I heard a shriek of delight.

"Look, Marisol! It's little Mr. Oliver Popp! Mr. Oliver Popp! Yoo-hoo!"

I froze for a second, my eyes wide, my cheeks flushed, before I could bring myself to look around and locate her. *Little* Oliver Popp? I was no towering giant, but then neither was she. In fact, I was fairly certain she was a few inches shorter than I was. But she had that big voice, the big hair, big lips, big boobs; she was small in stature, but everything else about her was big. Maybe in comparison, I deserved the diminutive.

She and the dark-haired young woman were standing alongside one of the benches facing the fountain in the center of the hall. The young woman held the camera in front of them, screen up, as though they had been reviewing the results of their photo shoot together when Mimi had spotted me.

As we veered off our course toward the women, I tried on a

smile to hide my panic. Through my teeth, I muttered to Ricky, "Do you think she knows? What do we do?"

"Play dumb," he whispered back. "And do something about your face. You look like you have hemorrhoids."

The stooped young woman stared at us blankly for a second as we made our approach, then returned her attention to her camera, but Mimi watched us with dancing eyes all the way across the room.

As we joined them, Mimi raised a French-manicured fingernail to my shirt collar. "Good morning, Mr. Oliver Popp," she giggled. "Did you burn yourself with the curling iron?"

I flushed red again and ran a hand unconsciously over my neck. "Good morning, Mimi. What a surprise, running into you here."

"Isn't it scenic in here, though! Kelsey-poo is back at his boring ol' hearings, so Marisol and I are back to work, too. This is my assistant, Marisol," she added, indicating the young woman, who grunted without looking up. "Who's your friend with the perfect curls of his own?"

"I'm *his* assistant," Ricky said smoothly. *My assistant?* He winked at me as he reached to shake Mimi's hand, which she offered out like a limp fish.

So whatever had happened to King last night, he was okay now. I decided to play dumb a little more aggressively.

"We were in the hotel bar last night and saw Mr. King being taken away in an ambulance. I'm glad to hear it wasn't too serious and he's back up and about today."

"He's so dramatic, isn't he. He ate something that didn't agree with him, left me all alone with those *boring* people at that restaurant, and went back to the hotel and called an ambulance. An ambulance! Can you imagine! And all he needed was his stomach pumped, and he was fine."

"He needed his stomach pumped? That sounds kind of serious," Ricky said, bemused.

She shrugged. "I dunno. He probably could have taken care of it himself." She mimed sticking a finger down her throat and throwing up, raising an eyebrow and never breaking eye contact.

Was I being paranoid, or was she baiting us? Trying to get us to admit we knew more than we were letting on? Was I imagining that hard, assessing glint in her eye? I was imagining it, right? *Play it cool, Oliver, but get away from this woman.*

"Well, I'm glad he's okay. And it was nice to see you. I'm afraid we have to run. We're on a tight schedule, and we need to see one more exhibit before we leave."

"Okay, well, kisses! Goodbye, little Oliver Popp. Goodbye, cutie curls. Be careful the next time you do his hair for him."

"Oh, no, he—" Ricky pulled me away by my arm before I could finish protesting. He was hunched over, moving double time, trying to keep down his laughter long enough to get away from Mimi and Marisol. As we entered the gallery, he doubled over and let loose a choking fit of giggles.

"I burned you with a curling iron! *Doing your hair for you!* That's the weirdest euphemism I've ever heard. Why does it sound so disgusting?"

"Is it really that noticeable?" I wailed.

Ricky tried to stifle his giggles as he craned to look at my neck. "Do you really want to know?"

We tried to focus on the last exhibit we had planned to see, but running into Mimi had thrown me. I was sure it was only guilt making me paranoid, but I had gotten the distinct impression that Mimi knew what we had done, and had been trying to trap us in a lie.

I turned to Ricky as we headed for the exit. "Don't you usually get your stomach pumped if you've overdosed?"

"Yeah, I think so. I'd be surprised if they did that for garden-variety food poisoning. What do you think? Driven to suicide by guilt over what he'd done to Elise?"

"You still think that? It makes no sense. And it makes no sense that he would OD in the middle of dinner in a restaurant."

"Maybe that's how he covers his tracks—by only doing things that make no sense on the surface."

"Huh."

Ricky grinned as he held the door for me. He was putting me on. "Okay, so what's your theory?"

"I think someone slipped it to him without his knowledge."

He put a theatrical hand to his chest. "Poisoned! How dramatic. Mimi?"

"I can't really picture it, but I don't know. I wonder who 'those boring people' were that she mentioned."

As we walked down the brick path from the museum entrance to the street, I noticed the slouching figure of Marisol sitting on a bench, sucking sullenly on an electronic cigarette and exhaling massive vapor clouds. There was no sign of Mimi.

I pulled up alongside her. "Hello again," I said.

"Oh . . . hi." She spoke in a flat monotone, glancing up at us for a moment before returning her gaze down toward her feet, which were armored up in a pair of thick-soled combat boots.

I was about to move on again when she gave a sudden start and said, "So, what, are you a couple of Mimi's fangirls?"

"Huh? Uh, no, I don't think so. I met her yesterday, when I was interviewing Mr. King."

"Hmm. We get lots of gay guys coming up to her all the time when we're out. Like, two-thirds of her followers are gays who think she's totally campy. You want some?" She offered us the vape pen.

We shook our heads. "I guess I could see how they might think that," I said without really thinking.

"Yeah, well, that hickey's pretty campy, too," Marisol said blandly.

"That's why I gave it to him," Ricky chimed in. "*Camp* is our byword. All hail Paul Lynde, the queen of camp." I elbowed him in the ribs.

"So you guys have been going around doing photo shoots like this while you've been here?" I asked. I was suddenly curious about the life of Mimi.

"Pretty much. We go to some dumb place, I take some pictures, she does a bump, and I wait around while she takes a dump."

She was staring at us now, defiant satisfaction in her eyes at being so frank, or maybe at the rhyme. This was more information than I had bargained for, but it did explain why Marisol was sitting out here by herself.

"So she isn't going to any of the hearings or to any events with Mr. King? Why did she come?"

Marisol shrugged. "I think she went to one thing with him a couple of nights ago. Some party they were throwing. I don't know, I had my own stuff to do. And the rest of the time, you know, different places to take pictures than we usually use. And they have dinner together."

Right—the press event at Hillwood. Had Mimi been there? I couldn't remember. No, Joey had mentioned her, she must have been. "Do you know who was with them last night when Mr. King got sick? That must have been scary if he needed his stomach pumped."

"I dunno. I mean, I was there, but I didn't know who those other people were. A couple of boring guys and a boring lady. I took an edible before we went, so I wasn't really paying attention, you know?" She blew another terrifyingly large cloud.

"Is that her real voice?" Ricky piped up.

She stared at him blankly for a moment, then shrugged almost imperceptibly.

"Well, we should go," I said. I didn't want to chance still being there when Mimi emerged from her ritual. "Nice talking to you."

"Yeah, okay," she said.

We turned to continue down to the street. "Hey," Marisol called after us. "She really thinks you're funny. If you keep it up, she's going to start following you around."

CHAPTER 13

The next stop on our itinerary was the National Zoo. I had expected Ricky to put up a fight about going somewhere as devoid of local significance or character as a zoo, but he was surprisingly sanguine as we took Metro across town to Woodley Park.

The reason why became clear as we walked up Connecticut Avenue from the station and into the zoo. I followed Ricky as, ignoring all the animal attractions and apparently assuming that I'd keep up, he made a beeline down the main walkway and strode purposefully right into the line for Carvel ice cream at the Panda Overlook.

"Ice cream, really?"

I tried to give him an exasperated eye roll, but he was impassive behind his sunglasses. "What? I thought this was why we came here. It's the only reason I ever come here."

As soon as we got our cones of chocolate and vanilla swirl soft serve, he was off again. I nearly had to run to keep up as he charged down the hill, almost all the way across the park. Just before we reached the ring road that connected the parking lots circling the perimeter of the zoo, he veered off the walkway into a grassy field. He kicked off his shoes and scrunched up his pant legs, then dropped down into the cool, soft, impossibly green grass and gave his cone a satisfied lick.

It seemed I had no choice but to follow suit, although I kept my shoes on. As I sank down next to his outstretched golden legs, he wiggled his toes at me. I followed them up to his face, where he was waggling his eyebrows, too, from behind his ice cream.

Ricky was starting to feel like the little devil on my shoulder again, egging me on to mischief and mayhem, but through it all, he always seemed so happy and goofy and full of zest for life that it was impossible to resist him. He bent my will to his without even trying, and I couldn't stay mad at him for it. Sitting here in this beautiful spot on this beautiful day with this beautiful, golden, curly-haired boy, enjoying the simple perfection of my ice cream cone in perfect, companionable silence, I suddenly found myself in a state of blissed-out zen. All the weird confusion that had come before was gone. I wanted it to stay gone, to live here, in this moment, forever.

But, as always, there was a tiny nagging thought at the back of my mind ready to intrude on my calm. This one was whispering, so quietly I almost couldn't hear it, *One more day. Today and part of tomorrow, and that's it.* It took me a second to figure out what the voice was talking about. It was reminding me that tomorrow I would go home. What then? The thought of life without my little devil seemed far emptier than a few days' acquaintance should have warranted.

I started a bit when the not-too-distant roar of a big cat broke the silence.

"The lions and tigers are up there," Ricky explained, pointing with his cone up the hill. "Where were you? Looked like you zoned out for a minute there."

"Nowhere. Enjoying the moment." Mostly.

"Well, I'm glad to hear that. It was a pretty good moment, I thought."

"We do need to go back and get some pictures and actually see some of the zoo, you know," I reminded him.

"Not yet." He bit into his cone. "I've got another moment on the way I want you to try out. I like seeing you relaxed."

"I can be relaxed. I feel most relaxed when I have my work done."

"No, see, you want to tell yourself that, but then your work is never done. And besides, you're ignoring some of your work, hoping it'll go away if you pretend it's not there, and I'm trying to get you mellowed out before I bring it up."

This was true, but by bringing up the intention of bringing it up, he had very decidedly blown any chance of more relaxation before he brought it up.

"Okay, I'll bite. What are we doing about the Moonshot piece? I'm so confused."

"No, no, here comes my other moment. Breathe it in."

I tried to play along, moodily taking the last bite of my cone as my mind swirled around the Moonshot mess, wanting to make sense of it, wanting it to be behind me, wanting to be home but not really wanting to leave. Ricky leaned back on his elbows and looked up to watch a fluffy white cloud float by. The moment I had wanted to stay in had passed so quickly; this one, which I just wanted over, seemed to last forever.

"Okay," he said finally. "I got an email from my buddy at NHTSA this morning. I read it while we were on Metro. The official word is that their investigation into the car that hit Elise is incomplete and is part of a larger investigation into Moonshot's self-driving software, so the details of this specific incident might never fully become public. Unofficially, he was a bit disturbed, so we do have some leaked info."

"Like what?"

"You were right—the data recorder had been wiped. There was no footage of the accident on the car's camera feeds. Someone tampered with it."

"That seems suspicious."

"Yeah. They also started going through the car's log of over-the-air updates. It looks like the last one, a few hours before the accident, disabled the pedestrian detection system. This isn't in the release notes for that update, and it doesn't seem like something Moonshot would intentionally do, so either there was a mistake in the update's code that turned it off or the update was hacked to disable it."

"Like Richfield was asking about at the hearing."

Ricky nodded. "Something is very rotten here."

I did a double take. "Wait, the pedestrian detection system? So it wouldn't register if a person walked in front of the car? You think whoever hacked the update did it *because they were planning to push Elise in front of our car?*"

Ricky kept a poker face. "It's still all very circumstantial. And the hack affected all Moonshots getting their updates from that particular server, which probably covers a big chunk of the mid-Atlantic, so even if it suggests premeditation, it only means that they planned to push Elise in front of *a* Moonshot, not necessarily *our* Moonshot."

My phone buzzed in my pocket, and I shifted to pull it out as I said, "So we're back to the possibility that Elise was murdered. We still don't know who would have done such a thing, or why."

"There's still her mysterious drinking buddy with the Brooklyn accent," Ricky reminded me.

"She could be anyone, as far as we know at this point," I mumbled distractedly, looking at the text message on my screen.

It was from Joey. Apparently, the news of our disgrace last night had been kept under wraps, and the hotel manager probably hadn't even told him that I had stolen his room key. It read: **Hey you! Hope you're feeling better. Do you really have a concussion? I was worried about you all night.**

I groaned and showed it to Ricky, who couldn't hide his amusement. "Hey, at least if he's not mad at you, we can still get information out of him," he said. "Like who King and

Mimi were having dinner with last night. I bet he knows."

"Great. How am I supposed to go from 'No, I don't have a concussion' to 'By the way, who was your boss having dinner with last night?' I don't want to keep playing this guy. I'm no good at it."

"Give it to me. I'll do it," Ricky said, reaching for the phone.

"No! Last time I let you text on my behalf, I ended up with this beauty mark," I said, rubbing my neck.

Ricky peered at my neck, then looked up toward the sun. "It's not too noticeable anymore. Maybe if you got a good tan . . ."

"Shut up," I said, without any real malice, but also not quite as playfully as I'd intended. I was staring at Joey's text, my brow furrowed, trying to figure out how to respond. Best to be direct, I decided, but not lead him on. I typed, **Thanks for thinking of me. I don't think it's really a concussion. I feel better today. Sorry I had to leave in such a rush.**

I studied the last sentence. I meant it to be polite, but I worried that he would read it as regret that our make-out session had been cut short. I decided to delete it, then sent the rest.

I looked back up at Ricky, who was watching me, still reclined back on his elbows, a thin smile on his lips. "Am I allowed to speak again?"

"Yes. Sorry," I said. I showed him my response. "Okay, I answered his question. How do I maneuver to our question?"

"A white lie." He shrugged. "Say, 'I saw King and Mimi at the restaurant last night. One of their companions looked familiar, but I couldn't place them.' If you're vague enough about it, the easiest thing for him to do is to list everybody who was there."

"We don't know what restaurant they were at!"

"He doesn't know that. It's not like you have to name it. You're overthinking it."

"Overthinking a social interaction? *Moi?* You must have me confused with someone else," I said in mock indignation. He grinned back and waved at the phone, urging me to compose the text.

I drafted the message, then pulled the phone to my chest and said, "I'll send this, but then we need to go back up the hill and do what we came here to do before we go rushing off to chase whatever he tells us. Agreed?"

"Okay, but I don't think I really need another ice cream."

"That's not what we came here to do!"

Ricky balled up his paper napkin and tossed it at me with a smirk. I sent the message and stood up. While I waited for Ricky to put his shoes back on, I got Joey's reply.

"He says they had dinner with Jeff Tannenbaum, his wife, Verna, and an assistant from his office. Do those names mean anything to you?"

"Jeff Tannenbaum is a representative from upstate New York," Ricky said, pulling on his second shoe and raising a hand for me to help him up. I took it, trying not to notice the charge of electricity I felt pass between us. *One more day.*

Once he was on his feet, he continued, "Talk about coincidences. You remember what I told you about Richfield's little aide Derek? His Republican sugar daddy? That's Tannenbaum."

We did a half-hearted lap around the zoo, desultorily taking notes and pictures in the lapses of our speculations about what had happened to Elise, what had happened to King, what was happening at Moonshot Motors, and how they all might be connected. We weren't getting anywhere with these problems, but even when I remembered my taskmaster role and tried to steer the conversation back to the zoo, Ricky grumbled about how inhumane and backward it was to put animals in captivity on display. I couldn't really disagree, so those gambits didn't go anywhere, either.

My resolve to get back to my original schedule seemed to be wafting away on the sweet spring breeze. When we were ready to leave the zoo, Ricky suggested exiting on the Rock Creek Park side and walking back to his place, ostensibly for lunch, but I suspected more for access to his car so that we could take off in pursuit of . . . well, we didn't know, but it seemed like there must be something to chase. I was feeling drawn back to the scene of Elise's fatal accident on Connecticut Avenue, a short walk from the main zoo entrance, so I suggested walking up to Cleveland Park for lunch, pointing out that we could figure out what to do next and hop on Metro to get where we needed to go, and that lunch in a restaurant and continuing to use Metro could conceivably be article fodder, while sandwiches in a basement apartment and riding around in a privately owned car couldn't. Ricky conceded the point, and we headed out onto Connecticut Avenue.

Ever since Ricky had reopened the Moonshot wound, and I had started picking at the newly discovered worry about my looming return home, my stomach had been twisted into a small, dark knot, which was outwardly manifesting as a sort of distracted, worried grumpiness. As we walked up the street, I noticed that it seemed to have spread to Ricky, too. Our silences often felt comfortable, but this one was taut and moody. His hands were stuffed into his pockets, and I noticed his brow occasionally twitching into a furrow as his mind apparently wandered. I was wondering whether we were covering any of the same ground when he broke the silence and answered my question.

"So you leave, what, midday tomorrow? That's not a lot of time left to figure all this out, is it."

"No, it's not," I agreed, wondering which "all this" he wanted to figure out—Elise's death and the Moonshot mess or what would happen to our friendship when I left. Maybe he wasn't worried about that. Maybe he didn't care.

I wanted to find out but wasn't sure how. I settled for, "Where do we go from here?"

"I wish I knew." Frustratingly vague, as answers went, but maybe what I deserved for being so indirect.

We had been crossing the bridge between Woodley Park and Cleveland Park and again found ourselves back at the scene of Elise's death. Without thinking about it, I paused for a moment, pulling off the sidewalk into the shade of one of the leafy trees bordering the street. I looked up at the apartment building, then turned and stared numbly at the cars rolling by on the roadway.

Ricky was next to me. "You okay?" He put his palm lightly in the center of my back. I nodded, and his hand fell next to mine, our fingers briefly grazing as it did. Almost unconsciously, I felt my fingers twitch outward, trying to find his, grazing them again. Out of the corner of my eye, I saw him glance down to our hands. I took a shallow breath, and—

"Excuse me?" The voice came from behind us, gentle and concerned. We turned to see an older Black woman on the sidewalk, a grocery bag tucked in the crook of her arm. "I'm sorry, I didn't want to startle you. Didn't I see you boys here the other night, when there was that car accident out here?"

"Yes, ma'am, you probably did," Ricky said.

"I thought so." She turned to me. "Are you doing better, honey? You looked pretty shaken up that night."

"Yes, thank you."

"Well, I understand. I mean, I didn't see it happen. I was just coming home—I live right here, you see," she said, indicating the building behind her, "and I saw all the police and the ambulances and the body covered up in the street and you sitting right there. It's all so upsetting. I was surprised I didn't see anything about it in the paper the next morning. Did you see the whole thing?"

"Yes, we did. It was very . . . frightening and upsetting," I said uncomfortably.

"Oh, baby, I'm sorry. I bet it was. Traumatizing, I think, to see something like that." She gazed absently down the side-walk, toward the bridge, as if looking into the past to recall the night of the accident. "You know, it's funny. It's usually so quiet here at that time of the evening. There's still traffic and all, but the sidewalks are quiet, you know. But that night, I left to go down the street to visit a friend, and when I left, there were those girls loitering out front, doing drugs, I think, and when I came back, you were here with all that to-do. Very strange night."

I didn't know what to make of this, but Ricky started a little. "Was it two women? About midtwenties maybe?"

"There *were* two of them." She seemed surprised at the specificity of the questions. "Midtwenties, you say? I suppose so. You gotta understand, honey, I'm seventy-nine. Everybody looks like a child to me. They were real pretty, though, and looked like nice girls. It made me sad, but the one especially, she looked like she was on heroin. She was really out of it."

Ricky turned to me excitedly. "Do you still have that picture of Elise?"

"I think so." I swiped my phone open and pulled up my Insta-gram bookmark, then showed the woman the photo of Elise holding her nephew. "Could this be one of the women you saw?"

"Mm-hmm, I think that's her. The one who was out of it. What a shame. Is that her baby? How did you know that girl? Well, this gets stranger and stranger, doesn't it?"

"Ma'am, I'm afraid she was the person who was hit by the car that night. And we think maybe she wasn't *doing* drugs but that she had *been* drugged. Could you tell us anything about the other woman, the one with her?"

"It was her? That's terrible!" She thought for a moment. "Well, the other gal was a white girl, or maybe Latina. Dark hair . . . You know, it was dark out, so I couldn't say what color, but it was long and straight. I think she had a brown sweater on or something. She was kind of plain. I guess the other girl stood out more, because she had on a pretty skirt, but she looked so doped up. Her friend was kind of helping her stay upright, and they were stumbling around."

This tracked with Kaitlyn the barbecue server's description of Elise's drinking companion but was every bit as vague and unhelpful.

"Thank you. That's very helpful," I fibbed.

The lady smiled. "Well, I'm glad you're feeling better. You were lucky to have your sweetie with you—he was taking real good care of you. Ooh," she pipped, bobbing in close and peering at my neck, her eyes twinkling. "Looks like he's still taking good care of you! That's a honey of a hickey. Well, you *must* be feeling better. You boys have a nice day, now. I've got to get these groceries inside."

She gave a little wave as she turned toward the building, and I suppressed a sigh as we waved back. I could tell Ricky was grinning again.

"Let's go get lunch," I grumbled.

We continued up Connecticut Avenue to the next block, to the Irish pub where we had started our attempt to retrace Elise's movements yesterday. Ricky assured me that the place was a neighborhood institution, of the type that travel magazines liked to spotlight out of obscurity, if not exactly a glamorous hot spot. It would do for a quick lunch, in any case.

Once our order had been taken, I faced down Ricky across the table. "Okay, so we're back to the woman Elise was with. Who could she be?"

"Well, like we said yesterday, she could be almost anyone. But if we start from the people *we* know, or know of . . . That's a really short list, isn't it."

"The description kind of sounds like Mimi's assistant, Marisol, doesn't it? Nondescript, with long, straight dark hair. Only problem is, she doesn't sound like Rosie Perez. She sounds like Daria."

Ricky laughed. "It could be Mimi in a wig, but I somehow don't think even then she could be described as 'plain.' And how old is she, anyway? I feel like she could be anywhere between nineteen and forty-nine."

"Yeah, I have no idea," I said. "I'm beginning to see the flaw with this approach. We don't know anyone. What about people we've heard of but haven't met? There's that van Veldt woman. And, and . . . that congressman's wife that Mimi and King had dinner with last night?"

"Now we're really grasping at straws," Ricky agreed. "I'm pretty sure Verna Tannenbaum is noticeably older than Elise. Should be easy enough to find out anyway, since she's kind of a public figure. You Google her, and I'll look up Lila van Veldt."

I did a search for Verna Tannenbaum. There were indeed hundreds of articles, photos, and videos of her online. I scrutinized a photo, of her with her husband. He was in his late forties or early fifties, and while she was possibly a bit younger than him, I didn't think she could pass for midtwenties. She was, however, a dark-haired Latina, and while her husband's district was upstate, an article informed me that she was a Brooklyn native. I sought out a video in which I might hear her voice.

"Listen to this," I said to Ricky as I turned up the volume on my phone and held it between us. We both leaned in. Verna Tannenbaum's voice rose tinnily to our ears. It was apparent that she'd had media coaching and was working to neutralize whatever accent she had, enunciating carefully and clearly, with little trace of Brooklyn to be heard.

"I don't know. I'm not getting anything distinctive," Ricky said after a moment, "although it's hard to know from that how she might sound when she's talking casually with friends. I still think she's too old, though. And in this town, the odds that someone might recognize her out in public are greater than zero, so she'd be kinda dumb to go out with someone she was planning to kill."

"Besides, why would she want to kill Elise? It seems highly likely that neither of them ever had any idea who the other was." I moved my phone aside as two baskets of fish and chips were set down on the table in front of us.

I removed the ramekin of coleslaw from my basket and stuck a French fry meditatively in my mouth. "What about the mysterious Lila van Veldt? What does she look like?"

"We still don't know," Ricky said. "I couldn't find a single picture of her. She seems to have a low online profile—her name on several publications, and listed as faculty at MIT, with no picture, but nothing personal. Are you gonna eat that?" He motioned to my coleslaw, and I invited him to take it.

"So we have one very weak possibility and one that's a total question mark. Plus Marisol and Mimi, both of whom seem like ridiculous candidates."

"Although they did have access to King the night he was, what, poisoned? So maybe one of them could have done it," Ricky said.

"So did Mrs. Tannenbaum," I pointed out. "And none of them has a clear motive to kill anyone, as far as I can tell—King or Elise."

"Okay, motive. That's a good angle," Ricky said, jabbing a forkful of coleslaw in my direction. I tried not to flinch as the soggy cabbage flailed creamily at me.

"Except we still have no idea what anyone else's motive could have been, either," I said.

"It still feels like Elise's congressman ex-boyfriend, Richfield, might have had the strongest reason to want to get rid of her," Ricky said. "And he doesn't have a strong alibi. But then who was the woman? An accomplice? I don't see him making a convincing drag queen."

"Or someone wanted to kill her because of her work on the self-driving technology," I suggested. "Remember, there's the hacking element, too, which suggests someone with a sophisticated knowledge of the system. Someone connected to LO-COMOTO?"

"Which brings us back to Lila van Veldt—maybe."

"You know, there is someone connected to Richfield and Tannenbaum and even LOCOMOTO, kind of . . . and you," I reminded Ricky.

"Aw, Oliver, no. I already had to talk to that little turd once this week. Isn't that enough?"

"So I have to keep playing Joey, but you get to be one and done with Derek? That doesn't seem fair."

He waved some more coleslaw in my face in a bid to change the subject. "So what's the deal with the coleslaw, huh? Didn't want to eat it, and it seems like you have kind of a visceral reaction to even looking at it."

"I can't tolerate foods that are white and creamy and not sweet."

"Coleslaw *is* sweet. Sweet and tangy."

I tried not to gag at the thought. "Well, it shouldn't be. White and creamy and sweet and tangy makes my skin crawl. Don't change the subject." I folded my arms and stared at him in defiant satisfaction. "You're calling Derek."

CHAPTER 14

After we settled the lunch bill, Ricky loitered outside the pub to call Derek while I went up the block, hoping to show Kaitlyn at the barbecue restaurant a photo of Verna Tannenbaum to either rule her out as Elise's drinking companion or get a positive ID. I was very much expecting to rule her out, but Kaitlyn wasn't working, and when I returned to Ricky, he was staring at his phone in mild irritation.

"He didn't answer. I texted him, and he hasn't responded yet. I'm worried he's screening me."

"It is the middle of a workday," I reminded him. "He might not be able to pay attention to his personal phone."

We stood in awkward silence on the sidewalk for a moment while Ricky continued to try to stare a response into being. I wondered wistfully if we shouldn't forget all this and go back to sitting in the grass together in the park while we still could. I'd take my shoes off this time, I decided.

"Well, should we go to Richfield's office?" Ricky asked finally, jolting me from my reverie. "I think Derek's low enough in the pecking order that he's more or less always there, unless he's out getting coffees or lunch for everybody else. He doesn't go to hearings or anything."

"Okay," I said, sighing a little for my shattered dream.

Ricky continued to monitor his phone as we rode Metro across town, but had still gotten no word from Derek by the time we emerged from the Capitol South station and walked to the Rayburn Building. When we entered Richfield's offices, he was there at his little desk in the anteroom.

He narrowed his eyes at us and heaved a dramatic sigh. "Really? I don't respond to one text, so you just show up? Look, I'm not interested, I'm not intimidated by you, and nobody here has anything to say to you about anything."

We looked around. The office beyond the anteroom seemed mostly empty, with a couple of bored-looking staffers—who might have been interns, as they looked even younger than me—staring vacantly at their computer screens. Derek appeared to have been doing a crossword puzzle in that day's copy of the *Post*. Ignoring his dramatically disdainful greeting, Ricky dropped into one of the chairs facing his desk and chummily asked, "So, where is everybody?"

I took the other chair. Derek's irritation was palpable, but he answered, "The Moonshot hearings. I'm telling you, there's nobody here for you to bug anyway, so don't waste my time."

Ricky continued to disregard Derek's hostility. He leaned forward and rested his chin in his hands, his elbows on the edge of Derek's desk. "Okay, so riddle me this: Kelso King. Your boss is presumably over there trying to rip him a new one again, but a little birdie tells me your boyfriend had an intimate double date with King and his lady friend last night. What's going on there?"

Derek looked around nervously. "Keep it down, will you? And how did you know I was there last night?"

I looked at Ricky. I hadn't been expecting this. "*You* were there?" I said. "We were told there was an aide from Tannenbaum's office, not you." Derek waved his hands to shush me as I said Tannenbaum's name.

"Well, it was me, okay?" he hissed in a whisper, his cheeks flushing.

"When I said 'double date,' I was talking about his wife, not you, dummy. My, my, my," Ricky clucked. "What will the Right Honorable Representative Richfield think of that?"

Derek's eyes were practically slits now. I was impressed at his control over his facial muscles to be able to hold this expression so fiercely for so long. He considered us for a moment, then said slowly, through clenched teeth, "Richfield knows. He sent me."

Ricky sat back in his chair. He seemed to be regarding Derek with something that almost looked like respect. "A double agent! I never expected you to be so loyal to Richfield. Or is it that you need more time here on your résumé before you jump over to K Street?"

"Maybe it's something like that." Derek shrugged, leaning back into his own chair and trying to look more confident than I suspected he was feeling. "Let's just say Richfield became aware of my . . . situation, and I wasn't ready to leave this job yet, so we came to an understanding."

"And what is it he wanted to understand about Tannenbaum's interest in King?" Ricky asked.

"Jeff—I mean, Representative Tannenbaum," Derek corrected himself, his eyes darting around nervously, even though there was no one to overhear us, "wanted to advocate for a couple of companies in his district that are Moonshot suppliers, that's all. He assured Mr. King that he would help the hearings go more favorably. He, uh . . . he was also a little concerned about the company's stock price dropping any lower."

"Class act," Ricky said dryly. "But why would any of that interest Richfield? Unless . . . Did he send you to keep an eye on King?"

Derek narrowed his eyes and said nothing.

"So what happened to Mr. King?" I asked. "He left early, didn't he?"

"Yeah," Derek said, his eyes darting again, betraying his effort to look and sound nonchalant. "That was weird. We were halfway through the entrée, and he started coughing and wheezing, like he was choking or something. Everybody thought it was an allergic reaction, but Mimi—you know, his girlfriend—told us he wasn't allergic to anything. We were about to call for an ambulance, but he got up and staggered off. I'm honestly kind of amazed he came back to testify today. I thought he'd be in the hospital at least—if not dead."

"You thought he'd be dead," Ricky asked pointedly, "or you hoped?"

Derek's lip curled up a bit at the corner in a small snarl. I wondered if Ricky had hit on something; certainly none of the others present at the dinner made much sense as suspects in what had happened to King. So if not Derek, who? "Did you see anybody else you knew at the restaurant? Or anyone who seemed interested in your party?"

His face relaxed a little; perhaps he sensed that I was looking for suspects other than him. "Not that I noticed. I mean, lots of people were kind of glancing toward us—Jeff and King and Mimi are all kind of famous in their own ways, I guess—but nobody was really staring or came over to talk to us."

"What about Tannenbaum's wife? Does she know what's going on with you and her husband? Maybe hates him enough for it to want to destroy him in convoluted ways?" I'd give Ricky credit for coming up with an angle I hadn't considered, but this seemed a bit too soap opera.

"Huh?" Derek seemed to agree with me.

"How is she with computers?" Ricky pressed. "Could she secretly be a hacker?"

"Wow. That's nuts, even for you. What are you even talking about?"

"Yeah, what *are* you talking about?" I shot Ricky a look of warning and gave his foot a little kick with mine.

"I dunno, just thinking outside the box." He shrugged, returning the kick, as if I had been trying to play footsie with him. "We keep forgetting the hacking thing."

"What hacking thing?" Derek asked. He seemed to have forgotten most of his irritation with us in his attempt to keep up with Ricky's convoluted stream of consciousness.

"The cars, man! Remember, they're getting hacked to sabotage the self-driving system? We heard about this from your boss. It's true, you know."

"Well then, maybe that batty old lady was on to something. Why don't you go bug her? She's the one who brought it to us. See what she knows. I don't know anybody, Jeff's tacky little wife included, who knows anything about hacking." Derek's face darkened as his bad attitude returned. "Now will you get out of here?"

I got to my feet, but Ricky apparently thought he was still on a roll. He leaned in over Derek's desk, jabbing a finger toward his computer. "You sure you don't know anything about it? Looks like you're quite the computer expert to me."

Derek reached for his desk phone. "I don't know anything about hacking, and that computer is US government property, so I'd have to be really stupid to use it if I did. I'm calling security now."

I grabbed Ricky by the arm and dragged him out into the hallway as he continued to gesticulate wildly and spout nonsense at Derek. As soon as we were out the door of the suite, he straightened up, stuck his hands in his pockets, and flashed me a sheepish grin.

I exploded. "What on earth was that? What is wrong with you? What happened to you?"

"I was trying to keep him off balance, see if he'd slip up on anything. I don't trust that little weasel."

I blew out an aggravated sigh as we got into the elevator. "Next time you want to try a tactic like that, would you clue me in beforehand?"

"Sure. That's a good idea. That way we can both be in on the act. You know, a good cop, nutty cop approach. I like it."

"That's not what I meant. But maybe it'd be more effective. We didn't really get much from him, did we. Other than to rule out the Tannenbaums, I think."

"Yeah, probably," Ricky agreed. "I'm not convinced we ruled out Derek, though. What if he poisoned King, acting on behalf of Richfield? And maybe he had a woman help him bump off Elise. I'm not convinced Richfield isn't involved somehow. This seems to advance his personal and political agendas."

I considered this. It was extreme, but not totally outside the realm of possibility. "What about the hacking angle you so loudly reminded us of back there?" I asked.

"That's still the missing piece," he admitted. "Maybe we did get something useful from Derek there. Maybe we should take his advice and pay a visit to what's-her-name from LOCO-MOTO and see what she knows about it."

We returned to Ricky's apartment, and I dug out the LO-COMOTO press releases from my bag and called Melba, the local chapter president and press liaison, who heartily invited us to come over for cookies and an interview. I took down her address; when Ricky saw that it was in what he termed "deep-est, darkest Maryland," he declared that we would have to take his car, although I was sure I remembered seeing the name of the town, Greenbelt, on the Metro map.

I was beginning to notice that when he was behind the wheel of his funky little old copper-colored car, Ricky's joie de vivre expressed itself through spirited application of the accel-erator and enthusiastic cornering. It seemed like he heard the engine's happy sewing machine hum and the occasional squeal of the skinny tires as the soundtrack to a chase scene from a seventies TV cop show. Watching him zip through the streets of DC, headed toward the Maryland suburbs, I wondered whether he fancied himself more of a Kojak or a Rockford.

He noticed me watching him. "Whatcha thinking?"

"Just picturing an old TV show with a lot of car chases where the main character drives a Corvair like a maniac," I grinned.

"Hmm," he smiled back. "That would have been something. I think Darrin and Samantha Stephens on *Bewitched* drove a Corvair for a while, but I don't think they were going on many car chases. Broomstick chases, maybe."

"Which Darrin?"

"No, Samantha was the witch," he cracked, giving himself a rim shot on the steering wheel.

"Okay," I laughed.

Greenbelt was a centrally planned garden city built by the federal government in the 1930s as part of the New Deal. It had spread outward a little in the decades since, but the original core of the town was still mostly intact, identifiable by its Streamline Moderne shopping center, movie theater, and apartment blocks.

Melba lived in a modest two-story attached house in the middle of a row that appeared to have been built in one of the early waves of construction. Some of the houses on her row still showed their original Art Deco detailing, with strakes of trim unifying the windows and doors into sleek cohesion, while others, including hers, had been cheaply facelifted with vinyl siding, rendering them blocky and formless.

She was watching from her door as we pulled up to the curb in front of her house. "What a cute little car," she called as we got out. "Haven't seen one like that in years. I bet it's a stick shift, too."

"Yes, ma'am," Ricky answered.

"Good. Car like that, no doodads, crummy brakes, manual transmission—you gotta pay attention to what you're doing to drive that car," she said approvingly. "I'm not anti-driving, you know. I just think it's something to be taken seriously."

"I agree," Ricky said. "I have to be very aware of my surroundings driving my car, and I think that's much safer."

I refrained from commenting on other aspects of his driving that seemed a little less safe. At least we had established that we were simpatico in Melba's mind.

She waved us into the house behind her, through a dark, cluttered living room, an even darker, equally cluttered dining room, and into the bright, cheerful, cluttered little kitchen at the back of the house. We sat down around a small Formica-topped round table, and Melba placed a plate of snickerdoodles on top of a stack of catalogs and other junk mail in the center.

"You boys want any coffee? Tea? I'd offer milk, but my grandson got home from school a minute ago, and I think he finished it off. I got coffee in the pot, it's still good, or I can put the kettle on. Maybe I'll have some tea myself. Lemme look in the fridge, maybe there's still milk." She bustled around as she spoke, banging cabinets open and closed without any apparent rhyme or reason, her big energy overpowering her short, squat frame to fill the space.

"Coffee is fine," Ricky said.

It wasn't clear at first whether she had heard him. She had her nose in the refrigerator, noisily pushing bottles and cartons around. "Aha! See, there is some milk! Wait, how old is this? I guess I gotta give it the sniff test. You want any of this milk for your coffee, honey? Any sugar? What about you, you want coffee, too? I'm gonna have tea, I think."

"Black coffee is fine," Ricky said, shooting me an amused look.

"If you're having tea, I'll have some, too," I said. "Black," I added hastily.

"You got it," she said, banging her way out of the refrigerator and into a cabinet, pulling out three mugs with such enthusiastic tinkling that it seemed certain at least one of them should have broken. She babbled on as she added water to the kettle and started the stove. "I didn't wanna sniff that milk anyway. Jason—that's my grandson—he'll probably drink it, no matter how old it is. He won't care. That boy should go live on a dairy farm. He drinks me out of house and home. Eats all my food, too. You're lucky you called before he got home so I had a chance to hide those cookies so I had some left for you."

"How old is he?" Ricky asked politely.

"Fifteen," she said, pouring his coffee and bringing the mug to the table as she joined us. "He's a good boy, don't get me wrong. He's still growing, that's all. He helps me a lot with my work, does all kinds of computer stuff for me. He's my tech support, my webmaster, my youth consultant—he runs all our online outreach, stuff I don't understand at all. I couldn't do what I do with LOCOMOTO without him. Speaking of which, you came here to talk LOCOMOTO. What do you want to know?"

"Well—" I started. I was interrupted by the whistle of the tea kettle, and Melba jumped back up to pour the water. I grabbed a cookie while I waited for her to bring our mugs to the table, then resumed. "We understand you met with Representative Richfield's staff and gave them some information about Moonshot's over-the-air software updates being hacked. We were curious to know more about that, how you found out about it, and whether you know of any way to track down who's doing it."

"Mmm," she said thoughtfully as she sipped her tea. "Now, see, I gotta have you boys talk to Jason. He knows way more about all that kind of thing than I do. Or Lila—maybe you can talk to Lila."

"That's Lila van Veldt?" I asked.

"Yeah," Melba beamed. "That girl knows that stuff inside and out. She's the one who first brought it to our attention, and she's probably told Richfield's people much more about it than what they got from me. I only talked to some little twerp at the front desk. He didn't have any time for me, not until I offered to have Lila come down and show them everything."

"Wait, she's been here? She met with Richfield's staff?" This was new and unexpected.

"Honey, she's been here for a week. I thought I told you that. I think she's still in town. I don't know when she's going back to Boston, but I suppose it's probably sometime soon. She was helping out with the hearings as an expert witness or something like that. Maybe I should give her a call."

She didn't wait for a response, jumping up and grabbing the old yellow slimline phone from the kitchen wall. She punched in the number and waited, the phone cradled to her ear, but we could hear it go to voicemail. "Lila, honey, it's me, Melba. Gimme a call back if you can. I got some reporters I'd like you to talk to about the hacking stuff. I'll have them talk to Jason, too. Okay, take care now, bye."

She turned to us and shrugged as she hung up. "Well, I guess she's busy. Maybe she's already on the plane back home. Anyway, I'll get Jason down here . . ." She turned and hollered toward the stairs. *"Jason!"*

"What?" came the muffled reply from above.

"Come down here. I got some people wanna talk to you," she called back.

"Gimme a minute. I'm in the can."

"Jeez," Melba said to us blandly. "Everybody's busy, looks like."

I wrapped my hands around my warm mug. "Well, in the meantime, what can you tell us about Lila? What's her background? What's her connection to Moonshot?"

"Well now, I gotta go back to when LOCOMOTO started a couple years ago, around the time the Moonshot self-driving software started showing up on the streets. This young woman,

Sharlene Wilkins, was T-boned in her car by a Moonshot and got a spinal cord injury and became a paraplegic. So she and her parents made the Facebook group. I think she might actually be the first victim, but soon there were more, and lots of people, like me, who were real concerned about this menace out on the streets, you know? So that's how LOCOMOTO was born, and we grew real fast.

"So I got involved and had Jason helping me run the Facebook group, and one day I got this message. From Lila, who I had never met or heard of before, but, you know, we get lots of messages from strangers who are interested. Anyway, she tells me she's working on her doctorate at MIT, and she's a software engineer, and when she was an undergraduate, she worked on a project that turned into the basis for the Moonshot self-driving system. If I remember correctly, one of the people she was working on it with got hired and took it with them to the company. She wasn't mad about that or anything, but she said they hadn't worked all the bugs out of it, and she was worried that Moonshot hadn't, either."

I went stiff in my chair. "Do you remember the name of her classmate? The one who got hired by Moonshot?" Ricky nodded eagerly. He had had the same thought.

Melba thought for a second. "No, I don't, and I'm trying to remember if it was only one person, or maybe it was more than one."

"Does the name Elise Perkins ring a bell?"

"Not really. That could be it, but I don't remember. Maybe she never even told me their name."

"Sorry," I said. "Go on with what you were saying."

"What *was* I saying . . . ?" Melba mused. There was a flush upstairs, a door banging open, and teenage feet galumphing down the stairs.

She seemed to regain her train of thought. "Right, so we had Lila come give a webinar—you know, so people all over the country could participate—and she told us all about it. And she sent us some papers, and some language we could use in press releases and stuff. She's real busy, so she's not actively involved with LOCOMOTO, but she was very helpful, and when I told that twerp in Richfield's office about her, I guess she was nice enough to come help them out, too."

Melba's grandson had entered the kitchen, plopping down into the fourth chair at the table, and grabbing a cookie from the plate with a hand that I was certain I hadn't heard him wash in the bathroom. Based on what Melba had told us about Jason, I had been expecting a pallid, scrawny computer geek, but this kid was shockingly tall and filled out for fifteen, rumpled and sweaty and ruddy cheeked and brimming with puppy-dog energy. He looked like the kind of boy you'd see at an after-school lacrosse practice. Smelled like it, too.

"Jason, be polite. Say hello to Mr. Oliver and Mr. Ricky here," Melba scolded.

"'Lo," he said, cookie crumbs flying. He swallowed and added, "How ya doing. Sorry I'm all sweaty. I just got home from lacrosse practice. Hey, Grandma, we got any more milk?" His chair clattered back across the floor as he bounded to the refrigerator. He was a comically oversized mirror of his grandmother's chaotic energy.

"Yeah, honey, there's some in the fridge." She winked at us. "Listen, these boys are reporters, and they were asking me about the hacking stuff on the Moonshots, you remember, like what Miss Lila gave that talk on a while back? I know you got real interested, so I thought maybe you could tell them what you learned."

"Mmm, mm-hmm," he nodded, chugging directly from the milk carton as he returned to the table. "We set up a webinar for what's-her-name, Miss Lila, like, last year, I think? And she was talking about how Moonshot sends updates to its self-driving software out over the air. But, like, the servers they use to send out the updates are super easy to get into. Like, she started telling us about it, and I was in the chat with other people in the webinar, and within, like, five minutes, some guy had gotten into one of the servers. She was totally right, man! Everybody in the chat was saying how to do it, and there's, like, dozens of these servers across the country, right, and we were getting into them left and right. I was the first one to get into the one here." Jason beamed proudly.

"Wait, *you're* hacking the Moonshot updates?" I hadn't quite been expecting this.

"Uh-huh," he said, putting another cookie into his mouth whole.

"You are?" Melba seemed as surprised as I was. "Are LO-COMOTO people the ones causing all these problems?" Her face drained of color.

"I mean, some of them, yeah," Jason said, the realization slowly seeming to dawn across his formerly cheerfully open face that he'd said too much.

"I'm a writer, not a cop," I told Jason gently. "I'll try not to get you into trouble, but it would be really helpful if you can be honest with me. Are you still accessing these servers? Have you interfered with any of Moonshot's over-the-air software updates?"

He shifted nervously in his chair, picking at one hand with the other on the table and studiously avoiding his grandmother's gaze. His voice was suddenly small. "Yeah. Sometimes, I guess."

I had an idea. "Let's say someone else got into the local server, the one that sends updates out to cars in the DC area and made changes to the code in an update that was scheduled to go out. Would you be able to tell? Would you be able to tell who had done it?"

"Like, could anybody tell or me personally?"

"You personally."

He shrugged. "Probably not, but maybe. Some people like

to try to be as sneaky as possible, but others like to leave little clues or calling cards, like a certain joke written into the code or something."

"Maybe you can help us," I said. "We know an update that went out to Moonshots in the DC area earlier this week, on Wednesday, was probably hacked. Is there a way we could access the server, find that update, and look through the code to see if we could figure out who had done that?"

Jason brightened. "We could do all that, but we don't have to. It was me!"

CHAPTER 15

A silence would have hung over the kitchen as the three of us gaped at Jason, but Ricky had just bitten into a cookie and now choked a little on the crumbs as Jason's words sank in.

"What?" Jason's bright face once again clouded with confusion. "Did I say something?"

"It was you?" I squeaked.

"Yeah," he said, as if it should have been obvious. "If it happens on the DC server, it's almost always me. Just like if it happens in Philly, it's usually Squidward47, or if it's Miami, it's ButtfaceKillah. There's, like, four or five guys who do New York, though, and a bunch in California."

"My press releases," Melba moaned. "All those press releases about the horrible problems, and all along it's coming from my own house!"

"I take it those are usernames of other hackers you talk to online," I said gently.

"What's yours?" Ricky wanted to know.

"Yeah, uh, those are their usernames," Jason said, blushing deeply.

"What's yours?" Ricky repeated.

Jason's eyes ping-ponged wildly around the room. He chewed on his lower lip and squirmed in his chair.

"C'mon, man, I'm curious," Ricky said, cocking a mischievous eyebrow.

Jason looked down and mumbled something inaudible.

"Huh?"

His voice was still small, but this time we could make it out. "Boobfan69," he said wretchedly.

A keening wail arose from Melba.

"Nice," Ricky grinned. He reached across the table to offer Jason a fist bump, but the only response he got was me swatting his fist away.

"Okay," I said, trying to bring us back onto productive ground. "So you're in contact with other hackers in other parts of the country, and each of you has a sort of turf that you cover?"

"Yeah, we have a chat server that a bunch of us are on. It got started after that LOCOMOTO webinar, so we could be, like, organized, you know? But people aren't territorial or anything. I wouldn't care if there was someone else messing with DC. It's just that I already know how to get in, so if someone else wants to do something, sometimes it's easier for them to ask me."

"Did someone else ask you to hack the update on Wednesday?"

He nodded.

"Did you know what the change to the update was?"

"Nuh-uh. They sent me the code and told me where to put it. I didn't pay attention to what it was."

Not exactly a solid legal defense, but at least the kid wasn't evil, just dumb.

Melba had briefly had her head down on the table. Now she was looking wildly around the room, anywhere but at the three of us, and when she broke into the conversation, her voice belied an extremely tenuous grip on her self-control. "Are they all LOCOMOTO people? Squidface and Buttface and Boobface? Is it all my own people who have been making a fraud of me?"

Jason shrank again. "Yeah, mostly," he mumbled.

She pushed back from the table so violently that our drinks all sloshed and one of the cookies fell off the plate. "'Scuse me a minute," she said in a near-hysterical tone, flying from the kitchen and stomping up the stairs.

The kitchen was silent again for a moment. I didn't know how to respond to this outburst. Jason was back to picking at his fingers and chewing his lip. Ricky reached for the pile of paper napkins in the center of the table and began sopping up the puddles of coffee and tea.

"So who asked you to go into the update on Wednesday?" Ricky asked as he wiped.

"Huh? Oh, that. It was kind of a big deal, I guess." Jason's ever-swinging pendulum of emotions was on its way back to bubbly and obliviously proud. "See, the chat server is run by MoonChaser. They were one of the first ones to start hacking Moonshot servers and help us get organized and everything. And they're the best. They can do really complicated code, way more than what I can do. They can get into almost any server, but they mostly hit Boston, sometimes New York or San Francisco. But when MoonChaser wanted to do DC, she asked *me* to do it."

"She?" I snapped back into focus. "Do you know who MoonChaser is?"

His face screwed up in uncertainty. "I mean, not exactly, not for sure. But I think I do."

He seemed willing to leave it there, but I wasn't. "Well? Who do you think it is?"

"I think it's Miss Lila."

"What makes you think that?"

"Well, she knew all about how to hack Moonshot, right? And she lives in Boston, right? And she said in that webinar how she wanted to talk to everybody who was getting into the servers, and then right afterward MoonChaser set up the chat server."

Ricky and I looked at each other, exchanging small shrugs. It wasn't conclusive, but it didn't sound too far-fetched, either. Melba stomped back into the kitchen. She had a laptop under one arm and an iPhone in her other hand. "Say goodbye to these, mister," she said, thrusting the devices toward Jason.

"Aw, Grandma, what are you doing with that stuff? Did you go in my room?"

"Yeah, I went in your room, and I'm confiscating these. You're lucky I left the TV in there. You're going back to the Dark Ages, boy."

"We should probably go . . ." I said this more to Ricky than anyone else. We began to pull away from the table.

Melba noticed us. "Yeah, boys, gimme a call before you print anything about any of this, okay? Sorry, but this wasn't what I was expecting. It looks like I gotta straighten some people out." She began half ushering, half rushing us to the front door. "Starting with my own dumb grandson. You better leave so I can whale on him a little. Don't print any of this, okay?"

"Thanks for the cookies," Ricky said as we hit the doorstep, but the door slammed shut so quickly behind us that I wasn't sure if she heard him.

Ricky's driving was uncharacteristically sedate as we motored away from Melba's house.

"MoonChaser, huh," he said thoughtfully.

"Yeah. At least it's something, I guess." I turned this new wrinkle over in my mind. "Do you think MoonChaser really is Lila van Veldt?"

"I don't know, but it's not the least plausible idea we've come across. I think it's time we tracked the elusive Dr. van Veldt down."

"I agree, but how do we find her? We don't know if she's still in town. We don't know where she was staying. I don't know if we can go back to Richfield's office."

". . . We go back to Richfield's office," Ricky said, our words almost perfectly overlapping. I sensed his foot dipping into the accelerator. The thrum of the engine deepened, and the car surged forward. His destination now locked in, Ricky's behind-the-wheel brio returned.

"Oh, boy," I mumbled.

He downshifted and executed a crisp lane change to zip past an inattentive driver sitting at a green light. He muttered something under his breath that sounded like, "Flippin' Maryland."

I watched suburbia streak by out my window, still pondering the mysteries of Lila van Veldt. Suddenly, I turned back toward Ricky. "Could she be the woman? The one having drinks with Elise?"

"Maybe. We need to find out what she looks like."

"And what she sounds like," I added.

I could see Ricky's wheels turning for a moment. His lips moved a few times, and he waved circles in midair with his right hand as he worked something out. Finally, he said slowly, "She's been working with Richfield for the past week. Since before the Moonshot team got to DC, it sounds like. What if she and Richfield planned everything together? She bumps off Elise, he uses Derek to try to get rid of King, nothing goes back to him directly, but he's solved some big personal and political problems."

"What's in it for her?"

"Can we connect her with Elise through their time at MIT? It seems likely—she was working on software that formed the basis of the Moonshot system that Elise helped develop. Maybe there's some personal beef between them. Elise got the Moonshot job and Lila didn't, Elise took what they were working on and gave it to Moonshot. Maybe it's revenge!"

I pulled out my phone to see for myself if there were truly no pictures of Lila van Veldt online. I searched her name, and just as I was about to click over to the image search, the name Perkins caught my eye in the results. I gave a little yelp and looked closer: a citation of an academic paper on artificial intelligence, credited to "Gallegos, Perkins & van Veldt." I scrolled farther down the results. There were dozens of citations, to several different articles, all credited to the same three coauthors. I finally found an abstract of one of the articles that gave the coauthors' first names: Mercedes Gallegos, Elise Perkins, and Lila van Veldt.

"Well, you're right about at least one thing," I finally said to Ricky, who had been giving me sidelong glances since I had yelped. "Lila van Veldt and Elise definitely knew each other and worked together—a *lot*—at MIT. They coauthored a bunch of papers, all on subjects that look like they relate to the self-driving software."

"Ha!" he crowed, giving the rim of the steering wheel a celebratory thump. "I knew it! Let's go nail this broad." He weaved around a few more slow-moving left-lane hogs, cutting a path through the gathering late afternoon urban rush, which even I had to admit, through my growing terror, was remarkably efficient.

"'Nail this broad?'" I repeated, to distract myself from my white-knuckle grip on the armrest on my door. "Are we in some kind of hard-boiled noir now?"

"I dunno, kind of seems like it. I do wish there was an equivalent non-gendered term for 'broad,' though. I feel like I should be able to be hard-boiled without tipping into misogyny."

"Yeah, let's work on that."

Ricky's take-no-prisoners attitude followed him out of the car and through the now-familiar hallways of the Rayburn Office Building. I was nearly panting at his heels as we barreled toward Richfield's office door.

"Wait," I huffed, trying to grab his sleeve, hoping to strategize our approach, but he was too caught up in his own momentum. He charged in and stormed directly toward the inner office space, giving a startled Derek the finger as he passed. I shot Derek a frantic "Help me" look as I followed, as he scrambled from behind his desk to try to intercept us.

Ricky stopped short inside the door to the main staff office. I collided with his back, but he didn't seem to notice. Derek got caught in the traffic jam, trying to push past me but ending up stuck in the doorway.

"Who here has been working with Lila van Veldt on her testimony this week, please?" Ricky asked in a clear, pleasant, utterly unruffled voice. *How did he flip the switch like that?* I wondered, hanging on to his shoulder as I hunched over to catch my breath.

There were five or six people sitting at desks around the office, all looking toward us with expressions somewhere between blank and alarmed. It was hard to tell exactly how many because they all looked approximately the same. Gender and ethnic diversity disappeared under a unifying layer of conservative, corporate blandness in attire and self-presentation.

"I—I have," volunteered one young man hesitantly.

"What the hell! You can't barge in here like this," Derek finally sputtered from behind me, having given up on getting past.

Ricky ignored him, addressing the young man instead. "May we ask you a couple of questions about her, please? Nothing confidential, I promise. We're reporters working on a piece, and she's been a little hard to track down or get background on."

"Sure, I guess," he said, still peering nervously past us at Derek for guidance. Derek was in the process of returning to his desk, however, either giving up or, more likely, going for his phone to call the Capitol Police.

"What's your name?" Ricky asked, pulling a chair from an empty desk over to the man and motioning me to do the same. "Off the record, if you like," he added.

"Frank—uh, Franklin Chapman, I mean. And yes, please. Off the record."

"Sure thing, Frank," Ricky said smoothly. "Like I said, we've been having a hard time getting in touch with Dr. van Veldt and hoped you could help us with a few details."

Frank seemed to relax a bit. "Like what?"

"Like when did Dr. van Veldt arrive? Has she been working with only you, or with Representative Richfield or other staffers as well?"

Frank flicked his eyes to a calendar on his computer screen. "She arrived on Monday . . . that is, I think she might have gotten into town over the weekend, but she came here to meet with us first thing Monday morning. She did meet with Representative Richfield a couple of times, usually with me in the room, as well, but once one-on-one. They had dinner together Monday night, too. Otherwise, she was only working with me."

Ricky's eyes flashed. "Dinner together was just the two of them?"

"Uh, yes. Purely a courtesy, though, you understand."

"Sure. And when did you last see her?"

"She left about twenty minutes ago." Frank looked surprised. "I kind of thought you knew that."

"Twenty minutes ago?" I said. "Where was she going?"

"She was going to check out of her hotel and head to the airport to go home," Frank said, doubt creeping back into his eyes.

Ricky clutched at my arm urgently. "Do you remember which hotel?"

"The Monument, on the other side of the Hill," Frank said. "Wait, should I have told you that?"

"Probably not, but it's fine," Ricky reassured him. "Um, so this is weird, but we also haven't been able to find a picture of Dr. van Veldt. Could you give us a description of her?"

Frank looked conflicted but continued as if his mouth was

on autopilot. "She's, I don't know, about your age. Medium height, average build, long dark brown hair."

This was a pretty good match with the description of the woman at the bar with Elise. "Does she have an accent or anything distinctive like that?" I asked eagerly.

"Yeah, she has a pretty noticeable New York accent," Frank said, slightly and perhaps unconsciously pronouncing it *Nyoo Yawk*.

I knew Ricky would want a more concrete answer. He asked, "Could you narrow it down to any particular part of New York? A specific borough?"

Frank's previously mostly confused countenance took on a heavy-lidded, sardonic look. "Do I look like a linguist specializing in New York accents to you? No, I can't narrow it down. Can I see some press credentials or something?"

I dug in my pockets for a business card. Ricky nudged me and said, "We should probably get out of here and see if we can catch up to her."

I found a card and handed it to Frank as we rose. He looked at it quickly, then incredulously called after us as we headed to the door, "*Offbeat Traveler?* What's going on here?"

Derek glowered at us from his desk. "What was that?" he hissed.

"Nice try, buddy boy, sending us off to the LOCOMOTO lady," Ricky taunted. "Joke's on you, because she was super helpful *and* she sent us right back here."

I swear Ricky had his tongue out and was about to stick his hands in his ears, but I couldn't say for sure, because I was too busy pushing him out the door.

CHAPTER 16

"You know we can't go in there," I reminded Ricky as he pulled up to the curb across the street from the Monument Hotel.

"Aw, I knew you were going to say that," he said in a mock whine, winking at me. "No, I know. We won't invite trouble. I figure, if she's going to the airport, she'll come out to walk to Metro or grab a cab or something, so we can wait here until someone matching her description comes out."

"Just checking," I said warily. "Getting kicked out of somewhere doesn't always seem to stop you from going back in."

"Well," he said thoughtfully, "I was the one who got us kicked out of Richfield's office, and I don't care, but you were the one who got us kicked out of the hotel, and you do care. So I'll respect that."

"I don't know that I'd claim full responsibility for getting us kicked out of the hotel," I said. "But . . . thanks, I guess?"

We settled down into our seats to wait. The late afternoon sun was waning quickly, and the air was getting cool. I cranked my window up until it was barely cracked.

"I hope we haven't missed her," I said after a few minutes. "And I hope she comes out soon. Too much longer, and we won't be able to see anything in the dark."

"Yeah," Ricky said. After a few seconds' thought, he piped up again. "I wish Frank had been able to give us a better description of Lila's accent."

"I suppose that would have been helpful," I said absently, still staring out my window toward the hotel. "But I'm not surprised he couldn't. I mean, I don't think I could tell one New York accent from another. Could you?"

He thought about this for a moment. "Maybe not," he finally conceded. "But it feels like the most concrete thing we have to go on in our description of Elise's drinking buddy."

The hotel's exterior lights came on to counter the gathering dusk, illuminating the sidewalk, the ever-present row of blue Moonshot sedans parked on the street in front, and the small semicircular driveway before the entrance. Vehicular and pedestrian traffic in this strange, quiet downtown neighborhood were both light. The first car to pass by in several minutes, a red, white, and green Toyota Camry taxi, pulled into the driveway.

Ricky's left hand tensed around the steering wheel, and he reached to the dashboard with his right and hovered over the key in the ignition. "Grab your phone," he said with quiet urgency. "See if you can get a photo of that cab's license plate and number. If she gets into it, see if you can get a picture of her, too."

I zoomed my camera toward the back of the cab, clicking off a couple of photos. I held my breath as the cab came to a stop and the front doors of the hotel slid open.

A lone woman stepped out toward the cab, pulling a wheeled suitcase behind her. She was neither short nor tall, neither particularly fat nor thin. She could have been in her twenties or thirties, or even her early forties, but I guessed she was on the younger end of that spectrum. Her clothes were sensible and tastefully nondescript. Her dark hair was pulled up with a clip at the back of her head, and a pair of gold hoop earrings glittered in the hotel's lights.

"Bingo," said Ricky. He turned the key, and the car rumbled to life. I snapped a few more photos as Lila van Veldt—she *had* to be, right?—put her suitcase in the trunk and slid into the back seat of the taxi. "Keep your camera ready, and keep eyes on that cab," Ricky said as he pulled away from the curb, slowly enough to let the taxi turn out of the driveway ahead of him.

We made a series of turns as we wound through the blocks of anonymous office buildings and hotels looming gray and institutional over us. The corporate office buildings were partially illuminated, but the windows of the government offices were mostly dark; the bureaucracy had gone home at five o'clock.

I had been keeping close tabs on the multicolored Camry, even as the volume of traffic around us grew, and I was startled when the cab took a left turn into what looked very much like the underground parking lot of one of the dark federal office buildings, not more than a few blocks from where we had started.

"Odd place to take a cab," I remarked. "Ooh, is this like *All the President's Men*? Some kind of Deep Throat parking garage rendezvous?"

Ricky grinned as he cranked the wheel to follow the cab—and a curiously high number of other cars—onto the downward ramp. "It's not what you think."

It certainly wasn't like any parking garage I'd been in before. There was no gate, no place to take a ticket, and we were going awfully fast down the surprisingly brightly lit, surprisingly long ramp. As we finally reached the end of the descent, I was startled to see the ramp open up to join several lanes of interstate highway, zooming along underground, where you'd never know it was there.

"That was a freeway on-ramp?" I was incredulous. "I've never seen anything like this."

"We're currently directly underneath the National Mall, and only a few hundred yards from being underneath the Capitol building itself," Ricky said, still smiling, his eyes still laser-locked on the cab a few cars ahead of us.

The tunnel was well lit, making the task a little easier, but as I looked around, I noticed that the traffic around us seemed to be, oh, about 65 percent comprised of Toyota Camrys, and up ahead I could see the road rising back up aboveground. Distinguishing the cab by its taillights alone out on the open road would be challenging. I made a concentrated effort to lock it in.

Ricky seemed to be reading my mind. "You got her, right? That's her getting over to the left." He flicked on his turn signal to follow suit. "Which means . . . aw, crap."

"Which means what?"

"Which means they're headed to 695 North, which means they're going to BWI, which means we're going back to *Maryland*." He spat the last word out.

"What's the Maryland thing about? I noticed some . . . feelings about it this afternoon, too."

He thought for a moment as we arced along the interchange onto I-695. "Well, I mean, the main thing—relevant to what we're doing right now, that is—" He paused.

"Yes?"

"Maryland has the worst, most terrifying drivers in the world," he burst out. "I was trying to think how to be diplomatic, but I can't."

"What makes them so bad?"

"What makes them so *terrifying*," he corrected, "is that they're consistently inconsistent. Like, some places, you know that the prevailing culture is to, like, sit in the left lane at ten under or stop at the end of an on-ramp before merging or something, and that's bad, but you figure out to expect it. But no two Maryland drivers are bad in the *same* way, so you can never know what to expect. It's a friggin' free-for-all."

We were crossing the Anacostia River now, and overhead lights and headlights were so far allowing us to keep tabs on which Camry was the red, white, and green cab. Our little loose two-car convoy followed the signs for the flyover to Interstate 295 North.

"I suppose I should acknowledge my bias," Ricky continued. "I'm a Virginian, and people from Maryland think we're as bad at driving as *they* actually are. Which is to say, they're wrong, of course. But we're eternal sworn enemies, and so even if it weren't true, I might still say it. Opposite sides of the Civil War, you know. Virginia was on the wrong side, of course, but ever since, they've been so *smug* about it."

"Uh-huh. And how do DC drivers factor in?"

"They're caught in the middle, descended upon daily by tens of thousands of unhinged Marylanders and sensible Virginians and doing the best they can to dodge the carnage."

"Huh." So far, I wasn't seeing any evidence of any of this. Traffic was moving much as it had on almost every urban freeway I'd ever been on, running dense and a little frantic, mostly moving, but with occasional slams on the brakes that never seemed to have a reason behind them. But maybe that was the sensible and the unhinged canceling each other out while we were still in the District. I'd have to see how things changed once we left city limits.

In the meantime, another thought was creeping up. "So, uh, what's our endgame here? We're following this woman, who we hope is Lila, to the airport. What happens when we get there? We try to intercept her before she goes through security?"

"Yeah, I suppose so," Ricky said. He did a quick left-lane maneuver, overtaking the last car that had been between us and the cab and wedging himself back in directly behind it now. A sign above us indicated an exit for Quarles Street and Eastern Avenue. He pointed to it. "That's the last DC exit. We're about to enter enemy territory. Keep your camera ready. God, I wish I had a dashcam."

"Jeez, you really hate driving here."

"You don't know the things I've seen . . ."

We kept left to get onto the Baltimore-Washington Parkway, and almost immediately the city lights that had lined the freeway disappeared, replaced by a border of foliage. The traffic around us thinned enough that we were now keeping a steady speed, free of the urban stop-and-go. There were still occasional overhead streetlights, and Ricky's headlights kept the cab's livery in their beam as he left enough space to not appear to be tailgating, but not quite enough to invite anybody to cut in.

"Okay, so we catch her in the terminal," I resumed. "What do we say? What do we do?"

Ricky thought about this for a moment. "I think we play it straight. We're writing a story and Representative Richfield's office put us on to her, but too late to catch her before she was leaving the hotel. We ask her questions about Moonshot and the hacking and Elise and see if she cracks on any of it."

"Seems kind of weak," I murmured.

"Yeah, it is," he admitted. "It's not like we have any hard evidence to nail her on, though, so I don't know what else we can do. But I feel really good about this theory."

"I do, too," I agreed. "She matches the description of the woman at the bar with Elise, she seems to have a beef with Moonshot—and possibly with Elise, who we know she knew—and we know she has the hacking ability to have disabled the pedestrian detection system. Let's at least try to get a decent picture of her, so we can go back and have the bartender identify her. Then we'd have something at least a little more concrete."

"Good idea. Maybe even get a recording of her voice, see if the bartender thinks it's the same accent."

It was hard to get a sense of our surroundings in the dark. The trees bordering the road, and sometimes even dividing the north- and southbound carriageways, blocked out the world around us. The shoulder of the parkway was occasionally delineated by a low stone wall and at other times by an inky darkness between the road and the trees, which I guessed was a grassy verge. The glow of the taxi's taillights ahead of us was becoming hypnotic as we kept perfect pace.

"Hmm," Ricky said, seemingly out of nowhere.

"Hmm what?"

"On-ramp." He glanced to our right, where several cars were bearing toward our path. The taxi's brake lights came on as one of the cars merged in front of it, then another, a silver Camry of a dismayingly similar vintage, cut in between the cab and us. This Camry couldn't quite match the speed at which we had been cruising before, and I saw Ricky glancing in his mirror to see if he could pass, but the car behind us pulled out first and began to overtake us. It, too, was a Camry, this time in white. He kept watch on the mirror and swore under his breath.

"That white car cut, like, three people off, and now they're all bunched up. We're never going to be able to get over," he said. The silver Camry in front of us seemed to be slowing down. The white Camry to our left passed excruciatingly slowly, followed closely by a Nissan, a red Camry, and a beige Camry.

"Huh," I commented as I watched this convoy pass by. "I never noticed before how similar the taillights are between that model Nissan and a Camry."

"Swell," Ricky said, signaling to pull into the left lane to get around the silver Camry. As the cars ahead of us passed the slowpoke, some moved into the space ahead of it in the right lane while others kept left. One of the now-indistinguishable midsize sedans ahead of us briefly tapped on its brakes at one point, for no reason that either of us could see other than to incite a disorienting round of flashing brake lights all around us.

"Crap on a cracker," Ricky nearly shouted, banging the rim

of the steering wheel lightly with a fist. The road around us had become a sea of Camrys and Accords and Altimas, none of them the red, white, and green taxi, all of them plodding along at speeds just different enough, but still enough the same, that there was no getting through.

Finally, a gap opened to the right from which Ricky was able to maneuver around a few of the roadblocks through judicious use of lane changes, and after a few minutes we emerged at the head of the pack into a rather considerable gap in traffic that had been created by this onslaught of vehicular groupthink.

"I think that's the cab up there," I pointed.

Ricky leaned forward and squinted a little to try to make it out. "I hope you're right. Good thing we have a ways to go on this road."

"Yeah, how far is it to Baltimore, anyway?"

"Well, we're not quite going all the way to Baltimore. The airport's a little past Laurel. We probably still have about ten miles."

I opened the camera roll on my phone to look at the license number of the cab. We were closing the gap with the pocket of cars ahead of us, and at the tail end of the line I could see a red bumper reflected in the glow of the taillights that I hoped belonged to the taxi. Finally, we got close enough, and I compared the plate to my picture.

"That's it!"

"Thank god," Ricky sighed. "Let's not let that happen again."

I glanced back over my shoulder. "Gee, we really got separated for a minute there. Look how far back all those cars are."

Ricky flicked his eyes up to the rearview mirror. In that instant, there was a dark flash of motion behind us, something briefly coming between us and the headlights of the cars behind us.

"What the—" I twisted further in my seat to look. One of the sporadic streetlights dotting the parkway gave us a momentary burst of illumination, revealing a dark car coming up very quickly behind in the lane next to ours with no lights on.

Ricky saw it, too. "Turn your camera on," he said tersely. "Something is very wrong."

I aimed my phone at the dark apparition coming up on our left. As it drew alongside, I was able to make out that it was a Moonshot, but the color was indistinct in the dark, and I could see no illumination coming through the windows from inside the car. It glided silently past, then, without warning, lurched toward our lane, as if to wedge itself into the too-small gap between us and the taxi. The Moonshot's brake lights flashed, and Ricky had no choice but to give his own brake pedal a good stomp.

"What the hell," he shouted, downshifting and veering into the left lane to try to regain his momentum. We began to gain on the Moonshot, which was glued to the cab's rear bumper, following at an uncomfortably close distance. The cabdriver seemed to notice, first giving his brakes a quick tap to activate the brake lights, then, a second later, when the Moonshot apparently failed to take the hint, executing a quick lane change, cutting us off.

I still had my camera trained on the phantom Moonshot, now on my right, as our fractious trio raced along through the night. I still couldn't make anything out through the windows, which were tinted dark. There was now very little space between the cab and us, although Ricky eased off just enough to keep the cabdriver from thinking we were going to tailgate like the Moonshot had done. There was still not enough room for a car to get between us, and the Moonshot driver seemed momentarily uncertain of what to do. The car briefly lunged forward, as if to overtake the taxi, then fell back again until it was once again right alongside us.

Slowly, almost imperceptibly, the Moonshot began to drift closer and closer to my side of the car. *"Ricky,"* I shouted, and he yelped and gave the wheel a leftward tug. The Moonshot began pushing more aggressively to the left, its nose bobbing toward and away from us in a snaking motion as it gained speed.

"They're trying to run us off the road!" Ricky was frantically trying to wriggle his little car out of the Moonshot's path, but we kept drifting further and further onto the left shoulder of the parkway, toward who knew what in the darkness of the median. Suddenly, our headlights caught the edge of the pavement, which was bordered by a pronounced curb.

"*Yow*," Ricky yelped as his left front tire made sudden, sharp contact with the curb. The nose of the car bucked slightly as the steering wheel spun free of his grip. The camera flew from my hand to the floor as we ricocheted off the curb, our front corner barely missing the rear of the Moonshot, the car performing a sickeningly slow pirouette across the roadway toward the opposite shoulder. As the tires screeched around us, we were caught for a moment staring down the headlights of approaching traffic before we twirled away again, hitting the opposite curb as the oncoming cars whooshed past.

We lurched up over the curb onto the verge, the headlights catching a grassy blur as we barreled away from the road, thumping over the uneven ground. A stout-looking tree trunk rose up in the beam of the lights ahead of us. I scrabbled for something to hold on to, somewhere to brace myself, noticing for the first time, somehow, in this eternal millisecond of hurtling toward doom, that the dashboard was almost entirely metal, but that it didn't matter, because my head would hit the windshield before it got to the dashboard anyway.

And then we were stopped. The tree loomed inches in front of the front bumper, but we weren't moving anymore, and we weren't going to hit it. The engine had cut out at some point, stalled maybe, or maybe Ricky had turned it off once he had brought the car to a stop—I hadn't been paying attention to anything but my imminent demise.

But it was quiet. Quiet except for our breathing, both of us gasping coarse and ragged, and suddenly the sound started growing and wouldn't stop until it was screaming in my ears and each breath came out of me with a hoarse yelp and a heave of my chest and my eyes were as wide open as they'd ever been, but I wasn't seeing anything anymore, I was just pitching back and forth on the waves of my screaming breaths. My fingers clenched into my palms, the nails digging into the flesh, and as the adrenaline began surging into my limbs, I began to pound my fists against my legs in rhythm with my breathing.

Ricky told me later that there was never any sign of the Moonshot again. By the time we came to our resting place, it must have been a couple miles up the road—but the police cruiser appeared, as if by magic, almost instantly. He told me how we were ordered out of the car. I couldn't hear this, of course, and he tried to tell the officers what was happening, but one of them opened my door and reached for my seat belt.

I guess that's when I punched the cop in the nose.

CHAPTER 17

Nearly two hours later, I was huddled on a bench in a suburban Maryland police station holding cell, my back pressed into a corner, my feet up on the bench, my arms around my legs. I was pretty sure I had stopped crying, but my cheeks were damp and crusty with a mixture of tears, dirt, and grass stains from when the officer had pinned me to the ground, and my nose was running. I was exhausted, terrified, sore, hungry, and miserable. Footsteps coming my way told me that at least I soon might not be alone, but I wasn't at all sure if that would be a good thing.

To my great relief, the arriving company took the form of Ricky being brought to join me in the cell. I watched him, still in my protective pose, with shy trepidation as he slumped onto the bench next to me. His face was drawn and gray.

"I think they're going to bring us something to eat," he said after he had sat for a minute with his eyes closed and his head rolled back to the wall. He sounded spent. "I told them we hadn't had any food, and that low blood sugar might have been a factor in what you—in what happened."

"I'm sorry," I said from behind my legs. I could feel the tears, and my humiliation and hopelessness, rising again. Apparently, it didn't matter whether I stuck to a plan or went with the flow. Everything was going to go wrong no matter what, and the only thing I could count on was getting in my own way and blowing my chances—of writing features, of finding out what happened to Elise, of figuring out what I was doing, what I could do, what I wanted to do with Ricky. I tried and failed to contain a pitiful sniffle.

Ricky rolled his head to the side to look at me. He limply lifted his hand as if to pat my leg, thought better of it, and set it down next to my laceless shoe instead.

"It's okay. I mean . . . it's not really okay. Oliver, I know it wasn't exactly your fault, but you have to understand the position you could have put me in." His brow knit, and his eyes pleaded with me. "I'm a Black man driving in the suburbs at night, involved in what appears to be a one-car accident that seems suspiciously like the result of reckless driving. Who my mom is didn't matter in that moment—the minute the police showed up, I was a Black man, pure and simple. My life was already in danger, Oliver. And you had to go and punch the guy?"

The hurt and fear in his beautiful brown eyes was too much. I buried my face in my knees. "I'm so sorry. I didn't—"

"I know," he said gently. "I know. It was scary, wasn't it."

Tears streamed down my cheeks, but I realized I owed Ricky eye contact, for the position I had put him in and for the time he had had to spend talking to the officers on my behalf once we had gotten here. I put my head back into the corner, giving him the best bleary look of gratitude I could muster.

He noticed my green and brown cheeks. "Did you get hurt?"

"No."

His mouth turned up at the corners in a faint smile. "You know you broke the cop's nose, right?"

My stomach fell. "I didn't really, did I?"

He nodded slowly, the grin widening a little. I hated thinking I had hurt someone, but thrilled a little at Ricky's apparent pleasure that I had struck this blow against authority.

We sat for a few minutes in silence. I studied his profile as his eyes drooped closed again, noticing for the first time how long his eyelashes were and trying to memorize the soft curve of his nose. I had never spent so much time in close quarters with someone as ridiculously good looking as Ricky, and while he had been goofy enough that I had quickly gotten over my intimidation at his appearance, I still found myself, at least once a day, completely taken aback by it. And now it made me sad. Beyond being beautiful, he had been sweet and silly and kind and interested in me, and I had been fearful and panicky and had put his life in danger. I had definitely blown it.

Ricky opened his eyes and I roused from my brooding when an officer came bearing vending machine sandwiches. We tucked in hungrily, and I saw the color start to return to Ricky's cheeks.

"So, how much trouble are we in?" I finally asked.

He chewed and swallowed a bite of sandwich. "We'll probably be here overnight. They want to charge me with reckless endangerment and you with assault and resisting arrest."

"Overnight? I'm supposed to fly home tomorrow," I squeaked.

He shrugged. "They might set bail so we can get out in the morning. They can only hold us here for up to twenty-four hours. I don't know that you should count on making your flight, though."

"What happens if they don't set bail?"

"We'll get transferred to jail," he said blandly.

I blanched. "Do I get a phone call? Should I call my mom? What would I tell her?"

He shrugged again, taking another bite of his sandwich. "You probably can make a call, yes, but I doubt you'll get the chance before the morning. Try not to worry about it right now."

"Did you call anybody?"

"Yes. I called Drea. I figured she would be the best person to try to help us both."

My heart sank. "Was she mad?"

He gave me a strange half smile. "I think she was a little

amused. And she got very concerned about you, Oliver. She's not mad. She'll help us out."

I chewed meditatively on my sandwich for a moment. Another guilty thought flashed across my mind. "What . . ." I started hesitantly. "What happened to your car?"

"I think it got towed to an impound lot."

"Did it get all banged up?"

He looked at me quizzically. "We didn't hit anything. Did you think we had?"

"I couldn't tell what was happening!"

"At worst, it might have gotten a flat tire when we went over that second curb, but otherwise, I think it's fine."

"Well, I'm glad. I wouldn't want anything to happen to your car."

He grinned. "It is sweet, isn't it."

I smiled back. "Yeah. And it suits you." I had a sudden realization. "I dropped my phone in the car! Did anyone pick it up? I was recording video when that car tried to run us off the road. It could exonerate you!"

The thought excited me, but Ricky seemed unfazed. "I thought about that. I asked if they had your phone, and they said they didn't, so it must still be in the car. I asked them to look for it, but I don't know if they will."

His sandwich done, Ricky stood up and stretched, then got back on the bench. Before I knew it, he had laid down on his side and wriggled his head under my arm and into my lap.

I looked down at him. "I really am sorry."

"I know," he said, his eyes closed. "This is how you can make it up to me. By being my pillow."

"Okay." I smiled and, without realizing what I was doing, ran my fingers through his curls. He smiled, too, and nestled down further.

I rested my head back against the wall, thinking. "Ricky," I said after a moment.

"Mmm?"

"Where did that Moonshot come from? Who was in it?"

His eyes flew open, and he rolled onto his back so that he was looking up at me. "Huh. I don't know. I hadn't thought about that."

"Was someone else following Lila? Or were they following us?"

His eyes narrowed and flickered back and forth as he thought about this. I realized that at some point he had reached up and taken my hand that had been draped over his shoulders and was holding my wrist in one hand and playing absently with my fingers with the other.

"What if . . ." he said slowly, waving my own hand at me. "If Lila is MoonChaser, she's this really skilled hacker, right? What if *she* was driving the Moonshot?"

"Huh?"

"Remotely, from inside the cab. I've seen videos of this—where hackers can take control of a car's steering and controls completely remotely. Maybe there was nobody even inside the car!"

"That seems a little far-fetched," I said.

"Could you see anybody in there?"

"Well, no, but it was very dark."

"Exactly! Maybe she saw that we were following her, and controlled the car remotely to try to get rid of us."

"Why would she notice us? She's never met us. She has no idea who we are or that we even exist. And where did the Moonshot come from? We didn't encounter it until we had been driving for nearly half an hour."

Again without my noticing, Ricky had stopped playing with my hand and was now blatantly holding it, his warm fingers wrapped around mine. When I realized he had done this, I gazed at our intertwined hands in silent wonder, marveling at how suddenly, miraculously easy it was to do something I had never before been able to tolerate. He kept my hand in his grasp, pulling my arm over him like a blanket as he rolled back onto his side.

"Maybe someone from Richfield's office tipped her off? Like, before she even left the hotel. Maybe they told her about us, and she saw us and had that car following the whole time, until we got to a good place to get rid of us."

His words were slowing, interspersed with yawns, and his eyes were closed again. He seemed ready to drift from this fantastical theory into actual dreams, so I resumed stroking his hair with my free hand, tipped my head into the corner of the wall, and closed my eyes, too.

As I felt Ricky's warm body snuggle against the side of my leg and felt his shoulder rise and fall under my arm with his breathing, I smiled a little to myself. Maybe I hadn't entirely blown at least one thing.

I slept fitfully on the bench. Time passed formlessly. There were no windows, no clocks, and the fluorescent lights never went out, so it was impossible to tell how late it was or how long it had been. The hum of activity in the main precinct office down the corridor ebbed and rose throughout the night. My legs fell asleep quickly with Ricky's head in my lap, but I didn't have the heart to move him. Finally, after what felt like an eternity, he woke up long enough to let me up, at which point I went and curled up on the bench along the opposite wall and fell asleep for real.

When I woke up again, I was alone. I had barely enough time to cut through the disorientation and process this fact before a police officer came and opened the door of the cell.

"Come with me, please, sir," she said, without betraying any hint of why or where we might be going.

I followed her down the corridor. "What's going on? Am I going to jail?"

"No," she said tersely. "You're being released. No charges."

I saw Ricky, seated next to a desk, talking to an officer, as we entered the office area. Seated next to him, to my immense surprise, was Drea.

She stood as soon as she saw me. "Oliver! Are you okay?" She wrapped me in a hug, and I was so stunned that I let her pin my arms to my sides. I was really breaking down all my usual taboos against bodily contact, but as happy as I was to see Drea, it felt far less natural than it had last night with Ricky.

"I'm okay. What are you doing here?"

"I got myself on a red-eye as soon as Ricky called. It's been far too long since I've gotten to bail him out of jail, so I was happy to have the opportunity to do it again."

I looked at him and raised an eyebrow. His face was serene and impassive in response.

"Anyway," Drea continued, "he told me you had some video on your phone that would help, but he was worried the police wouldn't look too hard for it, so I dragged an officer to the impound lot, and we got everything cleared up."

"Thank you." I exhaled gratitude and relief.

The officer at the desk looked up at me. "Sir," he said, "we're dropping the charges against you, in light of what we now understand to have happened, and because of what your friends here told us about your . . . situation. But—" He was staring intensely at me, but his eyes clouded a little, as though he felt he needed to give me a stern warning, but he wasn't sure about what. "But let's see to it that this never happens again," he finished, with a little less conviction than he had started with.

I nodded. "I understand," I agreed, although I'm not sure I did entirely.

He handed me an envelope containing my shoelaces and the contents of my pockets, and after a few minutes of reassembling ourselves, we were free to go, and Ricky and I trooped out the door behind Drea. I looked shyly at him as we walked through the station, and he winked.

"Okay, boys," Drea said as she marshaled us onto a bench in

the morning sun outside the precinct door and pulled out her phone. "Here's the plan. Ricky, I'm calling you a cab to take you to the impound lot to get your car. Give me the keys to your apartment before you go. Oliver and I will go back there to get his stuff, and then he and I will head to National from there. I'll leave the keys in the mailbox. I was able to get a ticket on the same flight back as you, so we'll go home together," she said to me.

"Aye, aye," Ricky said with one of his mock salutes, then turned to me. "I guess this is goodbye for now, then."

I was taken aback by how casual he was about it. I looked at him in confusion. "I guess so? Sorry again about last night."

"Nothing to be sorry about," he said. "Your video got us out of it, so you ended up being the hero." He dropped his voice and pressed his leg against mine. "And parts of last night weren't so bad, were they?"

I gave him a small smile, cutting my eyes to Drea to see that she wasn't paying attention. I wondered what I should say. *I don't want to go?* I'm not sure that was entirely true—I was exhausted, and being in my own bed in my own room sounded awfully appealing. *I don't want to leave you?* That was getting closer to it, but it felt a little bit desperate. It had only been a few days, after all.

"I'll miss you." I'm not usually much of a blurter—my overthinking usually leads me to miss the moment and say nothing—but that one slipped out.

Two cabs pulled up to the curb, and Drea turned back toward us. "This is us," she said.

Ricky and I stood, and he pulled me into a hug. I tried not to cling to him too fiercely. He whispered into my ear, "Don't miss me too much. We have unfinished business." Then he pulled away with a smile and shot me another wink as he got into his cab and Drea and I got into ours.

* * *

I pondered our unfinished business as I settled into the cab with Drea. Ricky had meant the Moonshot story, right?

"You sure you're okay? That whole situation seemed very scary," Drea said as she fastened her seat belt.

"Yeah. And it was." I picked nervously at my fingers. "Am . . . am I in trouble?"

She chuckled softly. "No, you're not in trouble. Sending you off with Ricky, I was half expecting this. Only let's not mention anything about it to Ramona, okay?"

That would be no problem. I had no intention of mentioning anything about anything to Ramona if I could avoid it.

Turning to look out my window, I returned to my thoughts. Had Ricky meant something other than the Moonshot problem? Had he meant . . . *us*? What were we to each other at this point? I thought back to the night before, to the ways he had wormed into touching me, nuzzling me, holding my hand, without my even noticing until it was too late for me to deny how unexpectedly good it felt. He'd had a sneaky way of getting past my defenses. And then he'd seemed so unbothered by our parting—until that last comment.

It *had* to be the Moonshot thing, though, right? It had to be. That was driving me crazy, and I knew that meant it would be getting to him, too. We had seemed so close for a minute there yesterday. The Lila van Veldt and Representative Richfield theory hadn't quite solidified, but it had felt promising. And we had gotten so tantalizingly close, only to have that mysterious Moonshot horn in at the last moment to throw us back into the dark.

But maybe . . .

I must have been punchy from last night's fitful sleep, because I found myself doing the blurting thing again. "What did you tell him about me?"

Drea had been looking out her window, too, but turned to look at me in mild surprise. "What do you mean?"

"I mean that I know this was kind of a . . . a setup, and I'm wondering what you told him about me beforehand."

She looked sheepish. "He told you that?"

"Actually, it was my mother who told me."

"Yikes. Maybe I had too many coconspirators. I'm sorry, Oliver," she laughed softly. "What did I tell him? Well . . . I think I told him that you're really smart and cute, and that you need a little bringing out, but once you're comfortable, you're also fun and funny and sweet. Ricky's really good at drawing people out, so I thought you guys would be able to have some fun. And he's at his best when he has someone to care for, you know, be a little protective of. So maybe I thought in that way, you guys would be good for each other. Didn't work out, though, huh?"

I thought about this for a moment. "I don't know," I finally admitted.

"Oh," she squeaked. "So maybe I haven't failed yet?"

"I can take care of myself, though." I wasn't convinced that was true, but I felt the need to stick up for my independence. Ricky *had* taken care of me several times, but in situations that I probably wouldn't have been in by myself, so I wasn't sure how the math on that worked out.

"Anyway, he didn't seem too bothered that I was leaving," I said.

"That's how you know he likes you," Drea said.

"Huh?"

"If he's not bothered that you're leaving, it means he's made up his mind that he'll see you again. And then he'll pop up one day without warning. You might never be rid of him again. Man, maybe I really didn't fail." Her face broke out into a satisfied smile.

* * *

I was gathering my toiletries out of Ricky's bathroom when my phone buzzed in my pocket. I pulled it out to see who had texted me.

It was from Ricky. **What time is your flight?**

I called out to Drea in the living room. "What time is our flight?"

"Let me see . . . It leaves at twelve fifteen."

I relayed this to Ricky. His response came seconds later: **Perfect. We'll have to move fast. See you soon.**

CHAPTER 18

I tried a few times on the Metro ride to the airport to text Ricky to find out what he was planning, but the only response I received was, **Probably best you don't know too much. Trust me.**

Drea and I got off the train at the airport and crossed over the pedestrian bridge for the terminal. As we turned into the line for the security checkpoint, I was not too surprised to hear someone behind us call out my name, but I was surprised, and a little dismayed, when I turned and saw who it was.

"Oliver, what a surprise to see you again," Joey beamed, panting a little from running to catch up with us. "Are we on the same flight again going home? What a funny coincidence!"

"Hi, Joey. I guess maybe we are." He flashed his boarding pass at me, confirming that we were indeed booked on the same return flight to Oakland. "This is my editor, Drea Hollingsworth," I said, hoping Joey would be less chummy if he realized I wasn't alone. "Drea, this is Joseph Harris. He works in the PR department at Moonshot Motors. We met on the flight out here, and he helped me with parts of the story I'm working on for *Motor Mania*."

"Nice to meet you, Mr. Harris," Drea said politely, shaking his hand. I imagined she probably wouldn't be as bothered by the moisturizer as I would, but I felt bad for her nonetheless. "How was your stay in Washington?"

"It was a mess," he said happily, "but putting out fires is all part of the job."

I found myself annoyed that he could be so glib when the week had included the death of someone both he and I had considered a friend. "Has there been any update from the police on their investigation into Elise's death?" I asked sharply.

Drea raised an eyebrow at me, and Joey's face assumed an appropriately somber expression, though I doubted his sincerity. "No, I don't think so," he said. "I mean, I'm not sure there really is much of an investigation. Wasn't it a freak accident?"

I looked at him coolly. We had been moving steadily through the security line and were nearing the first checkpoint, where our IDs and boarding passes would be checked. I shifted my attention to gathering my documents and moving everything else from my pockets into my duffel to make my trip through the scanners more efficient.

As I zipped my bag closed again, I looked up and glanced around. My eye landed on a figure about halfway down the line behind us, a strikingly good-looking guy, his seemingly effortlessly fit physique clad in perfectly fitted dark-wash jeans and a lighter denim jacket over a cream-colored cable-knit sweater. He was doing a celebrity incognito impression with a baseball cap and sunglasses, which added just the right touch of ridiculousness to offset the hotness. It was hard to tell behind the sunglasses, but I was almost sure he was looking at me, too. I raised an eyebrow, and Ricky waggled his in response, raising a finger to his grin in a "shh" gesture.

I turned back to my companions and addressed Joey. "So, is the hearing over? Is the whole team headed back?"

"Yes, everything wrapped up yesterday. I don't think we're going to have a happy outcome from the hearings, but we'll deal. Some of those congresspeople are really out to make names for themselves by taking us down."

"Like Representative Richfield?" I suggested.

He shrugged and laughed. "I can never keep them straight."

We showed our IDs and tickets to the TSA agent at the head of the line and, to my annoyance, Joey trotted after me to the same line for the bag and body scanners.

For a moment we were busy with shoes and bins and removing extraneous layers of clothing, but then we were back in line, shuffling in our socks while waiting for our turn to go through the body scanner. Joey bumped me gently with his elbow, and when I turned to look at him, he was smiling shyly. "So . . . what are you up to when you get home?"

"Not too much, I guess. I have to work on my stories."

"Could I call you?"

Jeez. Joey was a perfectly nice person. He wasn't bad looking; he had a decent job. In another situation, I might have given it a try. I wasn't sure we had much in common, but in any event, a little experience wouldn't be a bad thing. Ricky had corrupted me. He had made me see Joey as nothing but a pawn, and I wasn't sure I could shake that—certainly not without feeling a lot of shame for how I had used Joey. Ricky had also offered—was maybe still offering—the tantalizing possibility of something much more fun and exciting than a few tepid starter dates.

But I didn't fully know how to extract myself, so I said, "Maybe, I guess. In a few days, maybe. I'll be really busy with this work when I first get back."

He didn't seem to get the hint. As we emerged from the scanner and waited for our bags and bins to come back down the belt to us, he kept close, saying, "I was going to see if you wanted to try to get together again last night, but at the end of the hearing, the whole team decided to go out and unwind. I kind of felt like I had to be there, you know?"

"Mm-hmm," I said, grabbing my duffel and my shoes. "Did you have a good time?"

"It was fine, I guess. People were kind of in low spirits.

Mr. King didn't even show up, but he hadn't been feeling well, so maybe he needed to rest." We had moved to a bench to put our shoes back on. He dropped his voice and leaned in close, back in Joey-the-gossip mode. "Between you and me, the night before last, Mr. King had to go to the hospital. He got his stomach pumped, and I heard—" He looked around, as if someone might be eavesdropping. "I heard that he had been poisoned. Like, straight-up *cyanide*. Isn't that wild?"

"How could that have happened?"

He gave an exaggerated shrug. Drea, who had gone through a different scanner line, rejoined us. "Looks like we're heading to gate forty-two," she said, pointing the way. Joey and I got up and followed.

"What seat do you have?" Joey asked me, walking entirely too close.

I consulted my boarding pass. "19F."

"What an amazing coincidence—I have 19E! We're seatmates!"

"Wow," I said nervously, trying to look for Ricky without being obvious about it. Where had he disappeared to? I didn't know what he had planned, but if it rescued me from Joey, I was ready for anything.

"Oliver! Wait!"

We all spun around to see Ricky running down the terminal toward us.

Drea gasped. I was pretty sure Joey rolled his eyes. My heart fluttered nervously. I had a feeling that a big, corny, rom-com-cliché-airport-declaration-of-love wasn't Ricky's endgame, but I couldn't quite piece together what was.

He was sure leaning into the big, corny, rom-com-cliché-airport-declaration-of-love vibes, though. "I couldn't leave things like that," he said dramatically as he reached us. He put his hands lightly on my arms, looking past me to Drea. "Drea, can I have a minute to say a proper goodbye?"

"Ooh" she said, fanning herself. She looked at her watch. "Baby, you can have exactly three minutes, but take it! Take it!"

"I'll catch up with you," I told her. "Gate forty-two. I'll be right there."

"Could you excuse us," Ricky said frostily to Joey. Then, before he could respond, Ricky wrapped me up in his arms and brought his face to mine.

Ricky was kissing me.

He caught me off guard, so for the first couple of seconds, my face was rigid with surprise, making the whole thing very awkward. But after a beat, I relaxed into it, tilting my head a fraction of a degree that seemed to make all the difference, locking us into place with each other, as though we were made to fit this way. His lips were soft, and I could feel the warmth of his breath flooding into me as they parted slightly. The tip of his tongue flicked tentatively between my lips, and—I swear, I don't know what possessed me—I met it with mine. It felt like the kiss went on for ages, which wasn't quite long enough, but then I felt his eyes flutter open.

"Ohh," I exhaled as he pulled his face away.

For a split second he shot me a devilishly cocked eyebrow and his most impish grin, the tip of his tongue poking flirtatiously between his teeth, before turning to give a quick look around the terminal. "Okay, they're both gone," he said, reaching down and grabbing me by the hand as he started to walk briskly down the terminal. "Let's boogie."

He pulled me around a corner, under a sign pointing the way to gates twenty-three through thirty-two, and picked up his pace a little. Over the PA system, a voice droned, "Last call for American flight 1642, with nonstop service to Boston Logan Airport. Last call for boarding at gate twenty-seven."

"That's us!" Ricky said, breaking into a run for the last few yards to the gate, still pulling me behind him. We barreled up to the agent taking tickets at the door to the Jetway, and Ricky scrambled in his inner jacket pocket and pulled out two printed boarding passes.

"Just made it," the woman smiled, scanning the tickets. "Enjoy your flight."

I was still catching my breath as we settled into our seats on the commuter jet.

"And . . . sent," said Ricky, tapping his phone. "There. I've texted Drea that I've kidnapped you, and she can go home without you. And now, good boy that I am, I'm turning my phone off for the flight."

"You're only turning it off so you don't see if she responds," I said.

"Maybe," he conceded.

"I take it we're once again going after the elusive Lila van Veldt?"

"Correct. I don't think we're done with her, do you? Either she was controlling that car last night, and she's our killer, or she wasn't and someone else is after either her or us. In which case, we warn her of the danger, or possibly draw the person out."

"Maybe," I said. "And back there, in the terminal? What was that?"

He cocked his eyebrow again, but his tone was almost exaggeratedly calm. "I had to get rid of Drea. She tried to set us up, so why not make her happy and make her think it worked? And that Joey guy bugs me, so I wanted to get one over on him. Two birds, one stone."

"I see," I said. "You know, that poor guy asked me out right before you showed up."

"Did you say yes?"

"Not really, but I couldn't figure out how to say no, either."

"Well, I doubt he thinks you're available now, so . . . you're welcome."

I was getting confused. *Was* I available? I tried to play it casual, but I'm not sure it worked. I couldn't bring myself to look at Ricky, and my words came out sounding more desperate than I intended. "So it was only a diversion?"

"If that's all you want it to be, sure," Ricky said slowly, not looking at me, either, but draping his hand over the armrest between us to trace a finger idly on my leg.

"What does that mean?" I finally lifted my face to look at him, and he met my eyes with an intense gaze.

"It means the ball's in your court. Always has been. I think I've been pretty open about my interest."

I blushed a little but didn't look away. "Even after my . . . performance back there, I still have your interest?"

"What, the kiss? You have nothing to worry about there. That was A-plus work." His eyes darkened a little. "It was hot."

My blush deepened, but I felt an odd rush of connection to Ricky that I had never experienced with anyone before. It took a few seconds for me to realize how comfortably I was sustaining eye contact with him. This was new. And . . . strangely comfortable?

Oof, things were getting too real here. And yet not in any way grounded in reality. We lived on opposite sides of the country. I was supposed to be going back home right now, and yet again, he had diverted me from my plans. What were we doing? Still playing detective, following flimsy leads to give us an excuse not to leave each other. Could he do reality? What would that look like? At some point, very soon, I would need to regain my sense of stability.

Ricky was still looking intently at me, though I had broken away to look at my hands to try to steady my swimming head. "I, um—what happens next?" I blurted. "I mean, I need to let my mom know where I am. She's expecting me home today. How am I getting home? When am I going home? Oh god, what am I doing?"

"Hey, it's okay," Ricky said softly. "Breathe." He still had his hand near my leg, and now he rubbed it gently, and strangely enough, I found that I *could* breathe. "We'll fly back to Washington tonight, and I'll get you on a plane home tomorrow, okay? I'll help you figure it out. And we can call your mom as soon as we get to Boston and let her know. It's not a big deal. I'm sorry, I probably should have let you in on my plans a little more to make sure you were up for it. I wanted to see this through and thought you would, too."

"Do you really think we can find out what happened to Elise?"

"I don't know," he admitted. "All of our theories have been kind of a stretch, and I don't have any special strategy to get someone to confess to murder. But I feel like we should follow whatever leads and hunches we have, no matter how flimsy, so that we know we did what we could."

I thought about this for a while and regained my cool. It was more than a pretense, I reminded myself. I very much wanted to understand what had happened to Elise. "How about—" I said at last, slowly and a bit uncertainly. "How about we simply approach Lila like it's an interview. We're working on a story, she's a source. No special strategy, just see what our guts tell us."

"I think that makes sense," Ricky agreed.

"Do we know where to find her? It's Saturday," I pointed out. "She's not likely to be at her office at MIT."

Ricky broke into a slow, sheepish smile. "I, uh, might have gotten in touch with a . . . friend, shall we say, at the *Globe* who worked a source or two and got me a home address in Cambridge."

I cut him a sidelong look. "Isn't it handy to have so many . . . friends."

"Stick with me, baby, and everywhere you go, you'll always have a hookup—er, so to speak." He blushed, and I laughed and lightly swatted his hand away from my leg.

* * *

The flight from Washington to Boston was only about an hour and a half, and when you factored in the ascent and descent, it felt like we were in the air a very short time. As we shuffled toward the exit of the plane, we both turned our phones back on. Ricky had missed two calls and a barrage of texts from Drea. I had one text, also from Drea, which simply said, **Have fun and be safe**, accompanied by a winking emoji.

"What did she say to you?" I asked Ricky.

"Well," he said, knitting his eyebrows and frowning as he scrolled through the texts, "there's a fair bit of irritation, a soupçon of 'Murder? What murder?' and, finally, a demand to be best woman at our wedding."

I showed him my single text. "At least I can rest easy knowing she's holding you solely responsible," I grinned.

"What a relief."

We found a deserted gate in the terminal where I could call my mom. Ricky wandered off as I listened to the ringing on the other end.

"Oliver?" My mom sounded puzzled when she picked up. "How are you calling me? I thought you were on a plane." I heard her moving around the house, and I pictured her walking to the magnetic whiteboard on the refrigerator door, where I knew she'd have my flight information written down. "Yes, you're supposed to be on a plane right now. What's going on?"

"Well-ll," I said, "I *was* on a plane a minute ago, but instead of coming home, I kind of flew to Boston."

"To Boston? What? Are you okay, Oliver?"

"I'm fine. It's kind of a lot to explain, but I started working on a second story while I was in Washington, and there was someone I needed to talk to for that story, but she left town and went back home to Boston, so we followed her."

"We? Who's with you?"

"Um. Ricky. You know, the photographer."

I could hear my mom's ears perk up on the other end. "So you must be getting along with him okay now if you went off gallivanting to Boston with him instead of coming home," she said triumphantly.

"Yes, we're getting along," I admitted.

"Well, that's great, but I'm still confused. You had to see this person in Boston? You couldn't have come home and called her from here?"

"Well, like I said, it's complicated. So, yes, I think we needed to see her."

"Okay," she said slowly, still sounding skeptical. "So when are you coming home? Or is this your way of telling me that you're running off with Ricky?"

"I think I'll be home tomorrow. I'll let you know when I know for sure," I said, ignoring her crack about running off with Ricky, because the thought was still nagging that he had something along those lines in mind—that he would keep dragging me from harebrained hunch to weak lead so that we never had to go our separate ways.

"Okay, well, keep me in the loop, and let me know if you want me to come pick you up at the airport. I'll bring the car if you're bringing Ricky home with you."

"I'm not bringing Ricky home with me!" At least, I was pretty sure I wasn't. Who knew what he would manage to talk me into next.

"You know your aunts still haven't moved out downstairs yet, right? The apartment's not quite ready to become your love nest yet . . ."

"*Mom!*"

"I'm just teasing. Have fun, and let me know what happens."

"Okay, bye," I said witheringly and hung up.

"You don't want me to come home with you?" Ricky piped up from behind me. *Yikes!* Where had he come from? "I'm hurt. After all those hints you dropped about your great new apartment."

I groaned. "Don't you start with me, too."

He came around the row of seats and handed me a bottle of water with a grin.

I looked at it. "What's this for?"

He untwisted the cap on his own bottle and took a swig. "Let's treat Lila like any interviewee, but let's not accept any beverages she offers. If she is the killer, that means she probably spiked Elise's drink, and maybe gave Derek the stuff to do King's. Seems safer to bring our own, in case she's some kind of serial poisoner."

I took a sip of my water. "It worries me that you're starting to make sense."

"Yeah, that probably should worry you," he said, hoisting my duffel onto his shoulder. I followed him toward the exit.

As we stepped out of the terminal and headed for the taxi stand, I was shocked by how cold it was. The weather in Washington had been beautiful, and, of course, I had dressed for a trip home to California. But here it had to be around forty degrees, with a bitterly sharp wind making it feel even colder. I shoved my hands into the pockets of my light jacket, worn even thinner with age, and hugged it around me, wishing I had known to layer like Ricky had, though I was sure even he was cold. As we stood at the taxi stand, waiting for a minute, he leaned into me so that our arms could share a little warmth. *Just a little warmth, right? That's all, nothing more.*

Soon enough, we were bundled into the back seat of a cab, and Ricky gave the driver Lila's address. Much of the drive after we left the airport was underground, until we emerged in time to cross the Charles River. Soon after, we exited the freeway and motored through a maze of streets on a route I could never have retraced. We ended up on a narrow residential street, lined with weathered clapboard houses and brick apartment buildings that came right up to the sidewalk, making the street feel even tighter than it was.

The cab stopped in front of a gray-painted house with three doors at the top of the front steps. We hustled through the cold, up the stairs, and Ricky rang the bell for the door on the left. I leaned into his arm again as we waited. *Just for the warmth.*

On a warmer day, the wait might not have felt so long, but today it seemed eternal. Considering how strange and spontaneous the day had been so far, I had remained surprisingly calm, but now, waiting to come face-to-face with the woman who might be our most likely suspect to have killed Elise, my stomach did a few nervous backflips. *Don't let your nerves show, Oliver,* I told myself. *Treat it like any other interview. She doesn't know that you suspect anything. And maybe it wasn't her, anyway.*

Eventually, we heard movement inside, and finally the door opened halfway. A surprisingly young woman peered out at us guardedly, glasses pushed up on top of her head, her long dark brown hair cascading over her shoulders.

"Yes?" she said. One word, not enough to catch an accent.

I was almost certain this was the woman we had seen get into the cab in Washington last night. The one who matched the description of the woman Elise had been drinking with the night of her death. I took a breath, shallow in the cold.

"Dr. van Veldt?"

CHAPTER 19

"You want Dr. van Veldt? Come back in three years," the woman said, with a wry half smile, her brown eyes softening a little, still wary but not unfriendly. Definite hints of Brooklyn in her delivery. "But, yeah, I'm Lila. What can I do for you?"

"Sorry to drop in on you unannounced," I said. "We've been trying to get in touch with you regarding a story we're working on about Moonshot Motors and its self-driving car technology. May we come in for a moment?"

"Jeez, yeah, it's freezing out there, isn't it." Lila was dressed casually in a sweater and jeans and stocking feet, which I imagined had to be feeling the cold about now. She stepped aside and ushered us into the small apartment. "What'd you say your names were?"

"I'm Oliver Popp, and this is my colleague Ricky Warner," I said as we entered the living room. She indicated an old leather couch for us to sit on and took an IKEA armchair facing us. If our names meant anything to her, her expression didn't betray it. "We first got your name from Melba, with the LOCOMOTO group, and then we learned that you had been advising Representative Richfield's staff for the hearings this past week. We tried to call and email but didn't realize until yesterday afternoon that you were out of town, so, again, my apologies for dropping in on you like this. But we're on deadline," I fibbed, hoping it explained why we were there.

Suddenly, there was a spark of recognition. "I saw an email come through . . . I think from you, right?" She waved a finger at Ricky. "Sorry I didn't respond. Like you said, I was out of town, so I kind of had to triage my emails and only respond to my boss and my students."

"Well, is this an okay time? We can be fairly brief," Ricky said.

"Sure. I got home late last night, so I'm having a lazy morning, trying to motivate myself to grade some papers tonight." She cast a wary eye toward her laptop, sitting on a side table next to her. I thought better of pointing out that it was well after noon. "What do you want to know?"

I wasn't sure how Ricky was feeling, but so far Lila had managed to completely disarm me. She seemed open, at ease, and utterly unthreatening. Still, I knew I needed to stay on my guard, and I suddenly realized how unprepared I was. I had to think for a second, then started slowly. "I understand that some of the basic design of the self-driving software originated as a student project you worked on, is that right?"

"That's more or less true, yeah," she nodded. "It was kind of like a senior thesis. I worked with two other girls, Elise Perkins and Mercedes Gallegos. Elise was the expert on artificial intelligence. I was the data architect, figuring out how to structure the program, you might say in layman's terms. And Mercedes was the coder who basically wrote the whole thing. You might have heard of Elise in your research—I hope you have, anyway—because she got hired by Moonshot right out of school and took our project with her, and that formed the basis of what they're doing today."

"I have heard of Elise Perkins," I said, watching Lila closely to gauge her reaction to the name. She merely nodded her approval. "In fact, I have known Ms. Perkins for a long time—she's part of what sparked my interest in this story." She seemed completely at ease, no hint of concern. "Was the fact that she used your work at Moonshot a source of contention with you or your other collaborator, Mercedes?"

Lila looked thoughtful. "I don't think I'd say that," she said slowly. "At least, not for me, not at first. I don't feel I should speak to how Mercedes felt about it. I haven't seen her almost since we graduated. It's been a long time. But I did keep in touch with Elise for a while and even went and visited her in California and saw some of what she was working on. And that's when I became concerned."

"When was that?"

She thought for a moment. "It must have been about nine months after we graduated? So, a couple of years ago now. I haven't seen or really spoken to her since."

Did she know Elise was dead? It almost didn't seem like it, but I wasn't ready to go there quite yet. "What was it that concerned you?"

"Well, she was showing me what they were doing, which was basically rushing our little student project to market on an extremely tight time frame and with very little additional development. I mean, I think the first cars with the self-driving system went on sale within about a year of her arrival? That's an insanely short development period. It basically told me that they hadn't done the testing or scaling necessary to really make our project work safely out in the real world, which it was never meant to do—at least, not the way we'd left it."

"So you felt the system wasn't ready?"

"No, not at all. And then I dug a little into their infrastructure, the servers and so forth, because the lack of care in their software development made me worry about their data security, as well. And I was right to be worried. Everything was so shoddily done, no concern for safety or security at any level."

"What did you do? Is that when you reached out to LOCO-MOTO?"

Lila laughed ruefully. "Not right away, no. LOCOMOTO

was pretty far down the list of people I tried to get to listen to me. I started with Elise, of course, but she was feeling a lot of pressure from above to deliver the product quickly, safety be damned, so she didn't want to hear it. I reached out to everyone at Moonshot I could find contact info for—I even joined Twitter so I could tweet at Kelso King! That got me a pile-on from his army of loyal fans. I had to delete my account and scrub a lot of other stuff off the Internet after I started getting credible doxxing threats from them. I tried NHTSA, I tried Congress. Richfield is my representative, so I'd called his office dozens of times, but until these hearings, they had no interest. When I went there this past week, they gave no indication that they'd ever heard of me before. Anyway, that's when I finally found LOCOMOTO. They were the only ones that would listen to me."

I kept my poker face on. "I understand you gave a presentation to LOCOMOTO, highlighting the data security vulnerabilities of Moonshot's software."

She frowned a little. "I gave a webinar for them, yes, but that wasn't the only focus. I shared a presentation that included what I felt were the major design flaws with the system, as well as the security problems. I do remember some of their members got especially excited about that part of it, though. I think somebody even tried hacking into one of their servers during the presentation, after I had mentioned it, which I found a little alarming."

Ricky's brow furrowed. "Haven't you hacked Moonshot's servers yourself?"

Lila looked at him sharply, as though in his uncharacteristic silence she had forgotten he was there. "No, of course not. I did enough research to confirm their vulnerability, but that's not really my area of expertise. It's also not particularly ethical."

"Didn't you express an interest in following up with the webinar attendees who had hacked Moonshot's servers?" I asked, a little hesitantly.

Her frown deepened, and she was clearly trying to think back. "I might have said something like that," she acknowledged. "Again, it worried me a little. I thought it was something they could lobby Moonshot to fix, but I was concerned they'd abuse the knowledge."

"Was there any follow-up?" I prodded. "Did you set up a chat server to communicate with them?"

She looked confused. "No, I didn't do that. I don't think there was any follow-up, now that you bring it up. I wanted to be helpful to LOCOMOTO, because they seemed to share my concerns and had more of a platform than I did, but I'm afraid I didn't have a lot of time to be involved with them."

I didn't consider myself very adept at reading people, but I still couldn't help feeling that Lila was being very straightforward and sincere with us. I looked to Ricky, and he gave me a faint nod, as if reading my mind and validating my take. I wasn't getting *hacker* or *conspirator* or *murderer* from Lila at all. I wasn't sure where that left us, but I decided that maybe she could help us sort things out a little more. But first, she would need to see more of the cards we were holding.

I took a deep breath. "Ms. van Veldt—"

"Lila, please," she said.

"Lila, I think you should know that your fears were valid. A number of the LOCOMOTO members set up a chat server following your webinar, to exchange information on how to hack Moonshot's servers. Several of these people have been responsible for corrupting the self-driving system's code and causing the cars to do unsafe things, possibly even to crash."

"Oh, my god," she said, recoiling in horror. "That's awful! Oh . . . this is so upsetting. I had no intention . . ." She had been sitting cross-legged in her chair; now she drew her knees up to her chin, looking as if she might cry.

"I believe you," I said gently. "And not everybody within LOCOMOTO knew what was happening, either. Melba was devastated when she learned of this yesterday."

"Melba," Lila said, somewhat absently. "She called me, too. Wait, was it you she wanted me to talk to?"

Ricky and I both nodded.

"And I have to ask you another question that might be upsetting," I said. She looked at me with a hint of fear in her eyes. "It's about Elise Perkins," I continued.

Her look turned to one of confusion. "Elise?"

I spoke softly. "Are you aware that Elise is dead?"

"Elise is—?" Her feet fell to the floor, her legs going limp with shock. She doubled forward in her chair for a moment and buried her face in her hands behind the shroud of her hair hanging down around her head. She let out three loud, shuddering breaths before she lifted her face, then, slowly, the rest of her upper body.

"*Seriously?*" she said in a half sob, not looking at either Ricky or me. "That can't be true. Are you being for real with me right now?"

"I'm so sorry to be the one to tell you," I said. "I feel terrible. I thought you might already know—that you might have heard it in Representative Richfield's office."

She looked blearily at me. "No, they didn't say anything. Why would they know about it? What happened?"

"Did you know that Elise was on the Moonshot panel at the hearings?"

"She was? I didn't go, wasn't watching them—I really didn't have time. When I wasn't working with Richfield's staff, I was still teaching and trying to keep up with my work remotely." She wiped her eyes and looked dazedly around the room. Her voice cracked as she asked, "We were both in Washington at the same time?"

"You were staying at the same hotel," I said. "You really had no idea?"

"No. I had no idea. *God.*" She pounded the arm of her chair with a fist. "God, I'm sorry. I really want to know what happened, but I'm struggling a little here. Can I take a minute?"

"Of course," I said.

She got up from her chair, still looking around the room, as if she wasn't sure where she was. "I'm gonna make myself some tea. Do either of you want any?"

I really didn't think we had anything to fear from Lila van Veldt, but all the same, Ricky and I both said, "No, thank you," nearly in unison. She left the room, her shoulders slumped.

I put my head in my hands, leaning forward on the couch. "Well, I feel kind of terrible," I muttered.

Ricky rubbed my back. "You shouldn't. You handled that fine."

I looked over to him. "That was genuine, right?"

"It sure felt like it to me, but I don't know."

"She'd have to be a really good actor for that not to be real," I said.

"Yeah," he agreed, looking off into space, his hand still making slow circles around my shoulder blades.

Over our whispered conversation, I could hear Lila in the kitchen, putting water into a kettle, lighting the stove, and then softly crying. The three of us hung in our respective poses of grief, worry, and care for what seemed like an eternity. Only when the kettle whistled was the spell broken. Ricky withdrew his hand. I straightened up. In a moment, Lila emerged from the kitchen, mug of tea in hand, clearly trying to regain her composure.

"Please forgive me," she said shakily, returning to her seat. "This has been quite a shock, but I would like to know more."

"I really am so sorry," I said.

She waved this away. "Please. Tell me what happened."

I wasn't sure how to lay it out. I looked to Ricky for help, and he jumped in. "This past Wednesday evening, the Moonshot team put on a press demonstration of the self-driving cars. The cars were programmed to follow a specific route around part of Northwest Washington. During the demonstration, one of the cars struck and killed Ms. Perkins."

Lila's hand flew to her mouth. "Oh, my god," she whispered.

"The thing is," I added, "Elise wasn't attending the event. As far as everyone knows, she should have been back in her hotel room, clear across town. And, according to a witness who saw her prior to the incident, she looked like she had been drugged. The police have been treating this as an accident, but we believe that she was lured to that area, drugged, and intentionally pushed in front of one of the self-driving Moonshots."

"You mean, you think she was murdered," Lila gasped.

"Yes, we do. An over-the-air update of the software had also been hacked earlier that day to disable the pedestrian detection systems."

Lila chewed on her thumb for a moment, staring thoughtfully at the floor. "Did this witness see anyone with her?"

I again looked to Ricky for help, but this time he only shrugged, so I forged hesitantly ahead. "She was seen with someone, yes. A woman. Elise and this other woman were seen together having drinks at a bar up the street, and then were seen on the sidewalk in the area where . . . it . . . happened. Honestly," I said, squirming uncomfortably, "the woman matches . . . your description."

Lila dropped her hand, and her mouth fell open. No sound came out at first, though she seemed to be trying to speak. Finally, she squeaked, "It wasn't me! I told you, I had no idea she was there. Do you really mean to tell me you think it was me?"

"Having talked to you, no," I said with conviction. "I don't think it was you. And I'm guessing you wouldn't have any idea who it could be, either. It just seemed like a strange coincidence."

"I really fit this woman's description? Like, one hundred percent?"

"It wasn't a very good description," Ricky offered. "We were told it was a woman around the same age as Elise, with long dark hair. We were also told she had a distinctive accent. It really wasn't much to go on."

"Distinctive accent? Do I have a distinctive accent to you?"

"Do you *not* think you do?" Ricky laughed a little, but I gave him a shot in the ribs. He wasn't entirely wrong, though—the question had come out sounding very Brooklyn, although now I wondered if the accent could be narrowed down even further to a neighborhood. I wasn't sure it would be the right one.

Lila stared intensely at us for a moment. I was starting to worry that we had angered her or, worse, that we had misread her. She was back to chewing on her thumb. When she finally spoke, there was a note of hostility, but it felt like it was directed somewhere other than at us.

She said, "Maybe I should tell you about Mercedes."

CHAPTER 20

"Hang on, I think I have a picture somewhere." Lila rose from her chair and padded up the stairs. This level of the apartment seemed to contain only the small living room and the kitchen, so I assumed the upstairs consisted of her bedroom and bathroom. We could hear her steps overhead, drawers opening, papers rustling.

A moment later, she came back down and handed me a slightly crumpled photograph. There were three young women and one middle-aged man in the photo, all dressed professionally and standing against a wall in what looked like a conference hall. I recognized two of the women: Lila and Elise. The third woman looked somewhat like Lila, if she was trying to do a Kim Kardashian impression. Her pose was practiced, one hand on a jutting hip, and her lips were puckered a little under smoldering, heavily mascaraed dark eyes. Her hair was long, dark, and straight. Dangly gold earrings peeked out from under the hair. She was about the same height as Lila, including the slightly too-high heels she was wearing, but thinner and more curvaceous.

I held the photo up, pointing to the third woman. "I take it this is Mercedes?"

Lila nodded. "Yeah, that was taken when we were presenting at a conference. The guy was our faculty advisor, now my boss, Harvey Rabinowitz."

I passed the photo to Ricky. As he studied it, he said, "She looks like she'd rather be at a nightclub than an academic conference."

"That's about right," Lila laughed. "Mercedes stood out at MIT. She was kind of a party girl and much more attuned to trends and fashion and stuff than most of us. I met her my first day at MIT, but everyone always assumed we already knew each other, because we were both from Brooklyn, and I guess because they thought we kind of looked alike. Anyway, we didn't have a lot in common on a personal level, but we became sort of friends because everyone assumed we were."

"You think Mercedes might be the woman Elise was seen with?" I asked.

"Well, I have no idea. Like I said, I haven't seen or talked to Mercedes in a long time. But I thought of it because you said the description matched me and that she had a strong accent. Everybody always said we looked alike and everything. And if you think *I* have an accent . . . Well, I'll put it this way, I think *she* has an accent. Definitely stronger, and more distinctive, I think. Someone would probably notice and remember it."

Ricky handed the photo back to me, and I peered closely at Mercedes Gallegos again. "What was her relationship like with Elise?"

"They were better friends than Mercedes and I were," Lila replied. "Elise didn't get as wild as Mercedes could, but she was an outgoing person and liked to have fun. I think when we decided to work together, Elise was kind of the linchpin. I wanted to work with her, and she wanted to work with Mercedes. And I really wanted to work with an all-woman team. MIT can be a really difficult place to be a woman, and Mercedes was a brilliant coder, so it worked out. But Mercedes did get more upset than I did when Elise joined Moonshot and took our work with her."

"Why do you say that?"

Lila thought for a moment, then spoke, choosing her words carefully. "As I said, Mercedes was a brilliant coder. Kind of a savant, really. She didn't seem to care that much about coding, but it came naturally to her to be so good at it. She told me that in high school she had done a lot of theater classes and really wanted to be an actress. I got the impression that maybe she wasn't very good at it, but what she really wanted was to be rich and famous. Her family couldn't afford to send her to college, and she didn't get accepted to any theater programs, but her coding ability got her a full ride to MIT. And she got it in her mind that she could at least get rich, if not famous, with her degree and her skills by landing some really cushy tech job. When the Moonshot people began sniffing around us, Mercedes really threw herself at them. She wanted to work for a shiny, sexy company like that, she wanted to go to California; she really thought that would be her ticket."

"What happened?"

Lila shifted to rest an elbow on the arm of her chair and prop her chin up in her hand. "I think what she failed to understand is that there are a *lot* of coders out there. You can be brilliant, and she was, but unless you create an app and sell it for billions or something, you're more likely to be just one of the crowd, making a comfortable living at a boring job. When you're starting out, a degree from MIT gets you only a little higher up the ladder than the guy who did a twelve-week boot camp. Whereas Elise's skills with AI are a lot more rare and lucrative."

"How did you and Mercedes feel about Elise getting chosen over you?" Ricky asked.

"I was fine—I planned to go into academia anyway," she said. "But I think Mercedes had really latched on to the Moonshot possibility, and when they passed her over, she hadn't made any backup plans. That part shouldn't have been a big deal—like I say, there are so many jobs for coders, so she really could have gone anywhere. But she also really felt that Elise had betrayed her, that she was getting screwed out of a lot of recognition and money, and she got kind of obsessive about it. She was—well, I probably shouldn't say it."

Ricky, ever the devil on the shoulder, asked, "Probably shouldn't say what?"

Lila again seemed to choose her words very carefully. "I haven't seen or spoken to Mercedes in over three years. I can't speak to her current state. But when I knew her, she could be very dramatic—mercurial and obsessive. There were times . . ." She coughed a little, bashfully. "There were times I really worried about her stability."

Mercedes was taking shape as an intriguing character. An unstable Lila look-alike with a stronger, more memorable accent, with grudges against Elise and Moonshot Motors. A coding savant . . . Could she be a hacker, too? Hadn't Melba's grandson, Jason, mentioned what a skilled coder MoonChaser was?

The only problem was, where was Mercedes? She seemed to fit the description of the woman seen with Elise the night she died, but otherwise there seemed to have been no trace of her. Now that we had her name, it felt like we'd have to start all over, trying to retrace her movements and track her down, and we didn't have time for that.

"I know you haven't kept in touch with Mercedes," I said, "but do you have any idea where she might be now?"

Lila shook her head. "I talked to her once after graduation, and she was still melting down over being passed over by Moonshot. It frightened me a little, and I realized I wasn't in a place where I could help her with those feelings. She talked about moving to California anyway, which I thought wasn't the worst idea—lots of other opportunities in Silicon Valley—but she was fixated on Moonshot. It didn't make sense, and I didn't understand what she thought she was going to do. I don't know if she really intended to move or not, or if she ever did. It almost seemed to me like she was tipping over into paranoid delusion."

Ricky had pulled out his phone while Lila was talking, and I looked over to see that he was searching the Internet for Mercedes Gallegos. He toggled back and forth between the Web and image searches. "There are a good number of people out there with that name. The only references that seem to point to the right person are to the papers the three of you published." He looked up at Lila with a wry smile. "She's almost as hard to track down online as you are."

Lila laughed darkly. "She strikes me as more likely to be a doxxer than a doxxee, so if she's hard to find online, it might be for the opposite reason than why I am."

We had taken up enough of Lila's time. I asked her to scan and share the photo with me when she had time, and with her permission, I snapped a picture of it with my phone as well. We asked for directions to the nearest coffee shop, then braced ourselves against the cold for the short walk.

I ordered a hot chocolate for myself and a coffee for Ricky while he used my laptop and the cafe's Wi-Fi to book our return flight to Washington. "I'll be glad to submit *that* to *Motor Mania* for reimbursement," he said cheerfully as I brought our drinks and joined him. "Booking a last-minute flight is no joke."

"What about my return home?"

"I'll do that one now," he said. "Do you mind leaving later in the day? Maybe we can spend a little time in the morning seeing if we can track down Mercedes. At least see if the bartender can ID her."

"That sounds like a plan," I agreed. "I don't know how far

we'll be able to get, but at least we can get started." I thought for a minute as I wrapped my hands around my cup to absorb its warmth. "If there's more follow-up to do than we have time for tomorrow, would you be willing to do a little legwork after I'm gone?"

Ricky smiled slightly over the top of his coffee cup. "Of course I will. I'll work with you anytime you want." He set the cup down and locked those soft dark eyes on me again. "Whatever you want our relationship to be, Oliver, I think we work well together."

"If a little chaotically," I smiled back.

"Yeah, well, that's part of the special sauce," he said with a wink, returning his attention to the laptop.

Whatever you want our relationship to be. What did I want? It wouldn't be true to say I didn't know. I just didn't know how to make it work. Ricky seemed to know what he was doing; he kept initiating touch between us, finding ways to be thoughtful or to keep a joke going. When we were together, I could follow his lead—and clearly, I would. I had followed him into all kinds of shenanigans I would never have done on my own, plans and schedules forgotten. But what would happen when we were apart? It would require more give-and-take, and I didn't know if I could navigate that.

"Okay," Ricky said, breaking into my thoughts. He looked up from my computer. "I got you onto a flight out of National tomorrow at three thirty. You gain three hours going home, so it won't be too late in California when you land. Sound okay?"

"Sounds great," I said. "Thank you."

"That one goes to Drea for reimbursement," he said. "Lord. My credit card is taking a beating."

"Hey," I said to get his attention, squaring my shoulders and gathering my courage and trying some soft, intense eye contact of my own. He met my eyes and smiled.

"Hey what?" he said.

"I, um . . . you said, whatever I want our relationship to be. Can—can I have some time to think about it?"

"Of course you can," he said, one eyebrow shooting up.

"Why do you look so surprised?"

"I didn't expect you to be so open to ambiguity."

I gave him a look that I intended to be enigmatic. "You'd be surprised at what I can be open to." As soon as I said it, I realized how it sounded and flushed scarlet.

He laughed heartily. "Oh, baby, maybe I don't want to give you any time, not if you're going to tempt me like that!" He tried to suppress his smile. "But I will give you all the time you need. Only promise me one thing."

"What's that?"

"Promise me we'll keep in touch while you're thinking. I don't believe in absence making the heart grow fonder. I want to talk to you as often as I can, so you don't forget how wonderful I am."

"Deal," I said.

"If it'll help you with your thinking, I'll kiss you again," Ricky said lightly as he took another sip of his coffee.

"Now you're trying to tempt me. How long until our flight?"

"About two hours. We can make our way back to the airport soon if you want."

"Might as well."

"You hang here for a second. I'll go see if I can get us a cab."

I texted my flight info to my mom as I waited. A moment later, Ricky waved to me through the window of the coffee shop, and I rushed out to join him as he bundled into the back seat of a yellow Ford Taurus taxi.

We both had our phones in our hands. I swiped mine open and pulled up the photo of Mercedes, then zoomed in and studied her face for a hint of familiarity. She was pretty, but there was nothing about her that stood out, no distinctive feature that I could definitively say I had seen before.

"You know," I said to Ricky in a low voice, "based on what Lila told us about Mercedes, don't you think she'd be on social media?"

"Probably," Ricky said eagerly, swiping his phone open and tapping the icon for the Instagram app.

He was about to start a search when I glanced at his feed and said, "Wait a second. Is that Mimi? Did you follow Mimi?"

He laughed, seemingly startling the cabdriver, whose eyes flickered toward us in the rearview mirror. "I did. She seemed like such a kook, I couldn't help myself."

Wait. "Let me see that." I took his phone and put it next to mine, holding the two pictures side by side. "Could she . . . ?"

Ricky leaned close, looking back and forth from one picture to the other. "Ho-lee mackerel," he whistled. "Maybe."

It was the pose. It was such a generic pose, one that seemingly every girl and woman between the ages of ten and forty had been doing on social media a few years ago: one hand on hip, the other leg strategically cocked with the foot up on pointed toe, the body at a forty-five-degree angle from the camera.

But Mimi and Mercedes held the pose identically, their heads at the same tilted-back angle, their non-hip hand resting at the waist with the fingers lightly pursed together. Mimi's hair cascaded down in loose golden-blond curls, while Mercedes's hair was dark and straight, but it could be dye or a wig. Mimi's eyes were that strange blue green, while Mercedes's were brown, but it could be contact lenses. Fillers had given Mimi the pout for which Mercedes had needed to purse her lips. What passed for a golden tan on Mimi could be Mercedes's natural complexion. Their makeup was nearly identical, although Mimi's showed a little more polish in the application, or maybe in Marisol's postproduction: heavy mascara, glossy pale pink lipstick, a bit of highlight and contouring on a matched set of cheekbones and jawlines.

I looked up at Ricky. "Do you remember seeing Mimi at the demonstration drive event on Wednesday? Joey mentioned her, but did you actually see her?"

"No. There were a lot of people there, though."

"Don't you think we would have noticed her?"

"Probably," he admitted. "She seems to like to be noticeable. Maybe she had slipped away."

"And she was at the dinner with King when he got sick, too!"

"Yeah, she was, and she didn't seem that concerned about it afterward."

Our route back to the airport had once again taken us underground, below Boston's North End, and now we emerged in East Boston, swinging our way over the interchange toward the airport.

I was excited. "Do you really think Mercedes could be Mimi? Is she our killer?"

"I think it's very poss . . ." Ricky's words trailed off as it registered for both of us that, instead of pulling up to the terminal for departures, we had entered the murky gloom of a parking structure. "Excuse me," he said to the driver, tapping next to the opening in the Plexiglas partition between the seats.

I looked out the window, a knot growing in my stomach. We were in the rental car garage, navigating up the ramp from level to level, flying past the lots for Avis, Budget, Hertz, Enterprise, National, and Dollar. The daylight gradually returned until we emerged on the uppermost deck of the garage, which was nearly empty except for a cluster of Moonshot sedans parked in one corner, plugged into chargers underneath an awning of solar panels. I flashed back to the article Elise and I had read in the in-flight magazine—the Independence Hub, your destination to rent a Moonshot with that impersonal touch.

The cab glided to a stop at the end of the row of Moonshots, and the driver turned to look at us, aiming a gleaming chrome revolver at us through the opening in the partition.

"Sorry, boys," Mimi, née Mercedes, said in a Brooklyn growl, all affectation gone from her voice. Her hair was messily pulled back into a ponytail under a ball cap, and she wasn't wearing the blue-green contacts or any makeup. "I'm afraid you're going to miss your flight."

CHAPTER 21

"We're switching cars," Mercedes said, waving us out the door with the gun. "Don't try anything. I know this thing looks stupid, but I know how to use it, and it will kill you."

The gaudy revolver did look kind of ridiculous, but also terrifyingly large. My heart was racing, but for once my brain was still, paralyzed by the threat of being shot. Ricky clambered out the door, and I followed, leaving my duffel behind in the back seat, as Mercedes exited the front. She again leveled the gun at us once we were all standing on the parking deck.

"Your phones," she said, holding out her free hand, and tossing them onto the floor of the cab as she closed the back door. We followed the gun around the car obediently as she opened the trunk and pulled out a large backpack.

Inside the trunk was a man lying on his side, his knees drawn up to his chin, his hands tied behind his back, and his mouth gagged. Probably the cab's usual driver. The ominous stillness in my brain deepened as his bewildered, terrified eyes locked with mine for a second before Mercedes lowered the lid, plunging him back into his dark prison.

The cold wind suddenly stung at my cheeks as it pierced the fear that had kept me insensible when we first emerged from the cab. I kept the gun in my peripheral vision but took a quick glance at our surroundings. The topmost deck of the garage was completely deserted. I knew the garage was surrounded by the roads servicing the airport and the low-lying terminal buildings, so there were no nearby buildings tall enough to offer a view of our predicament. And, of course, the Independence Hub was completely unstaffed.

Mercedes kept an impressively steady hand on the gun as she used her other hand to sling the backpack over her shoulder and pull her own phone from her pocket. Her one-handed phone technique was equally impressive: she used her thumb to scroll and tap while cradling the phone in her palm.

At the tap of her screen, the lights on the Moonshot at the end of the row flashed as the doors unlocked. "Looks like we're taking this one," she said, tapping the screen again to pop the trunk open. She dropped her backpack down from her shoulder to her hand, set it on the ground at her feet, and bent to unzip it. She pulled out several pieces of fabric and began to fold them into strips.

"Got any Hermès scarves in there?" Ricky asked. His tone was as light as ever, but I thought I detected the slightest quiver under the joking bravado. "I have high standards for my gags."

"Sorry, cutie," Mercedes said as she roughly pulled the gag over his head and into his mouth, tying it at the back. She gagged me next, then pushed Ricky toward the open trunk. With a prod of the revolver to his back, he climbed in. She had him lie on his side and face the back of the rear seat so that she could tie his hands behind him. She tied my hands while I was still standing on the deck, then grabbed the back of my jacket and gave me a boost while I climbed into the trunk and tucked myself in back-to-back with Ricky. I had one last look at the still-deserted parking lot as the lid swung down over us, shutting us away from the world in foreboding darkness.

A door thunked closed, and soon after, the electric motors

whirred to life directly beneath us as the car started to move. It was surprising how jarring the ride was from this vantage point. Without the benefit of seat belts or foam-cushioned seats, we were jostled at every imperfection in the road. A rogue speed bump, taken at what seemed like excessive speed, sent us both flying upward.

The events on the parking deck had seemed to happen very quickly, but as the car droned on, the pitch of the motors rising and falling with our speed, nothing to pierce the inky blackness but our own anxious speculation about our fate, time started to stretch out and slow down. I wasn't sure if it was my imagination or if the motors were radiating a bit of warmth up through the floor of the trunk. Ricky was certainly warm at my back, and as the air grew stale, I started to feel twinges of sleepiness nipping at the edges of my dread. But I was also achy—my knees were howling from being held in their bent position—and my arms and hands were going numb from the binding around my wrists. Adding insult to injury was the ticker-tape parade of anxiety itchiness marching up and down my arms, which I could do nothing to soothe. Where were we going? What was she going to do with us? Why did that stupid gun have to make its Chekhovian reappearance now?

Through the prickling numbness in my fingers and growing panicked numbness in my mind, I eventually became aware of another sensation. It took a moment to process it and realize that Ricky's fingers were poking mine, prodding and manipulating between them. For a second, our fingers interlaced perfectly, and, assuming some mutual comfort was what he was after, I tried to grab hold.

"Mmmph!" he protested sharply through his gag.

"Mmmph?" I guessed he wasn't in his jailhouse mood like I'd thought.

His fingers pried loose from and lightly swatted mine, then his hand started fumbling around again. Realization dawned:

the knot! He was trying to find the knot in my binding. I shifted my arms around a little until his fingers found their prize, and he let out a triumphant "Mmm!"

He worked at the knot for several minutes before I felt a slackening in the fabric, then my hands were free. I maneuvered my arms into a more comfortable position, rotated my wrists for a minute to get the feeling back in my hands, and rolled awkwardly from one side to the other so that I was now facing Ricky's back. I quickly located the knot in the binding around his wrists and worked it loose, then undid my gag. Ricky did the same, then wriggled his way around to face me, although we couldn't see each other in the pitch black.

"Well, that's a relief," he whispered.

"It is more comfortable," I acknowledged, "but what difference does it make? She'll still have that gun pointed at us when we stop. It's not like we can jump her or anything."

"No, I don't think it makes a difference in the long run—unless we can figure some way out of this before she can get to us."

I couldn't tell exactly where Ricky's face was relative to mine, and I knew he couldn't see it, but I raised a skeptical eyebrow at him anyway. "How are we going to do that, Mac-Gyver?"

"Shh, I'm thinking," he said, the movement of his voice suggesting that he was craning his neck to look around our inky prison.

"Can you see something?"

His voice still bobbed around, and a hand pressed on my shoulder as he lifted his torso as best he could to see over me. "Isn't there supposed to be a release handle inside the trunk?"

"Why would there be a handle *inside* the trunk?" I tried to turn my head to look around, too, but my face ran right into Ricky's chest hovering above me. "Mmmph!"

"Sorry," he said, his voice retreating back to his position against the rear seat. "I think I saw the handle down by your feet. It's for situations like this. If you get stuck inside the trunk, you can open it from inside to get out or get help. We can get help!"

I tried again to look behind me and caught sight of a faint glow in the direction Ricky had indicated. "So I pull that, and the trunk opens? What happens then? I could fall out at seventy miles per hour! Could I get *sucked* out, even if I don't fall?"

To my embarrassed annoyance, Ricky chuckled a little at my fears. "It's not an airplane. Nobody's getting sucked out, and you won't fall. Just be careful. Once it's open, we can try to flag down other drivers to help. She won't have time to do anything, and there will be witnesses."

It took a considerable amount of maneuvering, and repeatedly bonking Ricky's knees and accidentally jabbing him with my elbows, before I was able to reach the glow-in-the-dark plastic handle. I wrapped my fingers around it, gave a yank, and . . .

Nothing.

I pulled it again. Still nothing. At a third tug, the handle came off in my hand. "Ughhh," I groaned.

"Do you think she disabled it?"

"No, it seemed like she picked this car at random, right? I think we have lousy quality to thank for this. Lousy quality and lousy luck. Any other ideas for getting out of here?"

In the process of reaching for the handle, I had rotated so that my back was to Ricky. His voice behind me now was soft and weary. "Uh . . . not really."

The promise of escape had given me the slightest jolt of hopeful adrenaline. Now I deflated, my arms going limp on the floor in front of me, my face rolling into the scratchy carpet, which muffled my voice a little. "So what's gonna happen now?"

Ricky's response was equally quiet. "I think she's going to kill us. I don't know if there'll be anything we can do or not, but . . ."

But. But I didn't want to die. I didn't want Ricky to die. A sad, tired tear ran down my nose toward that awful carpet. I wanted to go home. I wanted to see my mom, and my room, and maybe even see what it would be like to have my own apartment. I wanted to see my story, my words, my name, Ricky's name, our experiences in print.

A watery sniffle escaped from my nose. I felt Ricky's arm cross my shoulder, and his thumb gently found my cheek and wiped at my tears. I scooted back a little, found his body behind mine, pulled myself into him, and his arm wrapped around me, holding me to him. He rested his cheek on my hair, and I felt his soft, warm breath pass by my ear.

I didn't want to die. I especially didn't want Ricky to die. I mean, as a rule, I didn't want anyone to die. I also usually wanted those not-dead people to more or less leave me alone. But I didn't want Ricky to leave me alone. All those other things I wanted . . . I realized that I would give them up if it meant I didn't die, and Ricky didn't die, and Ricky didn't leave me alone.

What was I supposed to do with that?

Fight, I guess. I had no idea how to fight—probably both Ricky and I were better off relying on our brains than brawn—but I realized that I was angry enough with Mercedes to want to fight her. Deeply, deeply angry.

"She killed Elise, right?" I was holding Ricky's arm, still pulling him around me like a blanket. It felt better to speak such ugliness from under his protective embrace.

"Yeah, it seems that way. And presumably she tried to kill King, and now she wants to kill us. She's really lost it."

"We can't let her get away with it—any of it," I said, channeling strength from Ricky's arms to feed my own defiance.

"No, we can't," he said, seeming to rally a bit himself. Then I felt his grip tighten slightly, and his cheek left the back of my head as he again craned, this time to listen. "Wait. We've stopped."

The vibration of the motors underneath us had been so constant, so all-encompassing, that its sudden absence felt nause-atingly final.

We waited, holding each other in tense silence, for the trunk to open, to be faced once more with Mercedes and her re-volver. We waited a long time. The moment didn't come. After an eternity, the car moved slowly forward for a minute, then stopped again. Another tense wait, and still nothing.

"Do you feel that?" Ricky asked another eternity later. "We're . . . rocking?"

I tried to feel what he was feeling. It took a moment, but I realized the car was indeed swaying slowly to and fro, even though the motors were still and the car was not moving for-ward.

"We must be on a ferry," he said. "Probably to Nantucket or Martha's Vineyard."

"Why would she be taking us there?"

"Beats me, but neither of those places are very big, so I would expect that once she starts driving again, we won't have much longer in here."

"How long is the ferry ride?"

"I don't know. I think Nantucket is a shorter trip than the Vineyard? Either way, this could be our chance."

"Our chance?"

"To get somebody's attention!" Ricky released his hold on me, nudging me toward the trunk lid. "If we kick and bang on the trunk, maybe someone will hear us!"

I gave a tentative bang with the heel of my hand, then fol-lowed it with a somewhat more convincing kick. Behind me, Ricky reached up and banged on the top of the compartment. Soon, I was in the swing of it, kicking and punching, until, panting, I needed a break.

Ricky paused for a second, too. "Can you hear anything?"

I listened but heard nothing at all. "No. Are we totally sound-proofed in here?"

"Not totally," came a snarl from behind us, accompanied by

a dim, diffused burst of light as Mercedes opened the pass-through behind the rear seat center armrest and peered in at us from inside the cabin of the car. "I can hear you bozos banging around back there, and if you don't cut it out, I'll stick my gun through this little hole and you won't like what happens next. So shut up!" The light disappeared as she slammed the plastic pass-through door closed.

Plunged once again into darkness, I felt my shoulders begin to shake, but was surprised this time to discover that the cause was laughter, not tears. I tried to muffle my giggles as best I could, but after a minute I could tell that they had spread to Ricky, too.

"Why are we laughing?" he finally whispered, choking back a laugh.

"I don't know," I whispered back, trying to gather myself. "She's scary, but also kind of ridiculous, you know? Like, I don't know how seriously to take her threats."

An edge crept into Ricky's voice. "Do you want to find out?"

I sobered up. "No, I guess not."

At that we fell into a nervous, contemplative silence. After a long while, the rocking seemed to stop, and then the motor spooled back up as the car moved forward under its own power. I fumbled around to find Ricky's hand and took it. This strange journey, possibly the last time we'd have alone together, was nearly at an end. I didn't want to think about what would come next.

"Thank you for . . . everything," I whispered. "This trip has been nothing like what I had planned on, but it was definitely memorable. And I'm really happy I got to spend it with you."

He squeezed my hand. "I've had a lot of fun with you, Oliver, and I've really grown to care about you. I'm sorry we've ended up here." His voice broke a little. I freed my hand, reached up to his face, and wiped a tear from the corner of his eye with my thumb.

"Don't be sorry. It's not your fault. And, hey, we've bumbled our way into this—maybe we can still bumble our way out. Mercedes is nuts, but for all her threats, it doesn't really seem like shooting is her style, so we just need to figure out her plan and try to get out of it."

"How very loosey-goosey of you," he said with a tremulous laugh. "I'm glad I rubbed off on you a little."

It was not long after we left the ferry that the car stopped moving again, and this time we heard the slam of the door and Mercedes's feet crunching toward the trunk outside.

"Well, don't you two look cozy," she said as the lid swung open. "And such freedom of movement, too. Naughty, naughty."

In the time we had been in the trunk, the sun had nearly gone down. The chrome barrel of the revolver glinted at us in the twilight, and the chill in the air slapped us once more as we climbed out of the trunk onto the gravel driveway of a large white shingle-clad house. We were surrounded by trees and lawns and what seemed like expansive grounds, though we could also hear the lapping of the ocean against a nearby shore, somewhere on the other side of the house.

"We decided to take a weekend getaway to our place on the Vineyard after such a stressful week in Washington," Mercedes said dryly as we walked toward the door, her revolver guiding us from behind. "It was so stressful, poor Kelsey-poo dropped dead from a heart attack—or, at least, he was supposed to. Anyway, I'm so glad you decided to join us. Last night I got worried you might not make it after your accident. That cute little old car . . . I was afraid you might get hurt. But you two sure do have some dumb luck, don't you."

We waited while she opened the door, then she waved us inside with the gun. "You were after us?" I gasped. "Not—not anyone else?"

"Who, Lila?" Mercedes barked out a laugh. "I wasn't worried about Lila until you two started sniffing around her. No, it was you I was following—ever since you started snooping around about Elise—but once I saw who was in that cab you were after last night, I knew you'd show up looking for Lila again. And sure enough, I staked out her place and there you were. Now I'm gonna have to take care of her, too, but one thing at a time." My heart sank at the thought that, in our zeal to follow a hunch, we'd endangered Lila.

Mercedes led us into the main hallway of the house, past an impressive staircase and doorways into living and dining rooms that were decorated in an understated but expensive-looking East Coast beachy-elegant style. We paused at a door halfway down the hall, which Mercedes now unlocked. This opened to a stairway down to the basement. Overhead lights were already on, and I was surprised on reaching the bottom of the stairs to see Kelso King and Marisol, both gagged and tied to chairs in the center of what otherwise looked like an ordi-nary, if tastefully appointed, basement family room.

"Look, honey, now it's really a party," Mercedes sneered to King, keeping the gun pointed at us as she pulled two more chairs from a card table and motioned Ricky and me into them. King's watery blue eyes regarded us sorrowfully, and I was a little taken aback to see from the mascara running down her cheeks that the normally acerbic Marisol had been crying.

Mercedes tied us to our chairs but didn't bother to gag us. "We're not going to be here long," she said, moving to a desk and setting the gun down. She pulled her laptop out of her backpack and opened it in front of her on the desk. "We're all going for a nice drive in a little bit. Won't that be fun? But I need to make a few little tweaks to the car first."

"You're like a modern hot-rodder," Ricky said. "Only you don't have to worry about ruining your manicure."

"I know, isn't it great? Did you notice my app earlier? I cre-ated it so that I could open any Moonshot I want—one digital key to control any car. I can even drive remotely with it. And now—" She stuck the tip of her tongue out of the corner of her mouth as she paused to type. "I can make a fun little tweak to the maps that the self-driving system uses, and the whole Atlantic Ocean disappears. Soon some idiot is going to tell their car to drive them to England, and the car will think it can. Isn't that cute?"

I processed this for a second, struggling a little to hear my thoughts over my racing heart. "Are we going to be those idiots?"

She smiled terrifyingly at me in the glow from her computer screen and kept typing.

Since she seemed to want to gloat about what she was up to, I decided to tear boldly on, riding the adrenaline. "Why did you kill Elise?"

She looked up again, a little surprised this time, and thought for a beat. "You know, I hadn't really been planning on it. I only ever planned to kill Kelso. And I probably shouldn't have done it—I realized that when you texted her while we were at the bar and then showed up the next day asking questions." So *that's* how she had known Elise and I were friends! "But I really thought nobody would miss that little backstabber. I mean, I had moved on to bigger and better things. Once poor Kelso here meets his maker, I'll have the whole company. But it just felt so *good* to get rid of her, you know? Like, I could have fired her next week, but that wouldn't have been as satisfying. So I made like her old friend Mercedes was in town, took her out for a drink, and, well, took her out."

"You really think you'll get to take over Moonshot if something happens to King?" Ricky seemed confused. I remembered what King had told me about hoping to make Mimi his successor, but at the time I hadn't taken it very seriously. Now I wondered if he had really meant it.

"Darling, I've had that in the bag for months. I whispered a little New Age spiritual mumbo jumbo into this bozo's ear and shoved my ta-tas under his nose, and he thought I was *God*." I glanced at King, whose eyes were cast down. "He has an honest-to-god succession plan, signed off by his lawyers, naming me CEO if anything happens to him, can you believe that? He was too easy. Honestly, if I'd known I could go this route in the first place, Elise would've had nothing to worry about. But I guess I wouldn't have figured it out if she hadn't screwed me over like she did. Huh." Mercedes seemed to have an epiphany. "I guess, in a way, I owe this all to her. May she rot in hell anyway."

She continued to tap away for another minute, then closed the laptop with a satisfied slam. "Besides, I can do everything she could do. With me running things, we won't need Elise. I'll prove it to you. I'll show you exactly how well I can program a self-driving car." She picked up the gun again, waving it menacingly at all four of us. "I'm going to untie you all now, then I'm gonna tie your hands behind your backs. And"—she shot me and Ricky a sly smile as she fished a couple more scarves out of her backpack with her free hand—"we're keeping our gags in this time. Anyone tries anything stupid, I shoot. Capisce?"

CHAPTER 22

Mercedes marched us all up the stairs at gunpoint and back to the car. When we got out to the driveway, she ushered King, Ricky, and Marisol into the back seat. "You're driving," she said to me, with a wave of the revolver.

Me? My first panicked thought was that I didn't know how to drive, but then I realized that Mercedes would be controlling the self-driving system and I would just be the body in the driver's seat—quite literally, if she pulled off her plan.

Sitting with our hands tied behind our backs was uncomfortably awkward. Mercedes whacked my elbow with the door as she closed it behind me, sending pain shooting up and down my arm. She came around and got into the front passenger seat and, as I had surmised, the dashboard and headlights lit up as she pulled out her phone and tapped the screen. Once the car was on, she switched to the central touch screen on the dashboard, keying in an address and hitting the steering wheel icon to activate the self-driving system. It counted down, *3, 2, 1,* and the car smoothly surged forward, down the driveway.

Our headlights cut a curving path down dark, narrow, tree-lined roads as we rode in tense silence. We passed no other cars, and there were few buildings visible, though I caught occasional flashes of light through the trees. Moonlight glowed and diffused through a light cover of clouds.

Trying to move extremely slowly so as not to attract Mercedes's notice, I lowered my foot onto one of the pedals, though I wasn't sure if it was the brake or the accelerator. In any event, it plunged lifelessly to the floor, and I remembered the video we had been shown at the Moonshot press event, a lifetime ago, about how the system operated. The main way to deactivate it was through the touch screen, and there was an emergency override button somewhere—on the steering wheel, right? There were several buttons on the wheel, with illuminated icons that were inscrutable to me. But it didn't matter; with my hands tied behind my back, I couldn't reach the screen or the wheel.

If Mercedes saw my leg moving on the pedal, she didn't say anything. She seemed to have lapsed into a moody reverie, staring intently straight ahead through the windshield.

As the landscape outside began to change, with the number of buildings lining the road slowly increasing until it became clear we had entered a village, she tensed, scanning for anyone who might notice us. Her luck held, however; even in the little town, the streets remained eerily quiet, with only our phantom car cutting silently through the night.

Up ahead, the lights of the town abruptly disappeared, and I realized that we were nearing the ocean. As the road we were on came to a T with the last street following the coastline, the car glided to a stop. "You have reached your destination," an electronic approximation of the weird Mimi voice announced from the dashboard.

Directly ahead of us, across the street, was a long wooden pier jutting out into the black Atlantic. I glanced down at the map on the dashboard screen. It showed the entrance to an interstate highway where the pier was, continuing off to the east through what should have been open sea. We were about to set off on our road trip to England.

"Well, folks, this is my stop," Mercedes announced. "I'm going to get into a good spot to see you off. Have fun!" She got out of the car, crossed the street, and walked down the pier so far that all I could see of her was the pinprick of light cast by the phone in her hand, and then even that disappeared. In the stillness outside, we could hear the waves lapping against the shore. I glanced into the rearview mirror and found myself looking directly into Ricky's eyes in the middle seat behind me. He looked worried but waggled his eyebrows in greeting.

On the dashboard, the steering wheel icon suddenly lit up, as though an invisible finger had tapped it. Mercedes's magic phone app. The screen dissolved into the now-familiar countdown.

3 . . .

There was a flash of movement on the road to our left and our right.

2 . . .

Lights suddenly began to penetrate the gloom, coming rapidly toward us, white and flashing blue and red.

1 . . .

The police cars were barreling toward us from both directions. Our motors spooled up and the nose of our car lifted slightly, as if it was springing from coiled haunches to launch itself across the street and merge onto what it thought was a highway at full cruising speed. One of the police cars clipped our right front corner as we sped toward the pier, but the cruiser spun away at the impact, while our car only wobbled a little on its course, then continued ahead as if nothing had happened.

We were rapidly gaining speed. How long was this pier? It stretched ahead in our headlights, the wooden planks creating a mesmerizing reel as we barreled over them, but I knew the end couldn't be too far off.

I caught Ricky's eyes in the rearview again, and as if a silent communication had passed between us, he nodded and kicked his leg up onto the console between the front seats, extending his foot to barely reach the screen. He kicked delicately at the steering wheel icon in the corner a couple of times, but it couldn't register the touch of his shoe.

"Mmmph!" he cried, and I understood. As he pulled his leg back, I stuck the crook of my right arm out into the space between the seats. He stuck his shoe through the opening in my arm, and I latched on, pulling the shoe off. His foot shot forward again, and his toe made contact with the button to deactivate the system. It flashed, and the screen dissolved into the numbers again.

We just needed this pier to last for three more seconds.

3 . . .

The lights of the police cars were still following us down the pier.

2 . . .

Our headlights caught the figure of Mercedes, standing to the side at the end of the pier.

1 . . .

The end of the pier! NO!

Unconsciously, I had already mashed my left foot onto the pedal, praying that I remembered correctly it was the brake. As the last number flashed on the screen, I felt the pedal under my foot engage, pressure building rapidly as the tires began to squeal. None of us were belted in, and we all pitched forward as the car tried frantically to slow, the end of the pier now almost invisible beyond the nose of the car.

As he flailed behind me, his leg flying around near my head, Ricky's foot caught the steering wheel. The car veered to the left, skidding into its final stop at a ninety-degree angle from our original trajectory. A nanosecond before it juddered to a halt, inches from plunging off the side of the pier, it struck something, and I watched in amazement as Mercedes was pitched into the cold Atlantic below.

* * *

After they had fished Mercedes out of the ocean and taken her into custody, we spent hours giving our statements to the police on Martha's Vineyard. Then they put Ricky and me into a police launch back to the mainland, where we were met by Boston cops who drove us back to the city. Ricky and I stole snatches of sleep here and there during the boat and car rides, but as exhausted as we were, we were almost as wired.

Back in Boston, we went over our story yet again, this time with a couple of FBI field agents in the room and the DC Metropolitan Police listening in via teleconference. By the time all was said and done, an officer was being dispatched to get us breakfast.

A security guard in the rental car garage at the airport had found the taxi abandoned on the top level about an hour after we had left. In the course of looking it over, he had heard the driver, still bound, kicking against the inside of the trunk. He had also found our phones and my duffel in the back seat, with my business cards and other identifying information inside. The cabbie had confirmed seeing us being held at gunpoint and had given a description of Mercedes, and a call to the support phone number listed on the Independence Hub chargers confirmed that a car was missing that hadn't been reserved or paid for, though the call center employee couldn't understand how that could have happened.

The Boston PD had moved quickly. A resourceful detective had scoured the Internet for someone who could help trace a rogue Moonshot; after peering into a few dark corners, he was put in contact with someone who we were somewhat red-facedly told went by the name Boobfan69 ("Nice," whispered Ricky, while I broke into a smile), who was able to pinpoint the location of our stolen car while we were still on the ferry to Martha's Vineyard. From there, it had been a matter of coordinating with the local authorities and tracking our movements until the moment was right, although if you'd asked me, I might have suggested the moment was very nearly too late.

Now it was nearly noon, and we had been dropped off at the airport—actually dropped off this time, all the way to the terminal—to wait for a commuter flight back to Washington, where, after a short layover, I would catch another flight home. Ricky and I were slumped in side-by-side chairs at our gate, Ricky drowsily watching the passing parade on the concourse and me on my laptop, racing to ride the last of my adrenaline as I furiously typed out a draft of my DC article, which had somehow started emerging in fully formed snatches in my brain during the lulls in our police interactions over the past several hours.

I got the last of my thoughts out. The draft would need a lot of polishing, but I'd worry about that later. I shared the document with Drea, just so she'd know I was working on it, with a note not to look at it until I'd made another pass. Closing my laptop and slouching down in my chair, I turned to Ricky. "I know you probably want to go home when we land in DC. You don't have to wait with me at the airport."

"Of course I'll wait with you. Don't be silly." He shuffled his foot over to rub his shoe against mine.

It was probably the exhaustion rolling over me, but my mood was crashing, too, as I realized that the moment I had been dreading, for all of Ricky's harebrained attempts to forestall it, was almost here: I would be going back to my home, and he was going to his.

I gave his shoe a little kick in return. "Hey."

"Hey what?" he said, stifling a yawn.

"Where are we at?"

He thought for a minute. What was he thinking? What did I *want* him to be thinking? I realized I knew, and deflated a little when he finally said, "It's okay with me if you want to stick with just being friends for now."

Not the right answer. But given that we were about to be three thousand miles apart for the next who knew how long, I knew it was probably the right move. "Yeah. That's what I was thinking, too," I lied.

"Remember what I said, though. I want us to be *close* friends. *Very, very* close." This was getting closer to the right answer.

I smiled and kicked him again.

A pair of ornately tooled cowboy boots duded into view on the concourse, then stopped in front of us. I looked up to see Kelso King, accompanied by Marisol.

"Howdy, boys," he drawled. "Didn't get to say it, but I was mighty impressed with how you two got us out of that jam last night. Quick thinking, and good teamwork."

Ricky and I exchanged shy smiles before I turned back to King. "Are you headed home? I kind of thought you'd fly private."

He chuckled. "Usually do, it's true. But Mimi drove us up here last night. My jet's still back in Washington. So, yeah, this little lady and I are flying commercial—first class, of course, she deserves it after all that—and getting back home as quick as we can."

"And then I'm going back to Santa Clara," Marisol muttered in her dark monotone, "and, no offense, but I never want to see any of you people again."

"We'll try our best," Ricky said with a lazy mock salute, and they were off again.

After sitting for a minute with my eyes closed, I turned to Ricky. "Can you do me a favor? It's a big one—it involves braving the wilds of Maryland again."

"You would ask this of me when we're just friends?"

"Very, very close friends, remember? And, yes, I would."

He sighed. "Fine. What is it?"

"Take a cake or some cookies or something—something nice—out to Melba and Jason. Make sure to bring milk, too. I'll pay you back for it."

He grinned. "We'll go halvsies. I'm glad she let him have his computer back for our cause."

In a moment, our flight began boarding, and we joined the horde shuffling onto the plane to find our seats. Just as I was about to swipe it into airplane mode, my phone buzzed with a text from Drea. **You let Ricky kidnap you, I looked at your draft—now we're even. It's so *good*, Oliver! I can't wait to help you polish it up and then to see it in print!!**

I blushed deeply as I shoved my phone into my pocket, my head light and buzzy with exhausted, slightly embarrassed pride. *In print! With Ricky's photos,* I thought shyly, stealing a glance at him fumbling for his seat belt next to me.

Almost as soon as we were airborne, Ricky slumped into my side. "I'm so tired," he yawned, slowly inclining his head until it was resting on my shoulder and closing his eyes.

I didn't mind. I was tired, too, and again he felt like a warm, comfortable, welcome blanket draping over me.

"When did you say you were moving into your new apartment?" he asked suddenly from my shoulder.

"In a month or so."

"Let me know when you're settled, and I'll come visit you."

"I'd really like that," I said, surprising myself with how easily the genuine, unambiguous feeling came and was expressed. No second-guessing.

"You know," he said drowsily after a moment, "you're stronger than you think you are, Oliver. You're sensitive, and you think you're so flustered all the time, but you're tenacious and you follow your gut. I think you should give yourself more credit."

I thought about this for a moment. I wasn't completely convinced of my gut's trustworthiness—mostly because it seemed to follow Ricky's gut—but with Mercedes in custody and Drea's encouragement still buzzing around my head, I *was* feeling pretty tenacious. "Maybe you're right. And you—you're kind of a mess, you know that?"

I could feel his face stretch into a grin against my shoulder. "You're not so bad at being a little messy yourself. And I think you like it more than you realize. Admit it, we have fun being messy together." He yawned again, then continued. "You're pretty strong, pretty messy, and pretty."

"Pretty what?" I asked.

"Mmm?"

"You were saying I was pretty something, but you didn't say what."

"Oh, no, you're just pretty."

"Shut up," I laughed affectionately. "You're ridiculous."

"You could tell me I'm pretty, too . . . you know, tell me as a friend . . ." He trailed off.

After a few minutes, his breathing slowed and deepened. I looked down at his sleeping face. He *was* pretty, not that he really needed me to tell him that. He clearly already knew it. Maybe I should sometime, though—if for no other reason than to make him happy. Maybe I would.

Looking further down, I saw that his right hand lay open, palm up, on his leg, inches from my own left hand. Trying not to disturb him by moving my arm too much, I slowly lifted my hand, hovered it over his for a moment, then gently lowered it into his palm, loosely lacing my fingers between his. Slowly, his fingers curled up around mine, his grip tightening.

"Gotcha," he mumbled.

I didn't care. And I didn't try to think about what it meant that I was holding Ricky's hand. I just knew I wanted to do it. So what if my resolve to be friends with him and avoid further complication never seemed to last more than twenty minutes at a time. I rested my head on top of his, nestling into his soft curls, closed my eyes, and held his hand all the way back to Washington.